**PRA**

AUTHOR KEN FITE AND ABUSE OF POWER

★★★★★ "Riveting…"

★★★★★ "Fite never disappoints."

★★★★★ "This is his best one!"

★★★★★ "Grabbed me from the beginning."

★★★★★ "Another great Blake Jordan thriller!"

★★★★★ "As good as it gets for this genre."

★★★★★ "Absolutely captivating from cover to cover."

★★★★★ "I couldn't put this book down."

★★★★★ "Abuse of Power is a winner."

★★★★★ "Fast-paced and draws you in right to the end."

—Amazon reviews

## WANT THE NEXT BLAKE JORDAN STORY FOR $1 ON RELEASE DAY?*

*KINDLE EDITION ONLY

I'm currently writing the next book in the Blake Jordan series with a release planned soon. New subscribers get the Kindle version for $1 on release day.

Join my newsletter to reserve your copy and I'll let you know when it's ready to download to your Kindle.

kenfite.com/books

## THE BLAKE JORDAN SERIES
### IN ORDER

*The Senator*
*Credible Threat*
*In Plain Sight*
*Rules of Engagement*
*The Homeland*
*The Shield*
*Thin Blue Line*
*Person of Interest*
*Abuse of Power*

This is a work of fiction. The characters, incidents, and dialogues are products of the author's imagination and are not to be construed as real. Any resemblance to events or persons, living or dead, is coincidental.

December 2022
Copyright © 2022 Ken Fite
All rights reserved worldwide.

*For my writer buddies Jason and Creston,
who made me do the paperbacks.*

# ABUSE OF POWER

## A BLAKE JORDAN THRILLER

### KEN FITE

# 1

Washington, DC, was, for the most part, exactly the same whether it was daytime or night. But the biggest difference between the two was the population. During the day, it swelled to well over one million. It was considerably less at night. Less than half. Only Manhattan beat DC in day versus night population.

This random fact came to him as he was punched hard once more in the face. It struck him as odd the kinds of things people thought about when they knew they were about to die. His head moved to the right in response to the blow. He could taste something metallic in his mouth. The man standing in front of him stepped forward to punch him again, and as he did, he spit on him.

His attacker stepped back, surprised, then offended, then somewhat amused. He wiped the blood off his face with the back of his hand and turned to his left. Another man stood there in the shadows. Older. Grayer. His hair slicked back and perfect. A second man stood close by, ready to take over if he grew tired. The older man stepped forward, and the first guy moved away in deference, giving his boss room to work.

"I'm going to ask you one more time," the silver-haired man said patiently. "Who else did you talk to?"

The large man strapped to the chair stared up at the guy in charge, but said nothing back.

"We pulled your file. Impressive career. You've accomplished a lot." He paused. "Pity how it will end."

He didn't respond.

"The stress of the job. The endless nights away from home, away from your wife and your son."

He didn't speak. He said nothing at all and just stared out at the bright city lights through the windows.

"You didn't tell anyone you were married. Not part of your file. Now, why would that be?" The silver-haired man paused again. Longer this time. "I think I know why. I think it was to protect her. Same with your son. So someone like me wouldn't find out. So someone like me couldn't use it as leverage." He leaned in close and cocked his head to one side. "But people like me always find out, don't we?"

"Leave them out of this," the large man said, speaking for the first time.

The silver-haired man smiled and nodded to himself once and stood up straight. He said, "Last chance."

He stared at the lights. Unwavering determination. He said, "I'm not going to tell you anything."

The older man smiled. He didn't try to hide it at all. It was the response he was hoping for. Because the response was telling. He said, "The problem is, people like you are good at what you do. Very physical. You can take men down. You have a tactical mind. But you're not so good with the psychology of things. Because if you were, you'd see that your response means that, in truth, no one else knows. Only you know."

He didn't reply. A bead of sweat streaked down his face. Nature's lie detector. Hard to suppress.

"My guess is recent events didn't sit right with you. Maybe you tried to raise the concern. In a subtle way. To your superior. Maybe he told you to drop it." He paused again, eyeing him a moment longer. Then he shook his head slowly. "But that's not right, either. I can tell, son. Just by looking at you. Believe me. You didn't tell him anything. You didn't tell anybody. Did you? No. You were just doing your job. But now I have a mess to clean up. Now I have to make this go away. And believe me, son, if anyone can—it's me."

HE MUST HAVE BEEN HIT AGAIN, BECAUSE AS HE OPENED HIS eyes, he saw his head was hanging low, and when he lifted it, the guy with the silver hair was on the phone, and the other two men were gone. Silver hair spoke in low tones, staring out the windows, looking out at the glimmering lights of Washington, DC.

He tried to pull his wrists away from the chair they were strapped to. He was a large man and used all of his strength, but it was no use. The zip ties dug into his skin and pressed his flesh tight, but they would not break. He turned his head slowly, first left, then right, as far back as it would go. He sensed nobody behind him and wondered where the others had gone to. He turned his gaze back down to his wrists and looked at his watch. It was one thirty-seven a.m. Early Saturday morning. The world was asleep. But not for long.

Then he had another thought.

Did the men who disappeared leave to find his wife? Did they go to get his son?

He wasn't an interrogator, but he knew the basics. He was an Army man, after all. He knew how these things worked. The rules of engagement the United States military employed were very clear when dealing with the enemy. But there were other rules. Things commanders would allow with a nod, without words, when not on US soil, when what you were doing wasn't working, when you ran out of options and your captive wouldn't talk, when you had a deadline and the clock was ticking, and when you were desperate.

He wasn't sure how long he'd been out. Hard to tell. Maybe twenty minutes. Maybe less. Either way, the men wouldn't return with their prize for at least another hour. Because Tamara and Marcus lived thirty minutes away. It would take them at least an hour total to get there and back. Maybe less at this time of night. But they'd need time to knock on the door and convince her to go with them. She would know better. They would force their way in. There'd be a struggle, and they'd hurt her and drag her away. They would run upstairs and find Marcus asleep. The boy slept through everything: loud TVs playing old reruns of *Magnum P.I.* he'd watch in the next room, fireworks set off by neighbors on the Fourth of July. Only the sounds of his mother sobbing in the car would jolt his son awake, back to the land of the living.

He figured he had time before they arrived. Not much, but some. Enough time to come up with a plan. Enough time to lure silver hair over to him, enough time to get close enough to do something to him. Maybe with his legs. Or maybe the zip ties were loose enough to slide past his wrists up to his forearms. Maybe the leverage along with pure adrenaline would allow him to break free and take the older guy out.

Then he realized he was wrong.

About everything.

Because a door behind him that he could not see opened hard and fast, and he heard two sets of footsteps. The men were back, faster than he expected. But he didn't hear Tamara struggling or Marcus crying. He heard nothing at all. Just the sound of heavy breathing, men who were back from completing a task and waiting for their boss to give them his next assignment. Which the silver-haired man did one minute later.

He ended the call and looked at his men from across the room and said, "Is it done?"

One of them said, "The cameras are taken care of. And we'll have someone handle the historical footage."

The man in charge dropped his phone into a jacket pocket and brought his hand back out holding a pistol. He looked across at his men and nodded at them once. They came into view, one on his right with another weapon, one on his left with a knife; then the zip ties were cut from his wrists. But there was nothing he could do. Not yet, anyway. Three against one. One gun and one knife against nothing but two closed fists. The silver-haired man said, "Since no one else knows, I have no need to keep you around. These men will see you down." He looked at him and smiled. Something in his face. His men started to laugh as he left.

## 2

His men acted fast. They were alert and seemed to be ready for anything, but had tired eyes and clearly had sleep on their minds. The pressure was off. Their boss had left the rest up to them. One of them cut the zip ties and said, "Get up."

He got up. Slow and easy, pushing down on the armrests, steadying himself as he stood for the first time in hours. The city lights outside the windows caught his attention again. They glimmered and glinted as he slowly moved his gaze from the outside world over to the man holding the knife, then over to the one with the gun.

The one with the knife said, "Now turn around and step out of the room. Nice and easy. No heroics."

He thought about that. He was larger than them. Much larger. He had restrained plenty of thugs like them in the past, using his knee along with the weight of his body to keep men on the ground while he fished out handcuffs. But his height and bulk would do him no good. A draw against a knife. A loss against a gun.

"Don't think about it, hero," the man said again.

He thought about Marcus, wondering if his son was still alive or if the men had killed the boy and his mother.

He turned and moved toward the door and pushed it open. The men were maintaining a safe distance.

He waited until he got through, and then he kicked backwards and heard it click shut.

The whole thing was ludicrous. He knew that. Especially when a shot was fired through the door, shattering glass, the round buzzing an inch from his head, the bullet lodging into the wall as he turned and sprinted down the long hallway. But he had to do something. He'd only bought himself a few seconds. Five tops. A second by kicking the door closed. Another for the men to register what was happening. A third for the one with the gun to decide whether or not to take a risk. A fourth when he made his decision and fired the weapon. A fifth when the one with the knife stepped forward and pulled the door open again.

By then he was only fifteen feet ahead of them, scanning desperately for a stairwell, realizing there wasn't one. Not along that stretch of the hallway. There were no other doors, either. They were near the corner of the building. He only saw two things: an elevator bay directly in front of him and the two men directly behind him, looking at each other, then looking at him, and walking slowly in his direction. They laughed to themselves like they had when their boss had told them to escort him down. Some kind of shared understanding. Maybe that he wouldn't be able to use the elevator for some reason. Maybe because that wasn't an exit and the only way out was to get past them, which he was clearly not going to be able to do.

He considered trying it. Maybe waiting for them to approach and rushing them. Then he reconsidered.

So he ran toward the elevator bay.

It was directly in front of him now. He sprinted and pressed the down button. It turned a pinkish color as he pressed it again and kept pressing it repeatedly. He turned back and saw the men approaching slowly. They looked at each other as they moved. Then they faced forward, and the one with the gun lifted it high.

"Where do you think you're going?" the man asked.

He said nothing back. Just stared and watched helplessly as the men walked right up to him. A chime sounded behind him. A second after that, the elevator opened. The men stood in silence, staring some more as ten long seconds passed; then the doors closed. He said, "I thought you were going to let me go?" Which made the men laugh again. The one with the knife pressed the button.

But not the one to go down.

THIRTY SECONDS LATER THE ELEVATOR CHIMED OPEN AGAIN, and he was spun around and pushed forward. He turned back and saw the gun still aimed high and the knife held low. Then the one with the knife dug a keycard from his pocket and held it against a reader. The light on the reader changed from red to green. Then he pressed the top button on the panel. The doors closed, and they rocketed upwards, then it slowed. The elevator stopped. The doors opened. The guy with the knife moved on and climbed a set of stairs. He opened a hatch and disappeared. The guy with the gun rested it on the back of his head and said, "Move."

He moved, slowly and cautiously, and as he climbed the hatch, he could hear air conditioner units blowing hard and loud. Distant vehicles driving fast and planes flying overhead and all of the sounds ignored during the daytime that become loud and obvious during the night. Then he was outside. Out on the roof.

The man with the knife held out his free hand and beckoned him with it, glancing over his shoulder as he walked backward. As they moved, the large man noticed the sky. There wasn't a cloud in it. The stars were out, and the air was crisp. The moon shined brightly. It cast light on one side of the guy with the knife's face as the guy stepped sideways and pointed, then joined the man with the gun, and they boxed him in.

And then he understood: somehow, some way, he was about to die.

He said, "What are you going to do to me?"

The men smiled. He could see it on their half-lit faces. An inside joke. Like whatever it was they had planned they'd done before, maybe. But they said nothing back to him. Then the one with the knife motioned for him to turn around. When he didn't obey, the guy with the gun stepped forward toward him.

"Your boss is wrong," he said.

"Wrong how?" the guy with the gun replied.

"He thinks I didn't talk to anyone. He's sure of it. But he doesn't know for sure, does he?"

"He's good at reading people. He's spent his entire career doing it."

"I know who he is, and I know who you guys work for. I have friends who will hunt you down and kill you."

The man with the gun shook his head. A small little movement. He said, "Shut up and turn around."

The guy grabbed hold of the bottom of his weapon. Two hands on it now. One to keep it steady, one to pull the trigger. The one with the knife hung back, by the door, letting his partner do the rest. The large man felt loose gravel underneath his shoes. No sudden moves. He'd slip and skid, and it would be game over. He decided to give it another try. One last chance to save his life. He said, "Believe me or not. Your choice. But if something happens to me, you're a dead man. Both of you. Your boss and anyone else involved in this is, too. I called someone before I left," he lied. "I told them what I was doing and where I was going."

The man with the gun stared at him for a long moment. Then he said, "You're lying."

He said nothing back as he turned and looked out at the bright lights down below.

The man with the gun went quiet. Thirty long seconds. Thinking, deciding. He said, "Tell me the name."

Then the large man took a deep breath in and let it out as he stared back at him. Then he told him a name.

# 3

I was sitting in my office, eight a.m., drinking a hot cup of freshly brewed coffee and planning my day when I heard a knock at the door. I looked up and saw Emma Ross standing there staring at me.

"How'd you get in here?" I asked.

She pulled a keycard from her pocket and showed it to me. "My father asked me to stop by," she said, referring to Tom Parker, the guy who ran the covert black ops unit hidden deep within the Department of Homeland Security, where I work.

I pointed to the two chairs across from my desk and gestured for Emma to take a seat. "Coffee?"

Emma stepped inside and said, "I'd never turn down coffee," as she sat in one of the chairs and settled in.

I got up and walked to the corner of my office and found a cup and filled it high with the decanter. I said, "What do you want in it?" and she said caffeine, so I left it black and handed it across and sat back down.

"I like what you've done with the place," she said with a hint of sarcasm, taking a sip and glancing around. Her eyes danced around the room. There were stacks of notebooks piled high. Unpacked boxes. Only two pictures on my desk, a blurry photo of my wife, Jami, and me at a restaurant in Chicago on our first date, and a grainy, fifteen-year-old picture of my late buddy Jon Miller and I at Camp Rhino in Afghanistan in battle dress uniform. She picked it up and read the inscription Jami had made for the front of the frame. "Sometimes there's justice and sometimes there's just us." She glanced up and stared. "You believe that?"

"It's just a saying, Emma. And Einstein thought a messy desk was a sign of genius. He turned out okay."

"Cluttered office, cluttered mind," Emma said as she set the picture down and picked up her coffee again. She looked tired. I figured she'd been pulling double duty lately: late nights at the hospital with her father as he recovered from a gunshot wound, and long days at a new job at the CIA, working with their stateside agency, the Department of Domestic Counterterrorism, where Jami worked and where I'd worked a long time ago, in the Chicago field office, in a former life. I took a long sip of my coffee and said, "How is he?"

Emma became present and looked at me. "Okay," she said softly. "They think he'll make a full recovery."

"I'm surprised he's not back already."

She smiled and looked away. "If they'd let him out, he would be. He has a long road ahead of him."

"You can tell him everything's okay here."

"You should tell him yourself. He's asking about you."

I nodded. "Maybe I will. So why are you here?"

Emma thought for a moment. She took a breath and let it out. "We picked up a few searches for you. Someone was looking you up. We have alerts set up for a few key people. My father insisted you be added to it. Same with Jami.

When we get a hit, they call me. So I'm here to tell you. So consider yourself told. Watch your back for a few weeks. Look over your shoulder. Lock your doors at night. That kind of thing."

"What were the searches?"

"Your name," she said. "Blake Jordan. Chris Reed's name came up, too. Both of you had multiple hits."

I shrugged. "My name was in the paper. Just over a year ago, when the *Times* was trying to take down President Keller for putting together a black ops team. The first time. Before Keller hid us under DHS."

Emma stared at me again and shook her head. "It wasn't that kind of search. It was internal, Blake."

I narrowed my eyes. "What do you mean?"

"I mean the people looking you up were on an IP address tied to the Central Intelligence Agency."

I shrugged again. "So then you know who did it."

She said, "No, we don't. They used masking software. Sometimes we have to—" she lowered her chin and maintained eye contact "—intervene when other agencies are going off the deep end. Kind of like the military police who maintain law and order within their designated branch of the military. We do the same kind of thing for the Bureau, DHS, DDC, you name it. We have people who monitor their people. And as you can imagine, those people are untraceable. For deniability purposes. They'd have to be, right?"

I leaned back in my chair. "Maybe someone wants to promote me. Maybe they want to give me your job."

Emma forced a smile and took another sip of coffee and set the mug down. "Just watch your back, okay?"

"Always."

My cell phone rang. I dug it out of my pocket and looked at the caller ID. It was Chris Reed, my best friend who worked at the Bureau. I declined the call and set the phone facedown on the desk and glanced back at Emma. Then I started thinking about her father. Parker had taken a bullet just one week earlier. It was both the worst and the best thing that could've happened to him. It had taken him out of commission for a while, but it had also given him a chance to reconnect with his granddaughter after enduring a strained relationship with Emma for years, as she brought Elizabeth to the hospital to see him. "Anything I can do for him?"

"For my father? Besides making time to see him? No. Well, maybe try not to run his unit into the ground."

"Not much to run, just me and one analyst." I paused. "But tell him I have everything covered."

Emma said I should tell him myself as my desk phone rang, loud and shrill in the quiet office. It startled Emma. She stared at me, then glanced down at the phone. "Jordan," I said, answering on the second ring.

"It's me," a familiar voice said from the other end of the line.

"What's up, Chris?"

"We have a problem. And I could use your help."

I checked my watch and looked up. Emma was staring at me again. I said, "Where are you?"

"Hoover Building."

I nodded to myself and said, "I'm on my way."

# 4

Chris Reed set the phone down and leaned back in his chair. He looked up at the ceiling for a long moment, trying to make sense of things. Then he sat forward and checked his watch and did the math. Five minutes for his friend to get to his car. Twenty minutes to drive from DHS headquarters at the Nebraska Avenue Complex to the Hoover Building. But Blake would make the drive in less than that. Another couple of minutes to get through security. So in total he had twenty minutes until he had to be back in his office to get the call from the security desk. Or maybe he'd just go and meet Blake downstairs. He made a mental note of the time and stepped into the hallway and took the stairs up one flight to the fourth floor. Reed exited to an identical hallway. Identical to his in almost every way possible. Only up here, there were fewer people buzzing around. Fewer phone calls to take. Not as much paperwork to file. Not on a Saturday morning. Even the FBI let nonessential employees take weekends off. It wasn't like the movies. Field agents, such as himself, were a different story. He worked when he needed to, day or night.

And that was why he was worried.

Reed hustled down the long dark hallway and passed a joint workroom on his left. He saw a whiteboard, where twenty-four hours earlier he had stood and used a dry-erase marker to map out the plan. There had been an agreement. He'd shown what he'd drawn up to FBI Director Peter Mulvaney. His boss had made some adjustments, as every boss does, even if the plan was perfect in its original state. Because bosses had to show they were the boss. They had to show they still had it, that they were still capable. But Mulvaney wasn't worried about the assignment. Like he was just going through the motions. Dotting *I*s and crossing *T*s. So Reed made the adjustment, and Mulvaney approved the approach, and the plan was agreed upon.

But Reed's partner was late, which happened from time to time. The truth was, the specific time they'd planned to go in didn't matter much. They had a window. Zero dark thirty, they called it in the military. Just a humorous way to describe an unknown time in the middle of the night. Mulvaney was former military himself and declared it meant thirty minutes after midnight. But Reed didn't like specifics. Yes, details mattered, and yes, precision mattered, but he'd always attributed his success to his ability to be flexible. His partner knew that. They told their boss what he wanted to hear. But they did their own thing.

Reed arrived at the Hoover Building thirty minutes after midnight after a few hours of sleep. He'd gone to his office to get ready. But there wasn't much to get ready for. It was just a simple meeting with a former CIA employee. Someone who wanted to be discreet. Someone who wanted to meet when the world was asleep because they had information to share—damning information. But someone who was worried and wanted a clandestine meeting. He brewed a cup of coffee and sat in his office and thought through the details of the assignment. He played it out in his mind like an athlete would before a game, and he waited.

But his partner didn't show up.

At one in the morning he tried calling his cell. There was no response. At two he tried again. No reply. At three, he headed up to the fourth floor, much like he was doing now, and walked down to the man's office. Maybe he had misunderstood. Maybe he was sitting there waiting on him to show up. Maybe they'd have a laugh about it and head out. It was still dark out and would be for at least three more hours. And they didn't need three hours for their task. But the office was dark and silent. Nobody was waiting inside it.

The office light had turned on, like it did now as he walked through the doorway and the motion sensor caught him. Reed looked around, like he'd done hours earlier, and saw the same things that he saw now.

A jacket on the chair. A laptop docked but turned off. A notepad with sloppy handwriting he couldn't read.

CHRIS REED SPENT THE NEXT SEVERAL MINUTES LOOKING around the office, finding nothing interesting. There was an empty water bottle on the desk. He tried to open a desk drawer, but it was locked. The movement was enough to jostle the mouse, which woke up the laptop. A lock screen displayed. The FBI logo lit up bright on the screen for a minute, waiting for the laptop's owner to enter their password. Then the screen faded to black, and the computer went back to sleep. Reed stepped out and closed the office door behind him, partly out of habit whenever he left his own office, and walked down the long hallway.

He found the elevator and stepped inside and checked

the time on his watch and decided to go down to the lobby to bypass the phone call to his office from security and wait for his friend to arrive there.

As he stepped out, his phone buzzed in his hand. Reed answered. It was his boss, Peter Mulvaney, who asked for an update from when they'd last spoken. Reed told him nothing had changed; his partner hadn't shown up yet. He wasn't in his office and no returned calls from his work or his personal cell phones.

Reed said he was worried. Mulvaney asked if this had ever happened before, and he said that it hadn't. But Mulvaney remembered differently. He heard Mulvaney laugh on the line and said he seemed to remember one time when Reynolds had overslept. But only once, and it was for a low-priority assignment. So the oversight wasn't completely out of the realm of possibility. But in Reed's opinion it wasn't like his partner. Mulvaney said he was on his way in and would be there in ten minutes, and they would talk about it more when he got there. Reed clicked off and remained standing by the elevators and looked toward the lobby entrance. But he didn't see his friend. Not yet. But there was a woman standing alone on the other side of the security desk, looking tired, speaking softly but urgently, running fingers through her hair, frustrated.

He looked past the woman and out through the glass doors and saw his friend appear in the distance. Reed stepped forward so he could greet him as soon as he entered and get him through security quickly.

But when he got closer to the security desk, the man sitting behind it heard him coming and turned back. He stared at him for a brief moment and stood up tall and said, "Agent Reed, I've been trying to call you."

"I was up on the fourth floor."

"I realized that eventually," the guard said, pointing at a long row of black-and-white monitors.

Reed looked at the monitors and saw a view of the fourth floor. Nothing was happening. Nobody was there. The third floor had more action, even for a Saturday morning. An analyst walked across the screen from a cubicle to an open office door and spoke to someone, then turned back and disappeared.

Reed refocused his attention and looked at the two of them and asked, "What's going on?"

The security guard stared at him, then looked at the woman, then glanced back again, as Reed put it together and realized that what the security guy needed to talk about had something to do with her, too.

Reed's friend was making his approach. Reed made eye contact and nodded at him through the glass door. Then he turned his attention to the woman and said, "I'm Agent Chris Reed. What can I do for you?"

The woman said nothing. Just stared at him with puffy, bloodshot eyes.

Like maybe she'd been awake all night, just like him.

Reed's friend stepped closer. He got to the door and pulled it open; then he stepped through but hung back at the door, letting it close behind him, sensing that something else was going on. Waiting his turn.

The security guy said, "Agent Reed, this is Tamara Reynolds." He paused. "I think you need to talk to her."

## 5

I watched as my friend stepped forward and got the security guy to sign the woman in. The guard spoke to him in low, hushed tones. Chris nodded as he listened. I stood back and waited my turn. The woman was asked for identification. She handed her ID across to the security guy, who filled out some paperwork, and then he handed the ID back along with a temporary badge. Then the guy looked up and motioned for me to step toward him as the woman walked toward the turnstiles and stepped through.

I had my ID ready. I'd done this a million times. The security guy knew me. But this time he didn't ask how my morning was going. He seemed preoccupied with the woman and her situation. He kept glancing back at her, looking worried, as he wrote down my information and handed my identification back with another temporary badge. I nodded once as I took both items from him and stepped through the turnstile.

Chris addressed both of us at the same time as we moved toward the elevators along the far side of the wall.

Which I thought was strange. I didn't know the woman. He clearly didn't know her, either. But he said the three of us needed to talk; there was a conference room on the third floor where we could meet.

It was a short ride up to the third floor. Reed led the way. He got to the door and gestured for us to step in. The woman entered, and I followed. She took a seat at the head of the table, and Chris sat to her right. I took the seat to her left. Both of us sat next to her. I was directly across from my friend. He looked at me. "Blake, this is Tamara Reynolds." His voice was full of concern and worry and suppressed emotion.

I offered my hand, and she took it. "Blake Jordan," I said. "Homeland Security."

Her grip was firm. Her hand was cold. She nodded vaguely and in a soft voice said, "I've heard the name."

She let go and crossed her arms on the table. I glanced at Chris, then turned back. I said, "Who are you?"

Tamara took a moment to collect her thoughts. She had clearly told security something concerning and relayed it to my friend as I had hung back by the entrance doors. But for my sake she repeated herself. "I'm married to a man who works at this building. An agent." She paused. "His name is Mark Reynolds."

I nodded and said, "I know Mark," and glanced at Chris. "We both do. In fact, he's Agent Reed's partner."

Tamara glanced right and looked at Chris and said, "I know. That's why I'm here."

Chris furrowed his brow and said, "Tell us what happened," as the woman set her hands on the table.

Tamara took a moment to collect her thoughts. I looked down at her hands. They were trembling. She glanced at

Reed, then at me for a moment, and began. "We had dinner yesterday. An early dinner. Around four thirty. He said he had a lot of work to do at the office and that he had an overnight assignment, too, but he'd be home by the time I woke up. I had a bad feeling about it. I can't explain why." She paused. "I went to my mother's house. With our son, Marcus. We woke up and had breakfast; then I drove back home. We do this sometimes when Mark is going to have a long night. I feel safer that way."

Chris said, "Go on."

Tamara Reynolds looked away. "We got home. I thought it would be like every other time. I thought Mark's car would be in the garage. I thought he'd be in bed sleeping until noon after a long night." She shook her head. "But his truck wasn't there. I parked and called his cell. It went straight to voicemail. Marcus was anxious to get inside. So we got out and walked in." Tamara turned to look at me and said, "The door had been kicked in. I looked inside. The house had been ransacked. So I came straight here."

THE WOMAN WALKED CHRIS AND ME THROUGH THE REST OF what had happened. She said she got Marcus back in the car and left as fast as she could. She tried calling Mark's cell again, but he didn't answer. Then she pulled her vehicle to the side of the road and had an idea. She and Mark had set up tracking on each other's devices months earlier. It was Mark's idea so he could find her if anything happened to her and Marcus. But it also worked in reverse. She was able to see where her husband was at any given time. Usually it showed him at the Hoover Building. Because when Mark went out into the field, he'd leave his personal phone at the office. He'd only take his work cell with him. Tamara accessed the application and found his cell phone turned off, but last located here, at the Hoover Building, about twelve hours earlier.

Chris and I looked at each other from across the table. I asked where their son, Marcus, was.

"I'm not telling you that," she said. Then Tamara paused for a long moment and lowered her gaze like she was reconsidering her response, and she said, "I'm sorry. Mark just told me to be careful with these kinds of things. He's in the car with my mother. In the parking garage. Another thing Mark told me I should do. He said if anything ever happens, take Marcus to your mother's and stay there. Only I couldn't stay. I had to check on him." She shook her head and looked away at nothing at all. "Something's wrong. I can feel it."

I said nothing.

Chris said, "Mark was supposed to meet me here early this morning. Just past midnight. We had a job out in the field. But he never showed. I did the same thing. I called his phone. No answer. I went up to his office and found his laptop docked and a jacket on his chair, but he was nowhere to be found." He paused a moment; then he asked, "Did you say the tracker on your phone said he was last here twelve hours ago?"

She nodded.

Reed furrowed his brow and checked his watch; then he looked across at me. "That would've been three hours before we were supposed to meet up. So he was here before I arrived. Which explains the laptop." He paused. "We need to talk to security. The guy downstairs just started his shift. Maybe he can pull the logs and tell us about his badge swipes. What time he came and left. And we need to check the garage."

I said, "Spot forty-two?"

Chris nodded. "I didn't even think to check when I got here."

"It's not there. The space was empty. I walked by it on my way in."

Chris Reed glanced left to look at Tamara and said, "Let's go bring them in," referring to her mother and son out in the garage. "We can set you up here. Get you whatever you need while we figure all of this out."

I said, "How old is your son?"

She swallowed and took a breath and said, "Nine."

I pointed at a television mounted in the corner. "I'm sure we can find something to keep him entertained."

She nodded vaguely and looked away and whispered, "There's got to be some kind of explanation for this."

Then there were two loud knocks at the door. We all turned and looked. I looked right; Reed turned left; Tamara turned back. Peter Mulvaney opened the door and took in the room. First he looked at me; then he glanced at Tamara; then he stared down at my friend. He said, "Reed, I need to see you—right away."

Peter Mulvaney left as quickly as he had arrived. Chris said he'd be back in a few minutes, and I said I'd walk the woman out to the parking garage and bring the family inside. We stepped out and moved along the dark corridor and over to the elevators. Neither of us spoke. I pressed the button, and we waited. I said, "I'm sure he's okay, ma'am," as the doors chimed open, and I gestured for her to step inside.

She moved ahead of me and said, "Please call me Tamara. And I pray you're right. For Marcus's sake."

The doors opened out to the lobby thirty seconds later,

and we walked toward the security desk. I explained to the guard what was happening, how Tamara had her mother and son out in the car, waiting. He said he knew that already. The woman at the guardhouse had called him with a heads-up when Tamara had arrived. I explained that we needed to get them upstairs, and he said it wouldn't be a problem, so we stepped out and found the car and the family. The boy named Marcus was in the backseat, using his grandmother's phone, playing a game. The grandmother was in the passenger seat, eyes closed, deep in thought. Or prayer. Tamara knocked on the glass and spoke in Spanish, and her mother stepped out and got Marcus out, and they all looked at me. Tamara spoke another few words, a few I picked up on. She explained that I was a federal agent and we were going inside together. Tamara's mother asked for her phone back, and the boy became present and stared at me with wide, curious eyes.

I crouched down slightly and offered my hand. "I'm Blake," I said. "What's your name?"

The boy took it cautiously, and we shook, and he said, "Marcus Reynolds Junior."

I smiled. He had his father's eyes. "Nice to meet you, Marcus."

He nodded vaguely as I stood up and motioned for Tamara and her mother to follow me. Marcus and I led the way as the two women spoke in hushed tones behind me. I picked up a few more words here and there, thanks to a few Spanish classes I had taken over the years. I said, "Your dad ever bring you here?"

"No, sir." The boy paused for a long moment. Then he said, "Do you work with my dad?"

"Not very often, but sometimes."

"Is he here? My mom says she can't find him."

"I don't know where he is, but the people inside this building will find him."

"You promise?"

I glanced down as we moved and forced a smile. "Yeah," I said. "I promise."

Marcus nodded, and I looked over my shoulder. Tamara and her mother were still talking in low voices. I turned back and glanced at the boy. "So your dad never brought you here? To see where he works?"

Marcus shook his head and looked down at the floor. Then he had an idea. "Can you give me a tour?"

"Well, there's not much to see, but I can at least show you his office. You can see where he sits all day except when he's out in the field." I glanced over my shoulder again. "If it's okay with your mom, that is."

Marcus nodded again, but said nothing back this time. We got to the entrance, and I could see Mulvaney waiting for us through the glass. Chris Reed was on the other side of the guard desk, looking ghost white. I held the door open, and Marcus, his mother, and grandmother stepped through.

Mulvaney sighed heavily.

MULVANEY GESTURED FOR THE GUARD TO LET THE WOMEN AND the kid through, and the man obeyed. I walked slowly behind them and used my temporary badge on the reader. Tamara asked Mulvaney what was wrong, and he simply explained that they needed to follow him. Chris stared at me. He already knew what was wrong. That much was clear. There was a conference room on the first floor near the elevators. Mulvaney said he wanted the woman and her mother and Chris Reed to go in there to talk; then he turned back and looked at me and pointed at the kid, then pointed away. *Get him out of here*, he was telling me.

I nodded my understanding. I turned to Tamara Reynolds and said, "Can I show him his dad's office?"

She nodded vaguely and bent down to give her son a hug; then she followed her mother into the room. Chris Reed followed Tamara in, and Mulvaney closed the door behind them. I hurried Marcus to the elevators as quickly as I could. They chimed open, and we hustled inside, and I pressed the button for four. Less than a minute later, we were walking out into the dark hallway and headed to Mark Reynolds's office.

"Is that it?" Marcus asked, pointing to the door we were headed to.

"That's it," I said. "Go on in."

He ran up to the door and stopped. He turned the handle and pushed it open. The room was dark. He stepped inside, and the light came on automatically. That surprised the boy. He turned and looked at me. "There's a sensor," I said, opening the door the whole way. "It turns on whenever it detects motion."

Marcus nodded like he understood and started looking all around the room. I followed him inside and stepped behind Mark's desk. The first thing I noticed was his laptop. It was docked, and I heard it humming as it sat idle, but the screen was off. It worked like the light. When it wasn't detecting typing, it turned off and went to sleep to conserve energy. I reached across and used my finger on the keyboard. The screen came to life, and a big FBI logo came on the display. I sat down in the chair behind the desk and thought about the boy's father. Mark Reynolds wouldn't have just left his laptop here, locked or not. He would've taken it with him if he was leaving for the day. But he would've left it here docked if he was just stepping out for a while, like I'd done a million times when leaving the office for coffee or lunch or an errand when I wasn't working out in the field. I thought about the timeline Tamara had given us. She'd seen his personal cell here, at this building, twelve hours earlier. Then it went offline. Which would've been nine thirty last night. Chris said they were supposed to meet at thirty minutes after midnight. I looked away and wondered where Mark had gone to. Then I thought: *What happened during those three hours?*

"My birthday's in two weeks," the boy said, out of nowhere. "I'll be ten. My dad's getting me a cat."

"Dogs are better," I said as I moved stray papers and glanced around, looking for clues. "More loyal."

"Maybe," he said and paused, thinking hard. "But my mom says I have to take care of it, and cats are easier. Plus my dad had a cat when he was a kid. He said they're smarter than dogs. And it takes more to gain their trust." Marcus turned and noticed something on the desk. "I gave this to my dad for Father's Day."

It was a small golden trophy with the words *World's Greatest Dad* inscribed on it, facing me. I had sat across from Mark many times and noticed the trophy, but hadn't seen the words on the front. I had no idea he was a father. I figured there was a lot about Mark that I didn't know. Marcus smiled broadly and turned to check out another area of the office as I dug my cell phone out from my pocket and called Mark's number. It went straight to voicemail. I dropped my phone back into my pocket and pulled on a drawer. It didn't open. I studied the locking mechanism. It was cheap. Typical government quality. It looked like the lock to my desk drawer at DHS. I dug into another pocket and found my knife. I opened the blade with my thumb and eased it into the lock. I turned it slowly. The lock clicked. I pulled the drawer open and saw a cell phone. Not government issued. A personal phone sitting in the drawer. I reached for it and turned it on.

# 6

Mark Reynolds's desk phone rang loud in the silence. Marcus had been standing at a bookshelf looking over books his father had collected throughout the years about Navy SEALs and Army Rangers and all sorts of military-themed motivational books. The phone rang again. The boy turned back. His eyes were wide. I sat forward and picked up the receiver and paused. Then I said, "Mark Reynolds's office."

I could hear faint sobbing in the background. Then Peter Mulvaney said, "Come on down; bring the boy."

"Okay," I said as I kept the receiver to my ear and listened.

Mulvaney sighed again like he had done downstairs. Clearly upset about something. Clearly not wanting to have to do whatever it was he was doing. Which I was starting to get a pretty good idea of what it was. There was more sobbing and words being spoken in Spanish in low voices; then the line went dead.

Marcus continued to stare at me. I set the phone down, and he said in a soft voice, "Was that my dad?"

I shook my head vaguely. "No, buddy. It wasn't him."

He furrowed his brow. "Who was it?"

"Your dad's boss. The man we met downstairs. The one talking to your mom. He wants us to head down."

Marcus looked away, disappointed; then he turned and went back to the books. I closed his father's desk drawer and got up out of the chair. Then I walked around the desk and stood next to him. I said, "You like to read?"

He nodded.

"Do you want to pick one out and take it home with you to look at?"

He chose the one he'd been eyeing and then turned and looked up at me. "Will he be mad?"

I thought, *I hope so. I hope he yells at me for searching his office.* But I just shook my head no.

He said, "I just like looking at the pictures. When I grow up, I'm going to join the Army. Just like he did."

"What about the Navy?"

Marcus made a sour face. "My dad doesn't like those guys. He says they're all weak. We cheer for Army."

I thought about that for a long moment; then I smiled. "You're talking about football, aren't you?"

He nodded, and I took the book from the boy and thumbed through it. I didn't see any language Mark would be concerned with. There were plenty of pictures in the middle of it. Pictures of the author, who was himself an Army Ranger, in his younger days, posing with his buddies. I thought about the picture on my desk a few miles away from here. The one Emma Ross had picked up earlier. The one with the caption on it that my wife had added to the frame for me: *Sometimes there's justice and sometimes there's just us.*

I glanced around the office one last time and saw Mark

had his own set of pictures. None were of his family. For safety reasons, I guessed. But plenty of his own memories with buddies from the service. He was in one of them standing in fatigues with friends, wearing dark aviators, a younger version of himself. Before he joined the FBI, before he knew Chris Reed and me, and before he had met Tamara, I guessed.

I closed the book and handed it over. I said, "I think this is a good one to start with. Let's head down now."

WE GOT BACK INTO THE ELEVATOR, AND I FELT SICK TO MY stomach. I had a very bad feeling about the next few minutes and what would be said when we got downstairs. The elevator doors chimed open, and Marcus stepped out in front of me. His mom and grandmother were waiting there for us. Tamara bent down and called Marcus over to her. She hugged him tight. The grandmother had tears in her eyes. The three of them huddled together, and then Tamara stood back up and looked at me, then turned back. Chris and Mulvaney were standing behind her. Chris was as white as a ghost. Mulvaney wasn't quite sure what to do. So he just stuck his hand out, and Tamara took it. He put his other hand on top of hers and said, "I'm very sorry. You're welcome to stay here for a little while if you need to. Or we can have someone stay with you."

"Stay with me," she managed to get out. "For a few hours at least. Until I can make sense of it all."

"Of course," Mulvaney said. "I just need the address where you'll be staying."

Tamara gave him her mother's address. Mulvaney had security write it down. Then she grabbed Marcus by the hand and looked at her mom and said, "¿Estás lista?" and her mother nodded solemnly, and they left.

"What the hell happened?" I whispered once they were out of earshot.

Mulvaney kept his eyes fixed firmly on Mark's family as they moved toward the exit and said, "Wait."

We waited for the three of them to get through the turnstiles, for Tamara to return her visitor's badge, to pass through the door, to step into the garage. We watched them through the glass doors until they disappeared. I turned to my right, and Chris turned to his left, and we formed a huddle around Mulvaney.

Mulvaney said, "Agent Reed called me earlier. He said Reynolds didn't show up for his assignment today. I thought he overslept. He'd done that once. He's had a lot on his plate lately. So I just brushed it off."

The Bureau director took a breath to collect his thoughts, and I said, "Go on."

Mulvaney crossed his arms. He looked at Chris, then turned to me and said, "I made some phone calls. First to security. They pulled his badge swipes, confirming he was here, at this building, before he went missing. Which he was. Then I called the George Washington University Hospital to see if something had happened to him. Maybe he went out for food and had a wreck." He shook his head. "But he wasn't there."

I said, "Are you telling me that Mark Reynolds is missing?"

Mulvaney shook his head again. He said, "I didn't have to make any more phone calls. They called me. Metro PD, to be specific. They were called to the scene a few hours ago. They just identified the body."

I narrowed my eyes. "He's dead?" I asked, knowing the answer, but not fully believing it was possible.

Mulvaney said nothing. I turned to Chris. He looked down and away. Defeated. Still white as a ghost.

"I don't understand," I said. "Was it a shooting?"

Chris said, "No."

Then Mulvaney said, "They found him half a mile north of us, behind a building, sprawled on the concrete." The Bureau man paused for a long moment. Seeing if I would put it together. Then realizing I wasn't and needed help. "He took his own life, Jordan. Based on the wounds, they think he fell thirteen stories. Maybe more." He paused again, longer this time; then he ran a hand across his face. "And it's all my fault."

# 7

We asked Mulvaney what he meant by that. He shook his head and said he'd given Mark Reynolds too big a workload lately, and it had pushed him over the edge. He glanced up and looked at Chris, who was standing quietly, arms crossed, and admitted he'd given everyone too much work over the past week. There just weren't enough Bureau agents to spread the work across and make progress on their backlog of cases. Ever since the assassination attempt a week ago when Russian President Aleksander Stepanov had visited the US to sign a peace treaty with President Keller, it was as if things had shifted into a higher gear.

I thought back to the events of last week: the attempt on Keller's and Stepanov's lives, which Jami, Tom Parker, and I had helped thwart, along with the help of Chris Reed and Mark Reynolds. Parker's extended stay at George Washington University Hospital as a result of a gunshot wound, effectively putting me in charge of our covert black ops unit at DHS. The increased threats of terrorism every agency seemed to be dealing with now as a result of the peace treaty. Mulvaney was right about one thing: we all had a heavier workload lately.

Mark Reynolds was Chris's partner. Mulvaney stood up straight and seemed to come to that realization. So he told Chris he should take the rest of the day off. It was a Saturday, and even though the Bureau had a huge backlog of work, he needed Chris to take some time to come to terms with the news about Reynolds. In the meantime, Mulvaney would make some calls to the rest of the staff to make them aware. Chris tried to argue with him, but his boss wouldn't have it. Mulvaney held his hands up and insisted. Then he turned and headed for the elevators and disappeared as he headed to his office on the third floor.

I stepped aside and called Jami. My wife wasn't due in to the DC field office at the Department of Domestic Counterterrorism until tomorrow. I gave her the quick version of what had happened. She asked if there was anything she could do. I said I didn't know, but I'd be in touch if something came to mind. I clicked off and walked back over to my friend, who was standing alone, arms still crossed, thinking hard. "Jami sends her condolences." I paused a long moment and put a hand on his shoulder. "I'm sorry, man."

Chris said nothing.

I said, "Are you okay?"

He shook his head slowly and said, "I have to tell you something." He looked around. "But not here."

I nodded and glanced around and said, "Then let's go," and we walked to the parking garage together.

We took my vehicle and left the Hoover Building. I said there was a diner nearby. One I went to sometimes, before or after meetings I had with Bureau people since it was close by. Chris said nothing back. So I headed that way, and two minutes later, we were climbing out of my Tahoe and walking into Lincoln's Waffle Shop. We sat at the counter overlooking the street, and the waitress came by and asked what she could get us. We both ordered coffee, black. Chris wasn't in the mood to eat. But I'd lived by an old Navy saying for close to half my life: *eat when you can; sleep when you can*. I ordered breakfast, and she hurried off and reappeared a minute later holding two mugs with one hand and a glass decanter in the other. She set the mugs down and poured the dark brew and hustled away to offer a warm-up to other customers sitting around sipping coffee. Chris didn't take a drink. He just held onto his mug. He twisted it around, deep in thought, troubled, trying to make sense of the senseless, I imagined.

I took a sip and looked at my best friend. I said, "Chris, talk to me. Tell me what's on your mind."

He turned and looked me dead in the eye. "I don't believe any of this. Mark would never kill himself."

WE SAT IN SILENCE FOR A FULL MINUTE. THEN TWO. THEN three. I drank my coffee and looked around, watching the regulars being greeted by our waitress, getting their orders taken, then being served their own cups of coffee while they waited for breakfast. There were all kinds of people in the diner. Young, old, men in suits, women dressed up for a morning out, people who had gone out for a jog and stopped in. Mothers meeting other mothers with kids crawling all around, breaking free and playing underneath tables with their moms scolding them, telling them the floors were dirty. Young couples watching, admiring, looking at each other, then back at the kids, clearly wanting children of their own. Older couples past that part of their lives, looking on, maybe with grown kids of their own, glad to be in another phase of their lives. My thoughts drifted back to little Marcus and his wonderment as he looked all around his dad's office. A boy who had heard about his father's line of work but had known so little.

Chris broke the silence. He said, "We spoke yesterday. We made plans to meet up just past midnight. Someone who's going to kill themselves wouldn't do that. They'd be vague about plans. They'd be tentative. He was neither." Chris paused. "When I first called Mulvaney, he laughed about it. Because Mark had slept in once, a while back. Mulvaney seemed to think he'd done it again." Reed shook his head. "He never did. Mulvaney had him confused with someone else. Someone who left DC ages ago. He's at the Tampa field office or somewhere else. It wasn't Mark. He never stood me up. Never had and never would."

Chris took a sip of his coffee for the first time and set the mug down on the table and held onto it with two hands. Then he leaned back and glanced away again. We were sitting at the front of the room. We were both positioned well. I could see the entrance perfectly. He could see the exit. Our waitress came back and warmed up our coffees. She didn't have to ask. Just assumed and poured. Then she left again.

I glanced at my friend and said, "I searched his office."

Chris furrowed his brow and locked eyes with me. "You what?"

"When I took Marcus upstairs. I took him to see his dad's office, and while I was there, I looked around."

He stared and blinked. "What did you find?"

"A cell phone in a locked drawer. I used my knife to get in. I assume his personal cell. Not Bureau issued."

Chris thought about that. Then he said, "If he was going to kill himself, he wouldn't lock the drawer."

I said, "There's something else." Chris maintained his stare but said nothing back. "You don't see it?"

He looked away for a long moment, ignoring the children at the adjacent table, looking past them, through them maybe, thinking hard. Then he got it. He looked back at me and said, "Where's his vehicle?"

I nodded. "It would be near the building where they found his body. Somewhere in the area. Wouldn't it?"

"How do you know it's not?"

"You think something happened to Mark. I don't. So put your mind to ease: see if they've found the SUV."

Chris must've thought that was a good idea, because he dug into his pocket for his cell and made some calls while I drank my coffee and thought hard, wondering where Mark had been during the three-hour gap. Our waitress brought my food. Two eggs over easy, corned beef hash and toast, then she gave me a warm-up by refilling my coffee. I sat there eating and thinking and listening to one side of three separate phone conversations. Then Chris clicked off and turned to me. He said, "They can't find his SUV anywhere."

# 8

Emma Ross parked her car and stepped out and looked up at the two gigantic buildings at the Central Intelligence Agency's sprawling headquarters in Langley, Virginia. She walked toward the main entrance, where she'd have to pass through security before heading to her office inside the Original Headquarters Building, when her cell buzzed loud in her pocket. She saw the call was from her daughter, Elizabeth. Knowing she'd lose the signal once inside, she remained outside the entrance and answered, "Hi, sweetie."

"What time are you coming home? Suzie doesn't know how to make grilled cheese the way you do."

In the background, Emma heard her friend say that she *did* know how, and she was working on it.

Emma smiled. "You need to learn to make it yourself, baby girl."

"I know, Momma." Elizabeth paused a moment, and then she said, "Suzie wants to talk with you."

"Okay, put her on. I'll see you after work; I love you."

There was a rustling sound on the line, and then her friend said, "The hospital called again."

Emma tucked a lock of hair behind her ear and furrowed her brow. "About Tom?"

Suzie paused. "He's just trying to push himself instead of resting. Also, I hate it when you call him that."

She nodded knowingly. "Fine—my *father*, not Tom. I'm trying my best, Suz; be patient with me."

"I always have been and always will be. I know old habits die hard, but you need to make a real effort, Emma. For Elizabeth's sake." She didn't respond for several moments, so Suzie added, "She likes two slices of cheese. Just like her mother. I watched you make plenty of grilled cheeses at Yale. How could I forget?" Suzie laughed to herself. "Anyway, just wanted to check in. Take your time; we're doing okay over here."

Emma smiled again. "Thank you again for watching her. I'll pick up dinner, so don't go making anything." She clicked off and stuffed her cell back into her pocket and stepped inside. Emma got through security and reached the elevator doors. They opened on their own, and a group of half a dozen men and women stepped out and headed for the cafeteria. She checked her watch and saw that it was ten. Late morning. Emma wasn't hungry. She moved past them and entered the elevator and pushed the button for her floor.

The doors closed fast, and less than a minute later, they opened again. She made her way down a long corridor and to a door with a card reader. Emma swiped her badge and pulled it open and saw her assistant sitting dutifully at her desk. "Good morning, Samantha," Emma said as the woman turned around to greet her, and Emma brushed past her and grabbed the handle to her office door to pull it open.

"Ms. Ross, I need to speak with you for a moment."

Emma turned and stared back. She let go of the handle. "Of course, what is it?"

Samantha looked up at her with wide eyes. Something important to share. "Mr. Malone was just here."

"David Malone?" she asked. "He was here? In my office? Looking for me?"

Samantha nodded urgently. A fast little movement. "He said he needs to see you immediately."

EMMA SPENT THE NEXT SEVERAL MINUTES ASKING QUESTIONS. Why was he here? What did he want? And why was the man wanting to talk to her directly instead of communicating through her boss, Alex Gardner? The process had been made perfectly clear when she started with the Agency. She needed to follow the chain of command. Gardner had emphasized this point—never disobey an order, and never go over your boss's head. And if your direct reports had directs themselves, she shouldn't talk to them, either.

Emma didn't give a damn about office politics. She wasn't there to make friends. But she didn't want enemies, either. At least not yet. Not until she'd made it through her ninety-day probation period. She told Samantha her badge wouldn't work. Gardner always had to take her to the New Headquarters Building. Samantha said Mr. Malone took care of it. She stood and opened the door and motioned for Emma to go.

Which she did, slowly and cautiously, trying to understand what this was all about. Emma didn't take the elevator this time. She took the stairs. Gardner had escorted her to Malone's office once before, a week earlier, on the day Russian president Aleksander Stepanov was set to sign a peace treaty with President Keller. Emma stepped out and hurried past the cafeteria, through a courtyard, and to an inner entrance that led to the NHB. She reached for her badge and stretched her hand out to the card reader.

It turned green. There was an audible click. Emma reached for the handle and pulled it open and stepped through. She moved down the warren of corridors Gardner had taken her through before, trying to remember exactly where she had been led to. Emma found a set of managerial offices and looked at the nameplates outside each of them. She knew it was on the left. Emma found one that read D. MALONE.

SHE KNOCKED ON THE DOOR AND HEARD HIM CALL FOR HER TO enter. She turned the handle and pushed it open a foot and saw David Malone stand from behind his desk. Which was different. The last time she had been here, the man had stayed seated the entire time. A power move, she figured, sending a clear message: I'm important and you're not. He smiled and motioned for her to step inside and offered his hand and told her to have a seat. Emma closed the door behind her and sat on a chair in front of his desk.

"Ms. Ross, I never got a chance to thank you," Malone said.

"Thank me, sir?"

"Yes," he said. "The last time we met, I was under a lot of pressure. The situation with President Stepanov had us very concerned. Especially with the venue where he and Keller were going to sign that peace treaty. The president was hell-bent on having it in a place that was too exposed. We urged him to change the venue, but he wouldn't listen. Same with the Bureau. Even the Secret Service was telling him to move it." Malone smiled. "But somehow, you managed to get it done. Please, Ms. Ross, tell me—how did you do it?"

Emma looked away for a moment. "I just used my connections. I talked some sense into some people."

"And?" His tone of voice was telling. It said: I know what you did, so don't lie to me about it.

She glanced back and stared across the desk. Something in the man's eyes. "And I may have blackmailed someone. Ethan Meyer, to be exact," she said, referring to the president's current chief of staff. The role she'd once held for James Keller. "He wouldn't listen to me. So I alluded to the fact that I had dirt on him."

Malone smiled again and nodded approvingly. "However you did it, the point is, whatever you did worked. President Keller changed the venue. You did what you had to do. No complaints from me." The man paused. He leaned back and crossed his legs. "Do you remember our last conversation? About how the CIA works? I told you we take care of our people. Follow orders and you'll move up in the ranks. Don't and you won't."

Emma nodded. "I remember."

Malone said, "You followed orders. We had an impossible task, convincing a sitting president to do something we needed him to do. He wouldn't listen to anyone. But he listened to you. Indirectly, that is."

"Mr. Malone, with all due respect—we should've let the two presidents have their peace treaty signing at the original location. With what happened on the South Lawn, I'm not sure that location ended up being any safer." She paused. "I don't think I did anything to help that day. I may have even made things worse."

"A DHS agent was compromised. You're not to blame for what happened. Your *father's* to blame for that."

Emma narrowed her eyes and stared across.

Malone leaned forward and made a motion with his hands that said: Let's forget about that for a moment. He said, "Ms. Ross, the point is, I don't know you very well, but you appear to be someone I can trust. Someone who will find a way to get the job done, no matter what. A real team player. I like team players."

"I assume that's why Mr. Gardner hired me."

Malone pursed his lips and looked away as if the conversation had led him precisely to the point he wanted to make, a point that seemed to bother him, a conversation maybe he would much rather avoid. "Alex Gardner is no longer with us. The details aren't important. Just know that he wasn't a team player."

Emma fidgeted in her chair and tucked a lock of hair behind her ear. She said, "I don't understand."

Malone leaned forward some more, set his hands on his desk, and interlaced his fingers. "Your father, the Bureau, the Secret Service, even the president himself have told me to stand down over what Agent Jordan did. They've assured me there was never a real threat to the president's life on the South Lawn. They all tell me he was playing along with the terrorists, to figure out who their man on the inside was."

"And he did," she said. "He found out."

Malone nodded knowingly and said, "Yes, and no."

Emma shook her head slightly and narrowed her eyes again. "What do you mean?"

"The presidential motorcade. We had some of our own people involved. Jordan and your father took them out. Have you asked yourself how our people knew the path of the motorcade? We had assets on the ground. In that safe house. Turncoats. Clearly involved in the assassination attempt. But who told *them*?"

"I assume Agent Rivera is running that down," she said, referring to the presidential detail's lead agent.

"Don't ever assume anything, Ms. Ross. The Secret Service is good at one thing—protecting the president. They don't know how to investigate these things. They'll never get to the bottom of it. They need our help."

"Is Agent Rivera asking for our help?"

"No," he answered. "I am."

Emma made no reply. Just fidgeted in her chair again. Silence in the room.

"Ms. Ross, I want you to meet with the president. Come up with a plan. Figure out who leaked the route of the motorcade, allowing some of our people to make an attempt on Keller's life. So we can keep him safe." He paused a beat. "I've told you before, I know everything about you. You crave power. And you're an ambitious woman. First as Keller's chief of staff, then working for the former mayor of New York, now here at the Agency. Prove your worth and I'll have you replace Gardner. Fail, and I'll have you join him."

## 9

THE SILVER-HAIRED MAN PACED HIS OFFICE AND CHECKED HIS watch. He didn't have a window to look out of. A precaution. His cell phone didn't even work from where he stood. Which was perfectly fine with him. But his landline worked and was as secure as anything else. Maybe even more so than a burner phone or a satellite phone with encryption and cloaking mechanisms and anything else men like him might need.

News of the Bureau man made its way around Washington, DC, fast. But not faster than he expected it to. Devoting your life to one of service often meant living in cheap apartments, accumulating debt, living a life without luxury. Federal agents didn't do it for the money. They did their jobs for one reason and one reason alone—in service to the country that they loved.

But mental health was a known issue. Federal agents were prone to taking their own lives. More so than non-federal workers. That was what he was counting on everyone thinking. That was what he wanted them to believe, that the Bureau man had had enough and had come to the end of his rope and had simply given up.

But the vehicle was a problem.

So he had given specific instructions on what should be done with it.

His people had taken their time disconnecting the GPS device. That way it couldn't be located. The vehicle might be found eventually, but by then so much time would have passed, nobody would care anymore. The agent would be buried. Anyone who cared would've already moved on.

And there was another problem: the name the Bureau agent had given to his men.

The name of someone else who supposedly knew what the man they had killed knew: the man's partner. He believed it was a lie intentionally told as a message for his partner by way of involving him, a message telling him that something was amiss. A warning. The silver-haired man's people believed it was true. He did not. His landline rang, loud and shrill in the otherwise quiet office. He remained standing and lifted the receiver. "It's done," one of his men said immediately, not waiting for a greeting.

"Will they find it?"

"I don't see how," the voice responded. "I'm told it was hidden well. All precautions were taken, sir."

The silver-haired man nodded to himself and looked away. "Good work. Anything else?"

"I found Agent Reed," the voice said. "He went into a diner with another man. They're about to leave."

"Who's the other man?"

"Jordan, the one we used last week." There was a long pause on the line. "I can take them both out, sir."

The silver-haired man thought about it. "No," he said. "Only Reed. And not yet. We have plenty of time."

"If he really does know about us, it's a loose end. If we don't take him out now, when? What if I lose him?"

The silver-haired man smiled. "You won't," he said. Then he set the phone back down onto its cradle.

## 10

I wasn't expecting the vehicle to be missing. I was expecting it to be found maybe a block or two away, to prove my point that nothing was wrong. Which meant that maybe Chris was onto something. I dropped cash on the table as Chris stared out the window. He said, "Hey, see that guy in the black sedan?"

I shifted my eyes left, and I saw him. He was sitting in a black vehicle, dark-tinted windows, but not dark enough. Not at the front. And not with the late morning sun shining through at the perfect angle, illuminating the driver clearly. One person inside the vehicle, a man sitting behind the wheel. I said, "Yeah, I see him. Why?"

Chris kept staring out and said, "He's been there a long time."

"How long?"

"Since we got here."

I said, "Maybe he's waiting for someone."

He kept looking at it and said, "It looks government issued, the make, the model, the tint. This is going to sound crazy, but I have a feeling he's here for me."

"Did you pay your taxes this year?"

Chris said nothing back. He was still frazzled from the news about Mark.

I leaned to the side and reached into my pocket. I pulled my keys out and set them on the table. I looked at the saltshaker. It was tiny and wide but had a sharp point to it. I stuffed it into my pocket. I said, "Take my truck. Drive it around the block. Pull to the side of the road. Take your phone out and act like you got a call. Make a big show of it. Keep your window rolled down. See if the guy tries something. My guess is you're wrong." I turned and looked in the kitchen. I saw a back exit. "I'll meet you out there."

"And if I am wrong?"

"You're buying lunch."

CHRIS REED TOOK THE KEYS AND STEPPED BACK OUT OF THE diner, alone, toward the parked SUV. He didn't remember seeing the guy in the sedan when they arrived. He must've pulled up a few minutes later and then parked in a spot where he could watch the door, which seemed to be where he was looking and not inside the diner. Chris glanced over his shoulder and saw reflective glass from the outside. So no way of the guy seeing much inside anyway, unless it had been nighttime, in which case the fluorescents overhead would've allowed the guy to see everything inside. But it wasn't nighttime. It was a bright, sunny morning.

He fumbled with the key fob and unlocked the driver's door and climbed inside. The seat needed to be adjusted slightly, but he left it as it was. No need to make the guy wonder what he was doing. The guy didn't seem to be paying any attention to him now anyway, from what he could tell. For the next few moments, Reed thought he was just being paranoid. He thought about his friend awkwardly walking through the kitchen, moving between waitresses and cooks, maybe a manager yelling at him, stepping out the back door, orienting himself, getting ready to hustle down a back alley, only to find Chris parked there waiting on him. He thought: *I'm going to buy him dinner, too*, as he started the motor and shifted the gear. Reed threw it into drive and tapped the gas. He glanced up at the mirror as he drove.

Behind him the black sedan started to move, slow wheels speeding up, maintaining a necessary distance.

HE APPROACHED A STOP SIGN AND WATCHED THE REARVIEW mirror through his own tinted glass, seeing the sedan far behind, but there. Reed turned the corner without coming to a complete stop. *A guy in a hurry, not paying attention*, he thought as he dug into a pocket to find his cell phone. He accelerated and then slowed as he approached a second stop sign. Far behind, the sedan came into view and made the turn. Reed made another right turn and got halfway down the block and came to a stop on the side of the road on the other side of the diner. Same building, just parked on the north side of it now. He waited.

If he'd done it right, his friend would be headed right to him. He would've stepped out the back and moved fast, maybe crouched down low, between cars, waiting to step out. Hopefully watching him now.

Unless he wasn't. Unless there wasn't a northern exit from the back of the diner.

Reed glanced up and saw the sedan turn the corner and head straight toward him. But it wasn't a race. The driver wasn't speeding. It was more like a slow crawl, like the driver was deciding what to do about him being stopped. Like maybe he was looking left and looking right, maybe glancing over his shoulder both ways to make sure nobody was around. Reed saw the sedan still moving, a slow crawl toward him. Maybe five miles per hour. Making progress, but not enough to cause anyone concern. He grabbed his cell and pushed it to his ear and looked away, distracted, making a big show of it like his friend had suggested.

Then it happened. But not like he thought it would.

The sedan picked up speed, and it pulled a wide U-turn. Quick enough to get out of there fast, but not fast enough for its tires to squeal and attract attention. Chris looked up and watched through the mirror.

I HEARD THE TIRES TURNING HARD OVER GRIT AND THE SOUND of an engine revving hard. I stood from my kneeling position and watched as the black sedan to my left made a sharp U-turn and sped off, heading in the opposite direction. I stood fully and watched it disappear down a side street. My truck was on my right. I walked over to it and knocked on the glass. Chris unlocked the door, and I climbed inside.

"What was that about?" he asked.

"I don't know," I said as I shut the door.

"Do you think he saw you?"

"No," I said. "It was just a random person making a U-turn. I don't think it has anything to do with you."

Chris turned to his right and looked at me. "What were you going to do with the saltshaker? Season him?"

I reached below the seat for my gun. "I left it in the car. Had to use something. I was improvising."

"What do we do about that guy?"

"Nothing, Chris. You're overthinking this. Nobody's

following you. And there was no foul play with Mark. We're going to find his vehicle; then we're going to tell Mulvaney where he can pick it up." I dug into my pocket for my phone and dialed Simon Harris, my analyst at DHS. Simon answered on the first ring. I told him about Mark Reynolds. I said Chris and I were on our way, and we needed his help finding Mark's SUV.

I clicked off. Chris was staring. He said, "Mark was my partner, Blake. I knew him. He didn't kill himself."

## 11

CHRIS DROVE US TO THE NEBRASKA AVENUE COMPLEX AND called his boss on the way to make sure he knew about the missing vehicle. Mulvaney reminded him that he was supposed to take the rest of the day off. No need to come back to the Hoover Building. Mulvaney insisted that he take it easy and try not to think too much about what had happened. Not today.

But I knew Chris Reed. He was my best friend. And we had worked together for a long time, going back to when I ran the CIA's first Department of Domestic Counterterrorism office in Chicago. He was my number two. My assistant special agent in charge. We'd been through a lot over the years. We had both been fired after then-Senator James Keller had been kidnapped. Chris had landed at the FBI and moved out to DC. I wasn't too far behind, but took a job working for Tom Parker at Homeland Security. Even though we were now at different agencies, our paths still crossed thanks to joint task forces and interagency collaborations. As he drove, I thought about what he'd said about his partner at the Bureau: *I knew him*. And I knew Chris

Reed. He was a good agent. And he had good intuition. The problem was, he was wrong.

We pulled up to the guardhouse at the NAC. The guy stared at Chris; then he looked past him and stared at me. He had a confused look on his face, wondering why I wasn't driving my own vehicle. Then he shrugged his concern away and stepped back inside and pressed a button, and the big wrought-iron gate opened.

I showed Chris where to park, and we climbed out. He tossed my keys to me as we moved, and I stuffed them into my pocket. We got to the door of the long-forgotten building that was part of the DHS campus. I used a keycard to get us inside. We took the elevator up to the second floor, and I used my keycard again.

Simon Harris was sitting alone at his cubicle inside the large open space. A space Parker had envisioned would one day be filled with analysts just like Simon. And as his director of field operations, I wanted to help Parker get there. With enough funding and the right people, we could really make a difference.

Simon heard us step inside. He turned around in his cubicle as we approached his desk. He said, "I've already started looking at CCTV footage in the area." He turned back around and pointed at the large monitors on his desk. "There happened to be two cameras on the building directly across from the one Mark jumped from." Simon paused and looked up at Chris, realizing he needed to be a bit more sensitive to the situation. Then Simon turned to me. "I rewound it and saw him arrive. He parked a block away, but then something weird happened." He looked at Chris again. "I can explain it, but it's better if I show you."

Chris didn't reply. He just crossed his arms and nodded.

Simon turned back and rewound the footage. It

controlled the video from both cameras. The video was black and white. The action played backwards. Not much traffic in the middle of the night. A few cars moved in reverse across the two screens, each showing the vantage point from one of the cameras. The same vehicles entered one monitor and left the other as they moved across. Simon clicked on the rewind icon again, and the video moved faster as he looked for the section to show us. Then he paused the feed.

"There he is," Chris said, pointing at the monitor on the left. We watched as Mark Reynolds's vehicle moved across slowly and parked in front of a building a block away from where they found his body. His door opened, but nobody got out. Then the truck disappeared. It just completely vanished. Like the feed had been cut right then and there and spliced together with a new feed that started sometime later.

Simon fast-forwarded the feed. Black-and-white images of traffic flowing the right way moved across the screen. The occasional car or truck or bus became visible every now and then. Street lights changed quickly. The sky remained dark. Then Simon slowed it down, and the splice happened again, and then the sky was bright. No gradual transition with a falling moon to a rising sun. Just an abrupt switch from dark to light, from night to day. Simon paused the video and stared at the screens. "The feeds were tampered with. We're missing two gaps. A small one and a big one. Something happened they don't want us to see."

CHRIS AND I STOOD TOGETHER, ARMS CROSSED, TRYING TO understand why the tape had been altered. Chris said,

"Whatever happened during the two cuts, it involved Mark. Someone was covering their tracks."

I said nothing.

Chris turned and started pacing around the empty cubicles. Clearly frustrated. He ran a hand across his face. Then he stopped and looked out at nothing at all, just thinking, trying to come up with something. He said, "Any way we can get whatever was cut? Maybe we can go to the building and get another copy?"

Simon shook his head. "I don't think it works that way. It's not like there's an original somewhere. This is the tape. Whatever was cut is gone. There's no getting it back. We'll probably never know what happened."

"There's got to be something else we can do."

"There is." Simon reached for a can of Mountain Dew on his desk and held onto it as he thought about it. "I've got Morgan helping me. Blake, I hope you don't mind, but I brought him up to speed on your way over. We split up the work; I agreed to handle the CCTV footage while he figures out a different angle."

Simon was referring to Morgan Lennox, the Australian-born senior analyst at DDC, Chicago. *My* former analyst back when I ran the field office. Morgan was one of the best I'd worked with. Maybe the best. Simon was younger and newer to the job, but well on his way. Even though I was now working at Homeland, Roger Shapiro let Morgan help me out whenever Simon needed assistance. Or more like he looked the other way. Or maybe Morgan conveniently forgot to tell Shapiro from time to time. Shapiro was not an easy man to work for. I had learned that the hard way. But Morgan was good, and as any pointy-headed manager with half a brain knew, it was best to stay the hell out of a good employee's way.

Chris and Simon were both staring at me. I said, "What angle is Morgan working?"

Simon started to explain, but as he spoke, his landline rang, loud and urgent in the quiet open space. Simon reached over to his desk phone and punched a button to answer it on speakerphone. "Morgan?"

"Yes, Simon," he said in his unmistakable Australian accent.

"I've got Blake and Chris at my desk. You're on speakerphone."

There was a brief pause. A moment of thought, maybe of trying to find the right words to say. Then Morgan simply said, "Chris, I'm very sorry about Mark Reynolds. Please accept my condolences, mate."

Chris stepped close to me again, then nodded to himself and thanked Morgan.

Morgan said, "Simon, what have you come up with on your side? Any progress?"

"I was just showing the guys," he said. "I got access to the CCTV footage from two separate feeds. But both of them have sections removed from the record. Like someone had cut them out of the official recording. They must have cut a couple of hours' worth. It was sloppy. So we still don't know where Mark's truck is."

Nobody spoke. Silence on the line. I stepped forward and said, "Morgan, is there anything you can do?"

Morgan sighed from the speakerphone. A long, labored sound, like he'd figured out the hard way to get what he wanted but was hoping the easy way would've worked, then learning just now that it hadn't. "That's what I was afraid of," he replied. "But not to worry; I think I have something else we can try."

## 12

Emma Ross left Malone's office and took her time walking back to the Original Headquarters Building. She moved slowly, using the time to clear her head and think through the conversation she'd had with the man. He was right, of course. The mechanics behind the assassination attempt on Presidents Keller and Stepanov had bothered her. She figured someone had leaked the route the motorcade would take while Keller escorted his friend to the airport. But she thought it might've been someone within Metro PD. Maybe a bent cop had passed the details to the corrupt CIA agents involved in the attack. She hadn't considered that it might've been someone in the White House. Certainly not within Keller's inner circle.

Malone's concern made sense to her. Keller's administration wasn't new to having leaks. They had had plenty of them while she was working as his chief of staff. They had infuriated her. The leaks seemed to come from everywhere. As Emma made her way to the bottom floor and exited the New Headquarters Building, she walked across the courtyard and then stopped before she entered the cafeteria located between the NHB and OHB, and thought long and hard about the man who had taken her job.

Ethan Meyer was now the gatekeeper for President Keller. He maintained his boss's schedule. He made suggestions about where Keller should be at any given moment on any given day. Emma dug her cell phone out of a pocket and started to dial the man, and then she stopped. She knew how the conversation would go. She would ask to meet with him. He would make an excuse or straight out decline or not even answer her call. The last time she had tried to get to Keller, she'd lured Meyer out of the White House for a five-minute meeting at a nearby park. But that wouldn't work today, so she decided to try a different approach.

IT TOOK THREE PHONE CALLS, BUT MEYER'S DEPUTY CHIEF OF staff finally answered her call. Ethan's second in command. *Her* former second in command. Adam Stine finally answered, "Yes?" in a disinterested tone.

"I need your help, Adam," she said, calling the man from the courtyard.

There was a pause on the line. She could imagine the young man sitting inside his West Wing cubicle, working at a small desk with a legal pad in front of him. He always used the large kind. Eight and a half by eleven, canary, a full page of to-dos he needed to work on that day with anything not done carried over to the following day. Stine was extremely organized, which was why she had chosen him to be her top aide. He said, "I haven't heard from you in over a year. And now you call me out of the blue wanting my help?"

"I have something very important to discuss with you, Adam."

"You mean to discuss with Ethan. Wait just a moment, and I'll forward you to his voicemail."

"Adam," she said with the tone of voice of a mother reprimanding one of her children, offering a curt warning, telling him he'd better listen to her with just a single word and intonation. "Please let me finish."

There was another pause. Longer this time. Stine dropped the attitude and calmly said, "I'm listening."

Emma nodded to herself. She said, "I need to talk with you. Not on the phone. In person. It's important."

Stine said, "I can head over that way in about an hour."

"No," she said. "I'm coming to you. Right now. Put me on the guest list; I'll be there in twenty minutes."

Stine tried to argue, but she wouldn't listen. She just clicked off and headed toward her parked car.

## 13

THE SILVER-HAIRED MAN STEPPED OUT OF HIS OFFICE AND walked quickly across a walkway and to his car. He climbed into his vehicle as the burner phone he carried with him buzzed. "Yes," he said, answering it.

"I found him again," said his man in the black sedan.

"Where?"

"They drove together to the Nebraska Avenue Complex. Department of Homeland Security to be exact."

"They are smart men," he said. "I need you to stay out of sight until the time is right."

His guy said, "Do you think I'm an idiot?"

"You were almost caught before. In fact, I'm sure they noticed you. This is why only his partner was in the vehicle. It was a trap. They were trying to lure you in. You would've pulled up next to them, and Jordan would've surprised you. You are not dealing with stupid men. They are two very capable federal agents."

"I know what they are," said the man on the other end of the line.

The silver-haired man sat in his car, thinking. "You cannot take action if Agent Jordan is with him."

"I know this."

"So again, you must stand down. You have plenty of time to get to him." Then he paused, thinking hard. "Tell me—what do you think they're doing at the NAC?"

His man did not respond.

"I'll tell you what. They're looking for the dead agent's vehicle. We should've left it at the building. That was the better play."

"We drove it there," the man in the black sedan said. "Then we realized later that we shouldn't have."

"Why not?"

"The less you know, the better."

"I need to know that I have smart men working for me."

"Because we forgot about something. There's a GPS unit inside every Bureau vehicle. They use it not just for managing their fleet of vehicles, but to monitor where their people travel to, if they need to. For audits. They would've done an investigation. They would've checked the history. And they would've realized the guy had been at the residence last night. That would've raised questions." He paused. "And I don't think you want the FBI sticking their nose where it doesn't belong. Not now. Not while we clean up our mess. And before you disagree, you need to understand that the Bureau is very thorough. More than we are."

He thought about that and said, "Where is the GPS unit now?"

"In the SUV. Disconnected. And like I said before, the SUV won't be found any time soon." His man paused. "I'll keep my eyes on them. They won't see me. But make no mistake: Agent Reed will die today."

## 14

I stepped closer to Simon's desk. I said, "What's your idea, Morgan?"

We heard typing in the background as Morgan was working on it. He said, "Every Bureau vehicle has a GPS inside it. They use it as a fleet tracker, to know where every Bureau car is at all times."

"That's right," said Chris.

"So what we have to do, guys, is see if we can find it online still. Chris, what was Mark's car number?"

"Seven forty-two," he replied.

"Seven forty-two," Morgan said to himself, and we heard more typing in the background as he worked. "Simon, I'm going to share my screen. I'm sending you a link now so you can see what I'm doing, okay?"

Simon said okay. He went to his inbox, and after a few seconds, an email came through from Morgan. Simon opened the email and clicked on the link. After waiting a few more seconds, his screen came to life, and we could see what Morgan was working on seven hundred miles north and west of us, in Chicago.

Morgan had logged into the Bureau's fleet tracker system, which he'd been provisioned access to by Peter Mulvaney himself a week earlier. Not an uncommon thing, given how often DDC, and Morgan specifically, worked with the FBI. My former analyst had established and fostered a relationship with the Bureau director after the assassination attempt of the American and Russian presidents last week. Morgan had Mulvaney's trust. And I was happy about that, knowing firsthand how good an analyst Morgan was.

Chris and I remained standing behind Simon, and the three of us watched Morgan work. He navigated to a screen and entered Mark Reynolds's car number. An hourglass appeared on the screen as it worked. It spun over and over as it tried to locate the vehicle. Then a message displayed on the screen: OFFLINE.

"They did something to it," Morgan said from the speakerphone. "Ripped it out, maybe."

Chris said, "If they did, wouldn't it still be online? Does it have a battery, or is it tied to the truck's power supply? I would think it should show us where it is. Like on the side of the road or in a ditch somewhere."

Simon said, "Good question. I guess it depends on the model."

Morgan said, "I'll try to find out."

Chris said, "What if it's underwater? Would it still work? What if they threw it into the Tidal Basin?"

"Guys, please. None of this matters," said Morgan. "Whether it's offline and we can't get it to work, or it's in a ditch or a body of water somewhere doesn't give us answers as to what happened to Mark. But one thing I'm bloody sure of—between the missing footage and the GPS being offline, something happened."

None of us spoke for a long moment. Each of us thinking, imagining, wondering what had happened.

I didn't like where this was going. I had been convinced that Mark had taken his own life. I'd seen that kind of thing before. Stress, long hours, the things that men like Mark had seen. But now I wasn't sure.

Then Morgan said, "There is one more thing we could try with the GPS."

MORGAN NAVIGATED TO A DIFFERENT MENU WITHIN THE FLEET tracker application. He said, "Simon, I'm going to need your help. Do you guys at DHS have the capability to record something on your screen?"

Simon said that he did.

"Good. It's easier if I don't have to do both things on my end. Let me know when you're recording, mate."

Chris and I watched as Simon located a program and fired it up. It was an application that could take screen captures, but could also record a video when needed. Simon clicked on an icon and told Morgan that he was now recording everything the DDC analyst was doing and to tell him when to stop recording.

So far I had stayed pretty silent. But with the mounting evidence, I was beginning to think that maybe there was more to what had happened to Mark Reynolds. I said, "What exactly are you doing, Morgan?"

He opened a database and started combing through it and said, "Looking for the serial number."

"For the vehicle?"

"No, for the GPS device," answered Chris, catching on fast. "It's made by a private company who works with us.

When they're installed in a Bureau vehicle, they get tagged to the vehicle identification number."

Morgan picked up where Chris left off, adding, "And this database has records of all of the VINs and their associated GPS devices." He entered a search command. The hourglass appeared again. He said, "Got it."

"Now what?" I asked.

"Hold on and I'll show you. Simon, we've only got one shot at this. You're still recording, yes?"

"Yes, Morgan, it's still rolling."

Then Morgan went to yet another screen. It was a map of the greater DC metro area. He zoomed out. Morgan explained that he didn't want to zoom out too much. Because if this worked, he needed enough real estate on the screen to locate the device. But if he zoomed in too much, he might not see anything at all. He said, "Okay, Simon, I'm going to use my second monitor to ping the GPS so we can see where it is."

I said, "But, Morgan, I thought it was offline."

"It is, but there's a little-known feature with these devices. If our assumption is correct that someone tampered with the GPS and removed the power supply—whether it's a model with the battery or one using the SUV's power, what these specific devices do is maintain a slight charge, allowing a onetime ping. Think of it like your cell phone. When the battery's completely dead and you try to turn it on, there's usually enough juice to display a notification on the screen with a battery icon so you know it needs to be charged. Same deal here. It should have enough of a charge left so we can ping it at least once. Unless—"

Morgan's voice trailed off. Simon finished his sentence for him. He said, "Unless someone drove it out of DC. In which case, the ping won't show up on the map. So we have one chance to try to find the vehicle."

"Here we go," said Morgan as we all watched, holding our breath, willing it to work, praying he was right.

Morgan said he was about to enter the command to ping the GPS unit. He counted down: three, two, one.

## 15

Morgan clicked the button on his end. On ours, we saw a red pin show up, south and west of DC. But it disappeared as quickly as it had shown up. From the phone Morgan said, "Did you see it, Simon?" Simon told him that he did. Morgan zoomed in further on the general area. He was going to try it again. He clicked the button. Nothing happened. "Out of juice," he said. "Simon, stop recording. Rewind it back."

Simon took over the screen share. Now it was Morgan's turn to watch Simon work. Simon stopped the recording and saved the file. Then he opened it and pressed play. We watched the map and waited. Then we saw it again: the fast blip, the small red pin icon that showed up for a brief second, then disappeared. Simon paused the video and rewound it slightly until the pin showed up; then he paused it again.

"It's in Fairfax," I said.

Chris said, "Can you get us an exact address?"

Simon zoomed in on his recording. "Looks like a residential area. But yes, I think I can figure it out."

Chris turned to face me and said, "Let's go."

WE THANKED THE GUYS AND HEADED DOWNSTAIRS. CHRIS called Peter Mulvaney as we moved. He didn't answer. We figured he was tied up with delivering the news about Mark Reynolds, calling colleagues and holding meetings. Chris didn't leave a message. He just said he'd try his boss again later. I called Jami. I figured she might be able to help us. She, Chris, and I worked well together. We always had, along with Morgan, going back to our DDC Chicago days, where we all had met.

Jami answered on the first ring as Chris and I stepped out of the building and headed to my vehicle. I brought her up to speed on what had happened with Mark, what we'd found, and what the plan was. Which wasn't much of a plan, other than to head over to Fairfax and look for Mark's vehicle and see where that led us. Jami didn't know what to say. The news about Mark hit her hard. She agreed to help, but it didn't make sense for us to pick her up. We'd be backtracking and needed to head out as fast as we could. So Jami said she'd meet us there and asked me to send the address as soon as I got it from Simon.

Chris and I climbed into my SUV. I drove this time. My vehicle. Which seemed to confuse the guy in the guardhouse as I waited for the wrought-iron gate to open. I drove on, past him, following the directions from the GPS. My thoughts drifted back to Mark Reynolds and the many operations I'd worked with the man, realizing that Chris was right after all, and remembering what he'd said: *Mark was my partner, Blake. I knew him.*

. . .

I MADE THE FORTY-MINUTE DRIVE IN JUST UNDER THIRTY. Simon called right as we entered Fairfax city limits. He said he was sending the address to my phone. I asked him to send it to Jami, too, who was on her way. I clicked off, and a moment later, I saw the text message come through. I tapped the screen with my thumb, and the Maps application opened, and it started navigating us to the address Simon had managed to get.

Chris leaned over and glanced at the screen as we moved. His eyes grew wide as he stared at it.

"What?" I said.

"I had a feeling," he said. "I know the address. It's where Mark and I were supposed to go last night."

THAT CONFUSED CHRIS, AND MY MIND WAS RACING AS I TRIED to make sense of it. I drove on, drawing closer to the address Simon had found. Neither of us spoke. Chris just turned and glanced out the window, thinking. I was thinking, too. Had Mark come to the address on his own? If so, why hadn't he gone with Chris as they had planned? And if Mark had been at the place we were headed to, why did he leave his vehicle? And how did he end up miles away? I figured something was wrong. Morgan had gotten the GPS IDs mixed up, maybe. My phone buzzed. "Hey," I said, answering the incoming call on speakerphone.

Jami said, "I'm a block out, waiting for you guys."

"We're almost there," I said.

I clicked off and glanced right. Chris was still looking out the window, thinking some more as I drove on.

. . .

WE ARRIVED TWO MINUTES LATER. I SAW JAMI ON THE SIDE OF the road. I pulled up and parked behind her. Chris and I stepped out, and Jami followed suit. I walked to the back of my SUV and opened the hatch. I had a drawer full of weapons and tactical gear. I grabbed an extra magazine and stuffed it into my pocket.

Jami stepped up and said, "What the hell's going on, Blake?"

I moved to the side so Chris could take what he needed as I brought her up to speed, explaining everything we knew up to that point: Chris's phone call while I was in my office at the NAC, meeting him at the Hoover Building, the visit from Mark's wife, her mother, and their son. Peter Mulvaney confirming that Mark's body had been found and how he'd apparently taken his own life. The diner, the sedan, Simon and Morgan's assistance in helping us find the GPS unit. Chris finished grabbing what he needed, stepped back, and explained that he recognized the address. How Mark had been at the Hoover Building and then apparently left before Chris arrived. How they were supposed to be here, together, eleven hours earlier, meeting with someone at the very address that we were headed to now.

Jami asked Chris whom he was supposed to have met with, but he said he didn't have any of the details. They were supposed to learn more when they arrived. Then Chris's phone buzzed in his pocket. It was Mulvaney. There were plenty of yes sirs and no sirs, and a hint of desperation in his voice as Chris explained what he was doing, how we might have located Mark's vehicle, and seeking approval to enter the residence. Then his demeanor changed. He had clearly been given an order he didn't like. He clicked off.

I said, "What happened?"

"Mulvaney told me to stand down. He said he needs me to cool off. He's sending other guys out here."

"What happens if you disobey orders?"

Chris gave me a look that said: You know what. Chris glanced at Jami, and Jami turned to me. A question: What are we going to do? Not long ago, it would've been up to me. Both were working for me at DDC Chicago. It would've been my decision then. A different place and time. But not that different, in reality.

I said, "If Mulvaney isn't going to send you in, then I'm going to go in on behalf of DHS. Chris, you're welcome to follow me inside." My eyes shifted to Jami for a moment before I glanced back at my friend. "We need to find out what happened here, if anything. For Mark's sake. And for Tamara."

Chris said, "And for Marcus," and I nodded my agreement. Then we oriented ourselves and started walking.

IT WAS A SHORT WALK BECAUSE WE ENDED UP BEING ONLY HALF a block away. We'd parked five houses down. The three of us walked together toward the residence, and Chris asked what I had in mind when we got there. I said we'd knock on the door and take it from there. Hopefully they'd let us in. And if they didn't, we'd figure something out. Chris turned to me. "Not a good plan, boss. We don't know who's in there."

"I think the house is empty," I said as I turned to my right to look at my friend. "If you're right, if this is one big conspiracy and Mark is at the center of it, then these people wouldn't be dumb enough to leave his vehicle in the DC area. They would've sunk it in a lake or driven it out of state. At least out of the county."

"You still don't believe me, do you?" asked Chris. "I told

you, man. He was my partner. I knew him better than anyone. Hard not to when you spend so much time with someone. And I'm telling you, he didn't jump from the top of that building. Not willingly. There are easier ways to do it, but he never would. Not with Tamara and Marcus. I was the only one he talked to about them. There's foul play here. You'll see."

I nodded, but said nothing back. I just faced forward as we moved, and I looked at the residence. I said, "Chris, take the back. Jami, I want you on the side of the house. Pick one, doesn't matter which." I looked all around and said, "I don't see the vehicle. So if it is here, then it's in the garage." I thought: *But it's not.*

Jami said, "Unless only the GPS unit is inside. If they ripped it out and brought it here with them."

I said nothing.

Chris said, "What are you going to do, Blake?"

I said, "I'm going in through the front door." I thought: *Because no one's here.*

I TOOK IN THE STREET AS WE GOT CLOSER. TALL OAK TREES lined the sidewalks on both sides of the street. Spanish moss hung from the branches. The houses were older. Built in the sixties, maybe. But they held up well, and being so close to the DC bubble, there was no doubt that these houses were very expensive. Especially with the size of the homes and the land they were on. We crossed the street and moved quickly.

There was a long driveway on the left-hand side of the white-bricked home. There were large pillars out front. A big bay window to the left of the front door. Two side doors on the left of the house, just before the driveway wrapped around to the right with an away-facing garage door. Jami and Chris glanced at me as we made our approach. I eyed the home a moment longer; then I turned to them. I nodded once, and they split off, taking their positions as I had suggested. Jami splintered off to the left to take the side. Chris moved past the house and hooked around back and disappeared from view. I went to the front door.

I WAITED FOR JAMI TO MOVE PAST MY LINE OF SIGHT. THEN I waited a few more seconds, giving Chris enough time to get into position. I put my ear to the door. I heard nothing. No people inside speaking in low voices. No TVs playing mindlessly in the background. No feeling like someone was home.

So I knocked hard five times and rested my hand on my Glock, and I waited. No one came to the door. I listened hard and moved my head close to the door again, my ear by the jamb. I stood quietly and listened. I heard no creaking floorboards. I saw no moving curtains. Nothing at all. I turned around. No nosy neighbors watching from their windows. No cars on the street. I could hear a lawnmower somewhere in the neighborhood, but I didn't see anyone outside. So I gripped my Glock with my right hand and got ready to kick the door in, but out of habit, I used my left hand and tried pressing the latch with my thumb.

To my surprise, it gave. It clicked. It opened.

I STEPPED INTO A FOYER. THERE WERE ANTIQUES TO THE LEFT and to the right. Furniture passed on from generation to generation. Old pictures hanging on walls. Dull mirrors reflecting my image back to me. Antique rugs lining the floors and ancient furniture used as decoration. I cleared two rooms and moved to my left, through a dining room, and unlocked one of the doors on the side of the house for Jami. She stepped inside, and I pointed with two fingers toward the way I had come from. The direction I was going to double back through. Jami stepped to the left, from the dining room to what looked like an entrance to a kitchen. I walked back to the foyer and went straight through the center of the house and found myself in a family room with two recliners, a large sliding glass door, a TV, a big curving sofa, and a dead man.

JAMI STEPPED IN THROUGH THE KITCHEN, WHICH ALSO LED into the family room from a different direction. She glanced right and looked at the body, then looked at me, eyes wide, concern in her face, then a look of renewed focus, as we had the rest of the residence to clear. I pointed to my left, through the kitchen, to a door that led to the back. Jami nodded and turned to let Chris Reed inside as I made my way to the right, past a fireplace, down a short hallway that doglegged to the right with three bedrooms we'd have to clear.

I made the turn and stepped into the first room. Empty aside from a queen-sized bed with an old TV. Nobody hiding in the closet. I turned back and saw Jami and Chris appear from the family room and step up behind me. I pointed to the left as I passed room number two. Jami turned the knob and went inside.

I kept moving, straight ahead to the master bedroom as Chris Reed stepped up close behind me, then turned right to check out the bathroom as I walked forward and found a king-sized bed, a desktop computer, a TV, but no one inside.

Nobody was in the house, as far as we could tell. I lowered my weapon and turned back. Jami appeared in the doorway and said room number two was clear as Chris stepped out. I holstered my weapon, and they both followed me back to the family room to check out the dead guy.

"What do we got?" asked Chris as I stepped forward.

"White male," I said, looking him over, moving a suit jacket. "Mid-thirties. Single bullet to the chest."

"Identification?" asked Jami.

I felt his front pockets. They were empty. I carefully checked his back pockets, then his suit jacket. "No."

"We can check the house. I'm sure there's mail or a water bill or something."

I nodded and stood, looking the dead guy over a moment longer. Then I said, "After we check the garage."

Chris turned to his right and looked at the kitchen door. Jami faced forward, staring at it, too. I moved past both of them and stepped through, thinking about our friend, finding it hard to believe his vehicle would be here, trying to understand how that could even be possible. But it was the address Simon and Morgan had found. And it was the same address Chris and Mark had been planning on visiting. I decided if it was true, I'd do something about it; I'd search for the truth. But I didn't believe it. It didn't make sense for the truck to be here. It had to be a mistake. Then I thought: *Morgan doesn't make mistakes*. I got to the door and turned the handle. I pushed it open and stared. Parked neatly inside the garage was a black SUV.

## 16

WE STEPPED INTO THE GARAGE AND CIRCLED THE VEHICLE. I went to the driver's side door, Jami went around to the back, and Chris went to the passenger door. He opened it wide and looked inside. I figured he'd ridden with Mark enough times to know if that was the vehicle, and if it was, if something was out of place. He ducked his head inside and placed a knee on the seat and looked it over. Then he checked the backseat; then he climbed out. "It's his truck," he said as I shot Jami a look, then glanced back at Chris.

I said, "What do you think happened?"

Chris stood tall behind the open door, staring at the vehicle and shaking his head. He said, "I don't know."

Jami stepped around to join Chris and said, "What if he came here without you for some reason? On purpose, I mean. What if he knew something you didn't? What if he wanted to protect you in some way?" She paused, thinking some more. "So instead of waiting for you to arrive at the Hoover Building, he left early and came here alone?"

Chris shook his head and looked away. "That's not how we work. We were a team. Two is better than one."

Jami said, "I worked for the Bureau once; I know that's not always true. Sometimes one is better than two."

Chris didn't reply.

"What if he wasn't who you thought he was? What if he was working with them? And that's why his car's in the garage? What if he came here to meet with them but didn't want his vehicle in the driveway or parked out on the street. He had to keep it hidden. Maybe they let him park it inside?"

Chris made a sour face. "What are you saying, Jami? You think Mark came here by himself, without me, ahead of our meeting to talk to the guy? Because he was involved in something he shouldn't have been involved in? He came here to coach him and tell him what to say in front of me? It didn't go over too well, and they had a disagreement, and Mark shot the guy dead, then drove downtown to find a tall building?"

We all went quiet. Nobody spoke. I said, "I don't think that's it. Or his truck wouldn't be here."

Chris said, "Thank you."

"Maybe that's not exactly how it went down. But that doesn't mean Jami's wrong."

Chris slammed the door shut and stepped forward. He said, "Try again," visibly upset with our theories.

I held both hands out. "Look, I didn't know him as well as you did. He was your partner, Chris. Not mine."

"And I was *your* partner once, Blake. I was your second in command in Chicago. How well did you know me?"

"Not as well as I do now."

"You hired me for a reason."

I studied my friend for a spell. "Your track record, your references, your experience."

"And?"

I glanced past him and looked at Jami. Then I looked back at him. "My gut told me I could trust you."

He nodded slowly. "Well, my gut is telling me that you're both wrong. Something else happened here."

MULVANEY CALLED AND TOLD CHRIS THAT HIS PEOPLE WERE two minutes away. And Mulvaney was with them. Chris told him he was already inside the residence. He didn't enter on behalf of the Bureau. He explained that I had led the way on behalf of DHS, and Chris had followed me inside. Mulvaney didn't respond to that. He just asked if they'd be okay parking in the driveway, and Chris told him they would be.

Two minutes passed, and we heard the rumble of big motors outside. I turned and pressed the button for the garage door, and it started lifting slowly. Harsh daylight spilled into the dimly lit space, and as the door lifted, I saw two dark SUVs parked nose to tail in front of the other as the door lifted the whole way open. Bureau agents stepped out, glanced at Mark Reynolds's vehicle, then looked at each other. Chris Reed stepped forward and began talking with them as a third vehicle pulled up behind the second and parked.

Peter Mulvaney climbed out and closed the door as he glanced all around, taking in the whole expanse of the house, trying to understand what he was dealing with. Then he saw Jami and me standing by ourselves and walked past his men and Chris and extended his hand and shook Jami's first and then mine.

Mulvaney put his hands on his hips and stared at Mark's parked SUV. He turned slightly and listened to Chris as he brought the other Bureau agents up to speed with what we knew so far. Then Chris took a short pause and said there was something else he needed to tell them about. Something inside the house.

Mulvaney said, "What is it?"

I said, "I'll show you."

WE STEPPED INTO THE KITCHEN. I LED THE WAY. MULVANEY followed me in, and Chris followed Mulvaney. Jami let the other Bureau agents enter and hung back as I led the Bureau director into the family room.

"Good God," he whispered to himself, rubbing his face with his hand. "What the hell happened here?"

"He took a bullet to the chest," I said.

Chris said, "That's all we know. The rest of the residence is clear." He stared down at the dead man's body. Then Chris turned to look at his boss. "This is the address Mark and I were supposed to go to earlier."

"I'm aware," said Mulvaney.

"I didn't have any details of the assignment. Just a general overview. Mark was going to fill me in."

"I know."

Chris pointed at the dead guy and said, "So who is he? What were we supposed to be doing here?"

Mulvaney continued to stare at the body of the unknown man. He put his hands back on his hips again. Thinking hard, his mind racing, trying to put the pieces together, but ultimately unable to get there. He said, "I got a call last week from a man who said he wanted to talk to the Bureau. Right after the assassination attempt on the two presidents' lives. A whistleblower, if you will. I told him to come down to the Hoover Building, and we could have a chat, but he declined. I told him we could meet at a restaurant or a café, but he declined that, too. He wanted me to come to him. Not me personally, but my people, to speak off the record. He wouldn't give me his name, just an address. *This* address. He was a cautious man." Mulvaney turned to us. "I, of course, looked him up. He worked for DDC. His name was Gardner."

## 17

I didn't recognize the name, so I said, "Who was he?" but Mulvaney just shook his head slowly.

He said, "Not sure, Jordan. Didn't look that far into it, aside from making a call and learning he'd been fired. His boss is a CIA guy, in charge of stateside DDC operations. I figured the guy had a bone to pick and just wanted to talk to someone about it. You have to understand, this kind of thing happens all the time with former agency employees. They get let go; then they threaten to talk to another agency because their own agency's internal affairs division isn't going to give them the time of day anymore. Not after you've already been canned. It's like someone in corporate America filing a complaint with HR after they've already been fired. They're not even going to return their call, let alone look into any allegations."

Chris said, "Do we typically look into these kinds of things?"

Mulvaney said, "Not really. Usually we just have them come down, give them some stale coffee, talk to them for half an hour and take lots of notes; then we send them on their way. Ninety-nine times out of a hundred there's nothing there. But when it comes to the CIA, and specifically the Department of Domestic Counterterrorism, there's a little bit of a rivalry there. They think we're Big Brother, keeping tabs on them. Which we are and which we do. So we're more than happy to entertain those discussions, even if they want to meet at their home in the middle of the damn night." Then Mulvaney rubbed his face again, thinking hard. "Now we have two men dead from two federal agencies in less than twenty-four hours."

Jami said, "This is a problem."

Mulvaney said, "This is a big problem."

MULVANEY STEPPED AWAY TO MAKE A CALL TO A MAN CALLED Malone. Jami and I had heard of the guy. He was in charge of the entire DDC operation, which for the time being included the first field office for the new agency in Chicago and the newer one in DC that Jami now worked out of. As I understood it, Emma Ross reported up through the guy somehow, and since the CIA was DDC's parent organization, Malone's boss was the highest level you could get to in the DDC organization without entering into the CIA domain. So Malone was the top dog. I could hear his tinny voice from Mulvaney's phone as the Bureau man brought his counterpart up to speed. Then Mulvaney's eyes grew wide. He said he understood and rattled off the address we were at and told Malone he'd see him shortly. He clicked off and turned to look at us.

"He's on his way now."

"Why?" I asked.

Mulvaney pointed to the dead guy. "Apparently he was high up the chain. Maybe that's how he had my number.

Malone said he'd be right over. He wants to see this for himself. He's taking this personally."

"Does he know about Mark Reynolds?"

"Of course he knows. Every agency in DC knows. Word spreads quick when someone takes their own life."

Chris looked at me, but didn't say a word. He didn't have to. I already knew what he was thinking. I told Mulvaney I was going to head out. He said I needed to hang back and give an account for what had happened. Specifically how it had gone down when we entered the residence. But Chris said he could do that on my behalf. Mulvaney nodded vaguely as I stepped closer to Chris and shook his hand and said I'd be in touch.

Jami and I left through the open garage door. The Bureau men were huddled together, speaking in low voices. They nodded at us as we walked past them and the three dark SUVs parked back to back and headed down the street together toward our parked vehicles. By now, neighbors had noticed the commotion and were standing outside or sitting on their porches, watching with concern and curiosity.

As we moved, Jami said, "You still don't believe him, do you?"

I said nothing. Just kept walking.

She said, "What if he's right? How many more of us need to be taken out before you give him the benefit of the doubt? They killed a Bureau guy. Now a DDC guy. What's next? CIA? Maybe they'll come after DHS. Maybe you're next." She took a breath and let it out. Loose gravel crunched under our feet as we moved from the sidewalk onto the street. She grabbed my arm and pulled and said in a soft voice, "Blake, say something."

I stopped moving and turned to look back down the street. I thought for a long moment and said, "Something's going on. I do believe that. But I don't understand why Mark would've come out here alone. And I don't understand why the guy in the house was shot. And it doesn't make sense finding Mark's vehicle in that garage when he died miles from here."

We started walking again, slower this time, as we approached our parked vehicles. Neither of us spoke again for a long time, both of us thinking hard. Then finally Jami said, "What are we going to do about it?"

I thought back a few hours and remembered standing in Mark Reynolds's office, looking at photos of the man in uniform, arms draped across his army friends, with his son, Marcus, in the room. Then I thought back even earlier to Emma Ross visiting me in my own office. She had noticed a similar picture, old and dated, me with my SEAL buddy Jon Miller. I remembered Emma looking it over, then reading the quote Jami had put on the picture frame. Emma had read it out loud: *Sometimes there's justice and sometimes there's just us.* She had asked if I still believed that. I hadn't answered. Not directly. And when I left my office, I had turned the picture facedown on my way out. Because I didn't believe that. Not then or ever.

We got to our vehicles and stood together. Jami stared at me, waiting for me to answer her. Waiting on me to decide. I said, "What does Lynne May have you working on today?" referring to the DDC special agent in charge.

"Nothing. Day off, remember?"

I nodded vaguely and said, "Follow me back to the NAC; we'll try to figure out the connection to Gardner."

She said, "No, you follow me to DDC. Lynne will know who Gardner was. We'll have better luck there."

. . .

THE MAN IN THE BLACK SEDAN GOT A CALL ON HIS CELL PHONE. It buzzed loud in his pocket. "Yes?" he said.

"You need to leave the area," the man with the silver hair said.

He switched the phone to his other hand. "No, I need to take care of a loose end."

"I told you I would allow it, but not right now. We have a situation. You will make things worse."

"It could make things worse if I don't. We need to cover our tracks from last week before we're found out."

"They found the Gardner home, in Fairfax. And the vehicle. And the GPS. And the body."

The man in the sedan thought about that. He understood the implications and what the people in Fairfax would learn, eventually. He said, "Then you're right. I will stand down. For now."

## 18

Chris Reed was wrapping up his conversation with Mulvaney and the other Bureau men when a man stepped through the open garage door, through the kitchen, followed by one of Mulvaney's guys, holding his badge out for everyone to see. Mulvaney turned and nodded to his guy, letting him know it was okay. The man stepped through, approaching cautiously, dropped his badge into a pocket, and looked at the dead man on the couch. "Damn it," he whispered to himself, eyes wide, obvious concern all over his face.

He turned back and held a hand out, and Mulvaney took it, and the men shook. "David Malone," he said.

Mulvaney said, "Good to meet you, finally. Considering the circumstances." He paused. "One of yours?"

"He was," the man answered. "Unfortunately, we had to let him go about a week ago."

Mulvaney nodded vaguely. "Can you share any details?"

Malone shrugged. "I guess I can now." Then he paused a moment, thinking, reconsidering. He added, "First, do you mind telling me how you guys ended up here? MPD should've called my people, not yours."

"MPD wasn't involved," Reed said, speaking for the first time.

Malone shifted his gaze from Mulvaney to Reed. "I'm sorry, and you are?"

"Agent Chris Reed," he said. Malone made no reply. Reed continued, "If Metro PD had shown up, they would've figured out who he was, and they would've called you first. But MPD didn't find him. I did. About an hour ago." Malone looked at Mulvaney like he didn't understand, so Reed explained further. "I'm sure you heard of the Bureau agent who was found dead this morning? A man named Reynolds?"

"I have."

"Well—" he pointed through the kitchen and to the open door "—the vehicle parked inside that garage over there was his. Reynolds was my partner. We were able to track it down to this residence. Which is twenty miles away from where my partner died. We entered the residence when nobody answered the door."

Mulvaney said, "Agent Reed and the other agent who died this morning—they were supposed to be meeting with this guy. Actually, the meeting was supposed to have been today, earlier this morning."

Malone nodded and made a face like it all made sense to him now. "Let me guess, as a whistleblower?"

"Of sorts," answered Mulvaney. "He was worried. He didn't want to come to us. He wanted to meet here."

Malone nodded again. "Agent Reed, my condolences for your loss. I guess we should've listened to him."

"Why didn't you?"

"As I told you, we let him go. Had him escorted out once

we found evidence implying gross misconduct. Maybe even treason. Our people tried to get him indicted but said the evidence wasn't strong enough."

Nobody spoke. Reed stared at the dead man. Then he said, "So what was Gardner involved with?"

"We couldn't prove it, obviously. But we believed he was involved with last week's assassination attempt."

## 19

W E ARRIVED AT THE DDC WASHINGTON FIELD OFFICE THIRTY minutes later. We entered the underground parking garage, and Jami stopped at the guardhouse and talked to the woman, pointing back at me with her thumb as she spoke. The woman glanced at me and nodded. She pressed a button, and a bar rose, allowing Jami to drive through. I pulled up and was asked for my Homeland credentials, and I handed them over. The woman closed a clear window, picked up a phone, and made a call. I could hear her speaking with someone, asking a question, then nodding after hearing the response. She hung up and slid the window back open and said, "You're all set," as she handed my credentials back to me. "Follow her."

"Thanks," I said as I rolled my window up and followed Jami around a bend and found a spot to park in. Jami and I climbed out of our vehicles and walked together toward the entrance. We stepped through, and security stepped forward. They looked at her, then at me, and I said, "Blake Jordan, Homeland Security."

It had been a while since I'd been here, but they remembered me. Jami waited for me to get through the paperwork. It didn't take long. They issued me a temporary badge, and I had to sign a few things. Then I was free to enter, and Jami led me upstairs to her workspace. Unlike Chris and Mark at the Bureau, she didn't have an office. Just a small cubicle. Jami unlocked a drawer and pulled out her laptop. She docked it and turned it on. The screen came to life, and she moved the mouse to get it working, then she logged in with her username and password, and then she navigated to an intranet website. One I was familiar with.

She said, "Remember the org chart?"

"Yeah," I said. "Though I'm sure it's grown since we were in Chicago."

"It has, but they keep it current. I just want to check out the reporting structure with this Gardner guy."

As Jami worked, we heard the sound of someone moving behind us. Jami's boss, Lynne May, was approaching, with a concerned look on her face. "Blake, it's good to see you. They called from downstairs."

I nodded. "Good to see you, too, Lynne."

May glanced at Jami. She furrowed her brow and said, "I thought you had the day off?"

Jami gestured toward a small conference room. May nodded her understanding and moved toward it. Then Jami undocked her laptop and carried it inside with her as I followed both of them and closed the door behind us. Jami set her laptop down on the table as I adjusted the lights. We all remained standing, although Jami was crouched over her laptop, trying to multitask by navigating to the intranet page she needed to get to with the org chart while she brought May up to speed with what had happened so far.

Jami told her boss about Mark Reynolds. May said she already knew. She'd heard about it first thing this morning.

Then I told her about the GPS unit Morgan Lennox, out of her Chicago office, had helped us track down. How it led us to an address in Fairfax. How we found a dead man in the home. A man named Gardner. I told her that Jami was going to look him up so we could learn more about who the guy was.

Lynne May said, "You don't need to do that."

Jami said, "Why not?" just as she found the listing in the directory.

"Because I know who he is. First name Alex. He works for a man named Malone."

Jami pointed at the screen on her laptop. "And now we also know who reported to Gardner: Emma Ross."

EMMA ROSS PARKED HER CAR AT THE ELLIPSE, THE LARGE PARK just south of the White House. She climbed out and headed straight for a covered guardhouse so she could present her credentials and be escorted in. The Ellipse was the closest she had gotten to the White House in what felt like a lifetime, but in reality was more like a single year. Ethan Meyer, the president's chief of staff, had tried to keep his predecessor away. Sometimes he would meet her here, in the park, as he had done a week prior when Emma had tried to warn Keller about the assassination attempt. She had been successful in convincing Meyer to move the location of the peace treaty signing with the visiting Russian president. And that quite possibly might have saved Keller's life. Or maybe it had only delayed the inevitable, as things had eventually turned out. Either way, Emma had had to essentially blackmail Meyer to get her way and carry out what the CIA needed her to do based on the intelligence they had gathered. Meyer had complied, but since then, had not returned any more of her calls. She had never fully trusted Meyer. Truth be told, she didn't fully trust anybody.

Emma's cell buzzed as she stepped into the covered guardhouse. She took a quick glance and recognized the phone number. It was DDC's Washington field office. Emma sent the call to voicemail and dropped her cell into her pocket. She smiled, handed over her credentials, and said, "Emma Ross here for Adam Stine."

The lead man inside the guardhouse took her credentials and looked them over. "He's expecting you."

"Good," she said as the man handed her credentials back to her. Which was unusual. She expected him to spend at least a few moments looking them over, verifying their authenticity, writing down her name, documenting her visit on the logs, then ultimately giving the credentials back and gesturing for her to enter.

But that wasn't what the man did.

Instead he just moved on to another woman who was there to visit the White House, and started helping her. Emma raised her eyebrows, half annoyed, half confused, and crossed her arms as she stood to the side, waiting for the man to be done so she could step forward again and ask the guy what was happening.

That didn't happen, either. Because a minute later, she saw Adam Stine walking straight toward her.

The security guy noticed Stine over his shoulder and touched something inside the covered guardhouse, which made a buzzing sound. Stine nodded his appreciation, opened a metal gate, and stepped through. He patted the security guy twice on the back and stepped over to Emma and stretched out his hand.

Emma didn't take it. She just eyed him carefully and said, "What's this about, Adam?"

He lowered his hand. "You tell me."

Emma glanced past him, at the White House, then turned and started walking back toward the Ellipse. Stine walked with her, hands in pockets, like a couple taking a slow stroll together, not a care in the world.

She said, "Adam, I want to apologize to you."

"You? Apologize? For what?"

Emma took a breath and let it out slowly, determined not to let her former top aide get to her. When she had recruited him, Stine had been a bright-eyed recent college grad from Georgetown University. He had been eager to learn, eager to please, eager to listen to everything and anything she had to tell him. But Stine had spent too many years in the DC bubble. President Keller's first term was coming to an end. It hadn't even been two years, and Stine had already turned into a bratty know-it-all wannabe politico, hell-bent on changing the world, but too young and too naïve to realize that he couldn't do it all himself.

Emma said, "You must feel like I abandoned you. Adam, please understand, that was not my intent."

Stine said nothing back to her. Just looked away as they continued their stroll.

"You understand why I had to leave my position, right? There was a lot of fallout due to my actions. Stepping down was the best thing I could've done. Who knows? It might just help Keller with his reelection campaign. It all adds up."

Stine said, "I thought we were a team. You were teaching me a lot of things. Things Ethan won't show me."

"You have to speak up for yourself. If there's one thing I learned being in Keller's orbit, it's that if I don't stand up for myself, nobody else will. Adam, I've been very busy since I left the White House. You're aware that I went to work for former New York City mayor Bill DiBenedetto? And what I'm doing now? Working for the president was all I ever wanted to do. Now I have to try to change things from the outside."

Stine glanced at her and said, "What's your point, Emma?" A disrespectful tone of voice. A young kid who had up until recently referred to Emma as Ms. Ross. A kid who now saw her as nothing more than an equal. Or maybe even less than an equal. Maybe as a pawn that he could use somehow for personal gain.

Emma stopped moving. Stine didn't. She grabbed his arm to stop him. Stine pulled his hands out from his pockets and pulled away from her, but Emma stepped forward, toward him, getting up close and personal. She looked him straight in the eye and said, "Adam, I want you to listen very carefully. I need your help."

"Why don't you talk to Ethan?"

"Because he won't return my phone calls."

"And why is that?"

"Because he knows I have dirt on him, and he doesn't want to play that game with me anymore, I suppose."

"That's how you get things done in Washington? By blackmailing people?"

"If it comes down to it, yes."

"Are you going to blackmail me if I don't help you?"

She took a deep breath and let it out, trying to calm herself. "Adam, I know you have big dreams. And I'm sorry I'm not able to help you with them anymore. It's true, you don't work for me now. You work for Ethan. I get that. I do. But helping others isn't about what's in it for you. Think bigger picture. I told you many times, country over self. Remember? We're both in a unique position to make a difference."

He sighed. "What's your point?"

She stared at him intensely. She said, "You know those CIA men who tried to assassinate the president?"

Stine nodded.

"My superior at the Agency doesn't think they were acting alone. He thinks they were fed the route for the presidential motorcade by someone inside the White House. By someone close to the president."

"You should be talking to Agent Rivera. The Secret Service ought to know."

"Adam, I'm talking with you."

He stared back at her. Silence between them. A long moment passed. The only sounds either of them heard was the whoosh of the wind picking up, muted laughter from children playing at the park, and the low hum of Washington, DC, awake and alive and trudging on. He nodded reluctantly. Maybe resentfully. He said, "Fine. I'll help you, Emma." He paused for a beat, thinking long and hard. "But if I do this, if I help—then I want something from you."

## 20

CHRIS REED CONTINUED DISCUSSING THE SITUATION WITH Peter Mulvaney and David Malone. Mulvaney had a lot of questions for his agent. So did Malone. Understandably so. The dead man on the couch was one of his direct reports. He'd been relieved of his duties, but he was high enough in the chain of command that it caused a lot of concern that the man had ended up dead. Even more concerning was that Gardner had tried to talk to people within Malone's organization but had been denied that opportunity. The same with the Bureau. Peter Mulvaney rubbed the back of his neck and shifted his eyes from Gardner's body to Malone to Reed and back, thinking, wondering what had happened and who had done this as well as kicking himself for not taking the request more seriously and for brushing the dead man off.

Mulvaney said, "Of course, we will offer our full cooperation."

"I appreciate it," said Malone. "However, if it's all the same, I'd like the CIA to take over the investigation."

"David, I have a dead Bureau agent with his vehicle parked here, at this residence. So it's our jurisdiction."

"I could say the same," Malone said, pointing at Gardner's body. "For all I know, Reynolds shot him dead."

Stalemate. Both men now had not only a vested interest in learning the truth about what had happened hours earlier, but an obligation. Malone rubbed his face and looked away, thinking about it some more. Then he said, "Okay, you and your people can run point. Technically Gardner wasn't CIA when he died, and your man downtown was active when he killed himself. So I concede, your jurisdiction. But I want my people here alongside yours. You take the lead, but this will be a joint investigation." He paused. "Agreed?"

Mulvaney nodded and stretched his hand out. Malone took it, and the two men shook. Mulvaney said he was going to head out. He'd leave his Bureau men at the residence, and Malone was free to call his people over, too. But Chris Reed was no longer needed at the scene. He had brought the other agents up to speed. He'd done the same thing with Malone and answered all of the deputy director's endless questions as well. So Mulvaney asked Chris where his vehicle was, and he said it was parked back at the Hoover Building.

Mulvaney said, "Then come with me, Reed. I'll give you a ride back."

THE MAN IN THE BLACK SEDAN CHECKED HIS WATCH. NINETY minutes had passed. He was parked on the curb near one of two exits out of the neighborhood where Gardner lived, standing down as ordered, but not backing off. Not leaving the area. He was loyal, but not stupid. Even though the tracking device showed that Agent Reed had left, he knew he hadn't. The man named Jordan had. Which meant they'd split up. But he figured they'd be together again, eventually. Just a matter of time. As he sat in the silence, he saw movement. An SUV appeared at a stop sign, made a rolling stop, and turned his way. He leaned back in his seat. Just slightly. Not too worried about being seen. They wouldn't know who he was. Not with the tinted windows. Not by the make and model of his vehicle, which was very popular amongst the various agencies. Even if Agent Reed noticed him, there'd be no way to know if it was the same sedan that had been at the diner. The SUV rolled by. Light streamed through, and the front windows were lit up briefly by the sun. Lighter tint, allowing him to see who was inside. It was Reynolds's partner, after all, along with the Bureau director himself. He smiled as they passed by. Neither man seemed to notice him there. They seemed to be having a conversation. He did not engage. He wouldn't attempt to take the agent out. Not now. Not with Peter Mulvaney inside the vehicle. That would be too brazen. Too obvious. Instead, he'd bide his time and find another opportunity to take him out, but promised himself that it would be today.

His phone buzzed. It was a call alerting him to a situation in Fairfax. He said he happened to be in the area. He waited a few minutes, then pulled out and headed in the direction of the address he'd been given.

## 21

Jami waited five minutes and tried calling Emma Ross again. This time she answered her phone. Jami had it on speakerphone, and Emma's voice filled the room as Jami, Lynne May, and I stood together. Jami told Emma who was in the room and that we had tried to get a hold of her a few minutes earlier but got her voicemail. Emma apologized for not answering. She said she'd seen the call come through but had been at the White House for an important matter. Then she paused a moment and said, "So how can I help you?"

I stepped forward and said, "Emma, this is Blake. We need to talk to you about a man named Gardner."

"Alex Gardner?" she asked. "Yes, of course; I report to him." Then she caught herself. "I mean, I used to."

Jami said, "Blake and I just came from his home in Fairfax. He was shot and killed this morning."

There was an audible gasp on the other end of the line. Like that was the last thing on earth Emma Ross was expecting to hear. We gave her a moment to think, and then Emma said, "Do we know who did this?"

Lynn May said, "We were hoping you might have an idea."

"No," she replied. "I haven't seen him in about a week. I just learned this morning that he was let go."

I said, "Why was he let go?"

Emma started to explain. She said she didn't have details other than it seemed to be typical government bureaucracy. Play along and get promoted; don't and you won't. That was how her superior had explained it to her in the past. And that was what he'd alluded to being the reason Gardner was no longer with the Agency. She had been told that once you were in, you were in. You might get pushed all the way down to the mailroom, but you'd still be employed. She offered her theories on why. Maybe as long as you were working for the CIA, you wouldn't move to another agency and share secrets. Or speak freely as a civilian.

Emma said she was still coming to terms with learning her boss had been fired, and now he had been murdered. She said she was headed back to Langley to have a conversation with her superior about this. She hadn't heard from him yet and didn't want to make a call herself. Better to have a face-to-face conversation. Which she preferred so she could look her superior in the eye when discussing something like this. She found it odd that Gardner would lose his job and, less than a week later, would end up dead.

I asked Emma who her superior was. She said David Malone. I told her Malone was headed to the Gardner home in Fairfax. Emma said she was going to Langley, anyway. She started to hang up so she could call the man on the way, but I asked her to hang on. There was more we needed to discuss. Much more. Lynne May excused herself after whispering that she had to make a call herself. It was just Jami and me alone in the room. Jami looked at me as if she was wondering how I was going to explain the Mark Reynolds thing. I didn't know myself, so I just spoke straight to her, explaining how Mark had been found dead hours earlier.

"I'm aware," she said. "It's a domestic concern involving a federal agent, so I was alerted immediately."

Jami stared at me. A question in her eyes. I answered it by saying, "Emma, I don't think he killed himself."

Emma said nothing.

I explained how his vehicle had been found in Fairfax, how Simon and Morgan had helped me track it down, and how it was parked neatly inside a garage at the home belonging to Alex Gardner.

"How did he end up all the way downtown? That's twenty miles away? It would take him all night to walk." But before I could answer, Emma said she had another call coming through and had to go. Her superior was calling her, and she wanted to take the call. I asked if it was David Malone, and she said that it was. I told her to call us back when she was done, and she said she would. Jami and I spent two minutes in silence inside the room. Then Emma called back, direct to my cell phone. She said, "We have a problem."

THE PROBLEM WAS HER SUPERIOR HADN'T MENTIONED Gardner. Instead Malone just asked for an update on her assignment. Which Emma avoided giving us details about. At first. Jami asked what Malone had her working on. Emma danced around the question and simply said she had an important task to carry out. But when Jami pressed some more, Emma went quiet, thinking about it, deciding how much she should share; then she decided to tell us everything. She said, "A week ago, both of you helped us prevent an assassination attempt on not one but two presidents, Keller and Stepanov. You both understand that the Department of Domestic Counterterrorism rolls up to the CIA. And CIA agents were involved in the attack. My superior believes others were involved, and he wants me to find them."

"There was," I said. "A former Bureau guy."

"True," Emma said. "But David Malone believes there were more people involved. And I don't mean the FBI. I mean people in President Keller's administration. People close to him. People in his inner circle."

There was silence on the line. Then Jami said, "Why is it a problem that he didn't mention Gardner?"

"Because he should've. Don't you think? Unless he doesn't know."

"He knows," I said. "Mulvaney took a call from him just before I left the residence. He was on his way."

"Exactly. And I gave him an opportunity. After my update, I asked if he had anything for me. He said no."

Jami said, "Maybe he wanted to keep you focused. Maybe he wanted to tell you in person."

Emma said, "He's not like that. He shoots from the hip. He wouldn't wait for a good time to tell me."

I said, "Emma, there's more to the story with Mark Reynolds. Alex Gardner tried filing a complaint against the CIA. After he'd been let go by the Agency. But they wouldn't listen to him. I spoke with Peter Mulvaney earlier, and he told me that Gardner tried talking to them, too. But the Bureau didn't take him seriously. Not until it was too late. Mark and Chris Reed were supposed to talk to your former boss early this morning so he could tell them what he was concerned about. But apparently that never happened."

She said, "Why would he do that? Why would he want to talk to the FBI?"

"Because he had nowhere else to go. But he knew something. Maybe something tied to what Malone has you running down. Someone figured it out and decided to shut him up before he could talk. They took him out. Then they took out Reynolds because maybe he knew or maybe he had an idea. So they eliminated him as a concern, too. Better to be safe than sorry." Then I thought about Chris Reed and the black sedan. How the driver had been parked outside the diner. How Chris had noticed it. How it had then sped away. I said, "Emma, what are you going to do at Langley?"

"I need to kill some time. I'm waiting on my former aide to do some digging for me."

I glanced at Jami for a second; then I said, "Emma, we need your help. If Gardner really was a whistleblower, if he learned something he needed to tell someone, then we need to find out what he knew."

There was a long pause. Then Emma said, "Where would I look?"

I said, "Start with his office."

CHRIS REED STARED OUT THE WINDOW AS PETER MULVANEY navigated the concrete jungle downtown, heading back to the Hoover Building. He passed through the guardhouse quickly, rolling his window down, nodding at the person inside, who just glanced at the director, then at Chris, then quickly lifted the barrier arm. Mulvaney bounced across speed bumps and parked in the first spot next to the entrance. The spot reserved for him. He and Reed hopped out of the car and stepped inside and buzzed through security. They headed up the elevator to the third floor, which was the only thing slowing the Bureau men down some as they waited for the elevator doors to open. They finally did, and the men stepped inside.

Reed punched the button, and as the doors closed, he said, "Boss, I need to talk to you about something."

Mulvaney said nothing. Just glanced across at him, deep in thought himself, concerned with his own problems.

"I don't believe Mark killed the man in Fairfax and then killed himself. You know as well as I do the kinds of evaluations they put us through. Not just to get through the academy but ongoing. And I was his partner. I spent countless hours with Mark every day. If he was having mental health issues, I would know." Reed paused and stared at Mulvaney as the elevator slowed. "Something else is going on here."

The elevator chimed open. Neither man moved. Mulvaney said, "I've been thinking that all morning." Then he stepped out onto the third floor and headed to his office. But Reed stayed on and went up another floor and went to Mark's office to look around again, to see if anything seemed to be out of place.

JAMI AND I SPENT AN HOUR SITTING AROUND THE SMALL conference room table, looking at the DDC and CIA org charts, drinking coffee, and talking about Mark. She told me she had known him before she worked at DDC. Their paths had crossed once or twice back when she was with the Bureau. I asked Jami if she remembered New York, years ago, when I had tried to go after a Russian terrorist alone. I told her that Mark had been ordered to arrest me, and somehow I'd managed to get away from him. A hard thing to do. Mark had been a big guy, maybe sixty or seventy pounds heavier than me. All muscle and more height. Jami looked away solemnly. She said she'd never forget New York. I remembered her, Mark, Chris, and I teaming up in the end to take the terrorist out. Nobody else was going to do it, and it was up to us.

*Sometimes there's justice and sometimes there's just us.*

I had more than bent the rules between agencies when I had put Mark in a chokehold, knocked him out, and handcuffed the man to his steering wheel so I could get away. Things changed after that. There was a mutual respect between the two of us, and Mark and I had laughed about it eventually. No harm, no foul, he'd said to me after we had taken the Russian down and won in the end. He was a good guy. True to his word, loyal, and a good partner to Chris.

Lynne May eventually rejoined us in the conference room. She apologized and said she'd had to check on a few things. All of her DDC agents were either working their assignments or enjoying a quiet Saturday morning off. She asked if we had learned anything since she'd left. We said other than Emma Ross reporting to the dead guy in Fairfax, no. We told May about Emma getting a call from David Malone, calling us back, telling us about her assignment to figure out who might have leaked the presidential motorcade route a week earlier. How Malone believed there were people within the CIA, maybe even the White House responsible for the leak. How he needed Emma to do what she did best and figure out who.

Then we told her how David Malone hadn't mentioned anything to Emma about Alex Gardner. How we thought it was odd. But May didn't think it was odd at all. She said, "If the roles were reversed, I don't think I'd say anything about it, either. Not if I needed someone focused on getting something done. Especially if Gardner was no longer part of the Agency. I think I'd wait for a more appropriate time."

That made sense to Jami. But not to me. I had been in Lynne May's shoes once. Up in Chicago. And I would've said something about it. But everyone has their own style. And May's was working for her. She still had her job, and I didn't. Not with DDC. Maybe if I had done things by the book, I'd still be in Chicago and not in DC. May left again, and Chris called my cell and said he was back at the Hoover Building, across the street. He'd spent the last hour looking through Mark's office but wasn't making much progress. I told him we weren't either on our end. He asked if we were up for lunch, so Jami and I left to meet him at the diner again.

## 22

JAMI AND I ARRIVED FIVE MINUTES LATER. WE DROVE separately and parked out front. The sky had grown dark, and the temperature had dropped. The breeze was cool, and the air smelled like it was about to rain. We entered Lincoln's Waffle Shop and sat in the same spot where Chris and I had sat earlier, at the counter overlooking the street. Jami ordered lunch, and I ordered breakfast again. And more coffee. After the waitress left, I looked around the room. There was a whole new set of people at the surrounding tables. Jami noticed the missing saltshaker. I pulled it out of my pocket and set it on the counter, and she gave me an odd look. Then I saw her eyes shift. I turned and saw Chris step inside, and I waved him over. I looked out the window and saw his SUV parked next to ours. All three government issued. All three nearly identical. They were screaming *federal agents*. But that wasn't a problem. Special agents had to eat just like everyone else. Chris stepped up and sat down next to Jami. She scooted over in her seat so she was now on a corner so she could see us both. Chris sat down and said, "Did you guys order already?"

I nodded.

Jami looked at me and said, "Yeah, and he ordered *breakfast*."

Chris turned to me. "I said I'd buy lunch, not a second breakfast."

I shrugged. "Just be glad I didn't order the lobster."

Jami made a face and looked away. Chris waited for the waitress to look his way; then he motioned for her to stop by. He ordered a burger, fries, and soda. The waitress told him it would be right up as he handed the menu over to her. Then Chris looked at me, then at Jami, then back to me, and then he said, "What?"

"I'm not judging." I paused a beat. "Just don't come looking for a job when you fail your next physical."

"Here we go."

The waitress smiled at our banter and walked to the kitchen. I watched her place the ticket with Chris's order faceup on a window counter for the cook to see; then she grabbed a decanter. She returned a few seconds later and turned the mug in front of me over and filled it with the steaming brew. She paused and said, "Black?"

"Like his soul," Chris said.

She poured and shook her head and moved on to another table. Then the tone grew more serious. The three of us sat in silence, and I watched as Chris's face changed. He looked troubled. He was coming to terms with the fact that his partner was gone. Probably thinking about Mark's wife and kid. Or maybe the upcoming funeral. Or maybe he was thinking about none of those things. He confirmed it by saying, "The CIA showed up after you guys left. The guy called Malone. He told us that Gardner worked for him."

"He did," I said. "And Emma Ross worked for Gardner."

Chris narrowed his eyes and turned to me. He said, "Does she know the guy's dead?"

Jami said, "She does now." Jami crossed her arms and rested them on the table. "Emma actually spoke to Malone. Maybe he called her from the residence. She said he didn't tell her about Gardner. Not the right time, maybe. So we filled her in on the details. She said she was headed back to Langley, so Blake suggested she get into Gardner's office and figure out what the guy was trying to warn everyone about."

Chris nodded vaguely. He said, "Mark's office is clean as a whistle. Except for a locked desk drawer."

I dug into my pocket and pulled out a phone and dropped it on the table and pushed it over to my friend.

He spun it around to face him. He said, "Is this what I think it is?"

"I found it in his drawer. I turned it on, but it's locked."

Chris furrowed his brow. "How'd you get in?"

"I used my knife."

He narrowed his eyes again. "How does it help us?"

"It doesn't. I just don't want to carry it around anymore. I probably shouldn't have taken it to begin with." Chris nodded and picked up the phone and looked it over for a few seconds; then he pushed it back to me. He didn't want to carry it, either. So I pocketed it again and said, "How's Mulvaney taking all of this?"

"We're on the same page. He agrees that this thing with Mark isn't making sense."

"So what's he doing about it?"

Chris shrugged. "He's giving me a long leash. I think he'd prefer I took the rest of the weekend off. To clear my head and come to terms with what happened." Chris looked away. "But that's not going to help. Finding the people who did this is the only thing that's going to help. We have to do something about it."

I took a sip of my coffee. The waitress brought out Jami's food, then mine, then Chris's. First in, first out. I started eating and was halfway done when Chris took a bite of his burger and then almost spit it out. He stared out through the window. His eyes grew wide. He had a strange look on his face. He said, "You've got to be kidding me."

Jami turned to her left. I stared straight ahead. We were all seeing the same thing: an idling black sedan.

It all happened the same way as earlier that morning, only it was no longer bright out. The weather was changing fast. It looked like it might start to rain any minute. Jami turned back to us and said, "What?" but neither of us spoke. Chris and I just kept our eyes on the sedan, deciding what we should do.

There was a roll of thunder. A storm getting closer. Chris said, "That can't be the same guy, can it?"

I said, "Only one way to find out." I dug my cell phone out of my pocket and called Simon Harris back at the office. I told him I needed a favor. I asked if he could gain access to the satellite positioned twenty-four seven over Washington, DC. Specifically, I needed eyes on the area surrounding the diner. He said he needed a business purpose. I told him I was trying to avoid paying for lunch. He ignored the comment and said he'd make something up. I told him about the sedan, and he said he needed five minutes to reposition the satellite.

While I was talking, Chris brought Jami up to speed. He told her about earlier: the guy watching the diner, Chris taking my vehicle around the block, my walking through the kitchen, the guy in the sedan changing his mind and driving away. I clicked off with Simon, and Jami said, "I think you're just being paranoid." She stared out the window, watching. "There have to be a million cars in DC that look exactly like that one."

I stuffed my phone back into my pocket and eyed the sedan. Then I checked my watch to note the time. Chris dug into his pocket for his wallet and put cash on the table. He said, "I'm not buying you dinner."

I said, "Same as before, only with Jami this time. And don't drive anywhere. Just sit inside your vehicle." Chris nodded. I grabbed the saltshaker again and got up and walked through the kitchen to the back door.

## 23

I walked past confused kitchen workers and found myself outside. I moved around one of the building's corners as a flash of lightning lit up the sky, followed by another roll of thunder. The storm was closer now. The air was thick and heavy. It smelled like damp earth. Then the sky opened up. Just a light mist at first, then a steady sprinkle, then it became a straight-out downpour. I moved closer to the wall and worked my way around to the second corner and peered around it slowly until I saw the sedan.

It was parked facing west, away from where I stood. Parked in a way so the driver could glance out across the street and keep an eye on the door. Parked in a way so that whenever his target left the diner, he could pull out and follow them as they left.

But the position was in my favor. The driver was already facing forward and no doubt craning his head ninety degrees to the right to keep watch. And no doubt unable to maintain watch the whole time. Too straining on the neck. He'd much prefer to glance over every once in a while, or when he saw movement. My position was more like a hundred and twenty degrees to the right. Possible to see me out of the corner of his eye if he happened to be looking at the diner door. Unlikely if he wasn't. Very unlikely with the rain. Either way, I figured I needed to move because I heard the guy start the motor, and his brake lights lit up.

Rain was coming down at an angle now. Sideways, almost. Away from the building that was shielding me. I stepped out, and it started hammering at my back. The rain was cold, but it was my friend. It would make it harder to be seen. I fought the urge to run as I moved to the street. If the guy in the sedan was looking in my direction, no doubt fast movement in his peripheral vision or in the rearview mirror would catch his eye. Slow and steady was best. But I didn't take my time either. I looked both ways and crossed the street. I chanced a glance over my shoulder and saw Chris and Jami stepping out of the diner together. They were standing at the entrance, looking at Chris's SUV, watching me briefly; then they made a run for it. Chris unlocked the doors, and they both jumped inside, quick to avoid getting rained on too much. I heard Chris start his motor, then I saw him turn his headlights on, then his brake lights lit up bright red in the gloom, but he didn't move. He just kept it idling right where he was parked. "Good work," I said to myself as I got to the other side of the street and headed for the parked sedan.

It was facing the other direction. I was now coming up behind the left-hand side. The driver would be looking to his right, probably staring at Chris's vehicle now. Not worrying about neck strains. Now the worry was with losing the guy. His headlights were off, but I could hear the motor running. He was ready to go the moment Chris backed out and left. Ready to repeat the process from this morning.

Only there wouldn't be any backing out this time. There would be follow-through. This was going to be the real deal.

I moved faster.

The rain was now hitting the left side of my face. Still coming down at an angle. I squinted and held a hand up to block the rain as I moved. Twenty yards became fifteen. Then ten. Then I was just a few paces away.

I reached into my pocket and grabbed the saltshaker. I held it in my left hand.

Then I reached for my Glock with my right.

Chris put his vehicle in reverse. He didn't move, but the white lights lit up. Buying time. Sparking interest. I imagined the guy in the sedan was watching closely now. A hand on the steering wheel, the other on the gearshift. Ready to go. I got to the window and looked inside. The tint made it hard to see details, but the driver was doing just what I thought: he was looking away. Gripping the shaker, keeping the metal tip between two clenched knuckles, I pulled my hand back and launched it forward, punching the glass. I followed through, letting go of the shaker and grabbing the guy's collar. He flinched and recoiled, then turned to me as I shoved the Glock against his neck. I stared down at him and said, "Get out of the car."

BUT THE GUY DIDN'T GET OUT OF THE CAR. HE JUST STARED UP at me, two big eyes, one small brain, thinking, calculating, a hand still on the gearshift, the other no longer on the steering wheel, but that wasn't necessarily a dealbreaker. He said, "What are you going to do? Shoot me? Kill me in broad daylight?"

The rain was beating down from the left of me now. I said, "Not much daylight at the moment."

I was staring at the man's face. Specifically, his eyes. The eyes could tell you everything, and his eyes were telling me I didn't have a chance. They were telling me I didn't have the upper hand even if I thought I did.

And it was confirmed a second later when he flexed his right hand, and I saw his thumb depress the gearshift button. I kept the Glock tight against his neck but lowered my free hand and dug into my pocket. Because it was in that moment that I realized how he'd been following us. As soon as I found what I needed, the guy shifted into the drive position and stepped hard on the gas at the exact same time as I brought my hand out from my pocket. The guy's wheels spun on loose gravel. The tires struggled to catch onto the wet concrete. Then they did. The tires whined and screamed as they latched on and got traction, and the guy took off. Then I stood alone with the rain soaking me from head to toe, watching the sedan drive away, growing smaller, the driver taking a sharp turn up ahead and disappearing from sight. Jami opened the passenger door and looked back at me as I jogged toward her and Chris, checking for traffic as I crossed the street.

Nobody inside the diner was watching. Between the rain and the thunder and the fogged-up windows, there was nothing to see or hear. I could see the diffused figures against warm light through the glass as I approached. People eating, talking, reading newspapers, settled in, waiting out the storm. Jami closed her door to keep from getting wet as I stepped up close and opened the back door and slid in behind her. She turned around in her seat. Chris turned to his right and stared back at me blankly.

Jami said, "What happened?"

"I introduced myself."

Chris said, "We lost him."

"Maybe," I said as I dug my cell phone out from my pocket. "Maybe not."

They both stared at me. Neither of them spoke. Simon Harris answered my call. "Too soon," he said to me.

I said, "Simon, forget the satellite. I need you to access the FBI's Stingray program."

A long pause on the line. "Okay," he said curiously.

I put the call on speakerphone. I thumbed through my contacts list. "Write this down," I said and gave Simon the number I was looking at. He said he needed time to work and would call back in two minutes. I clicked off. Chris and Jami were staring back at me blankly. I was dripping wet and shivering.

Jami said, "Care to enlighten us, Blake?"

I said, "Before he took off, I tossed Mark's cell phone into the backseat. We can use it to track him down."

Chris thought for a moment and said, "You think that's how he kept finding us?"

"Doesn't matter," I said. "It's how we'll find him." Then we waited two minutes, and Simon called me back.

## 24

Emma Ross entered the Original Headquarters Building and headed up to her office. She walked into the hallway where her office was located but didn't step inside. She saw the faint outline of her assistant through the obscured glass, working diligently, facing the opposite direction. Emma thought it would be best if she didn't let Samantha know she was there. Plausible deniability, even though there would be a record of her being at CIA headquarters regardless. There would be timestamps of her driving through a checkpoint, swiping her badge at the door and again at the elevator. There would be video confirmation should anyone ever need to pull it. But she had no reason to expect anyone to need to do that. All she was going to do was look around. Nothing more, nothing less. So she kept walking past her office and moved to the far end of the hallway and to the corner office that Alex Gardner worked from.

Which was odd, because as soon as she walked inside, she saw his office completely untouched. It was exactly the same as she remembered it. Pictures hung from walls;

awards from many years of service were proudly displayed on his desk, outwardly facing, marking five-, ten-, and twenty-five-year milestones. Loose papers were scattered across his desk, but in neat, intentional piles. Emma walked around Gardner's desk and looked at them. The papers were bound with paperclips, with a single sticky note on top of each pile, marking what they were. But they didn't seem to be anything confidential. That was against policy. Especially with office doors that no longer had locks on them, due to another policy that had gone into effect years earlier. These documents were harmless, just meeting notes and things he needed to file the next day. A day that never came. Because Gardner had been fired for not being a team player. For not playing along.

The man's desk drawers were unlocked. She looked briefly, but there was nothing inside them. Emma sat down in his chair and looked around. The big corner office she dreamed of getting one day. The one Emma and her father had talked about only a week earlier. She was new at the Agency, very new, but had her sights set high. Why not swing for the fences? After all, Malone had said if she could figure out who had leaked what, if Stine came through based on what he'd learn, maybe the office would be hers one day.

But she didn't feel right about it. She didn't feel opportunistic. Maybe because Gardner hadn't left on his own, leaving a vacancy for the next best person to fill the job. Maybe because he'd been fired. Or because he was dead. Whatever the reason, Emma didn't like the feel of the office. It was dark. Almost haunting.

So she stood up from the desk and pushed Gardner's chair back in place. Just like he'd left it. Then Emma looked around the rest of the office. She spent five minutes opening books and flipping through pages, then another five looking through unlocked drawers and a credenza. She found loose change and a coffee club loyalty card for the café next to the cafeteria downstairs with five of the nine holes punched through.

She found lots of things in an office used for many years. But she didn't find any clues. Nothing that might explain what Gardner had been working on, or what he knew, or why he'd wanted to file a complaint, or why he'd want to talk to the FBI. Before she left, Emma sat back down at the desk again. Defeated, out of options. She glanced at the desk phone. It was just like hers. Identical in every way except the four-digit extension next to the receiver. His extension, not hers.

And one more difference: she kept current on her voicemails. And he hadn't.

There was a red blinking light indicating a new message. Emma stared at it as it flashed on, then off, then back on again every few seconds. Emma looked away, thinking. Then she pressed a button for a dial tone. The sound filled the entire office. A bright tone in an otherwise gloomy room. Emma dialed four digits. There was a brief pause, then a line started to ring, but it only rang once. The call was answered. Emma dialed a command to play the messages, but it was no use. It wanted a passcode, so she clicked off and sat there another long moment, thinking. Then she dialed an extension, and the call was answered. "Samantha, it's me." She breathed. "I need you to walk down to Alex Gardner's office right now. Hurry."

I PUT THE CALL ON SPEAKERPHONE AND ASKED SIMON IF HE'D been able to track Mark's cell phone. Simon had Morgan

Lennox on the line with him. He said Morgan would be able to help with using the Stingray program because it needed an authorization code that Simon didn't have because Parker wasn't there to give him one. Simon said he'd work the satellite angle and leave the Stingray usage to Morgan. Which I knew Morgan was more than capable of doing. Morgan told us he was accessing the program now. He'd already received approval to use it earlier from Roger Shapiro on something else he'd been tasked to work on. The authorization code would be valid for the remainder of the day, so he wouldn't have to ask for permission to use it again. He asked for the cell phone number we needed tracked, and Simon rattled it off.

Morgan repeated it back slowly. I could picture him writing it down with a pencil on the yellow pad he always kept at his desk. He said, "Just a moment," and we sat in silence as we listened to him typing. Morgan performed the search. He said it would take a minute; then he asked us what he was doing this for.

So I told him about the guy who was following us. I told him the direction the guy was heading in, and Simon spoke up and said he'd work on positioning the satellite for us. Then we all grew quiet, waiting on Morgan to get results from Stingray. I just looked out through the windshield at the foggy diner windows as the rain continued to beat down hard all around us. Then Morgan said, "Okay, guys, I got a hit. Blake, I'm going to add your cell number to the program. That way I can see both of your locations at once."

I buckled my seatbelt. Chris and Jami did the same. Chris said, "Where am I going, Morgan?"

Morgan said, "It looks like the target's about a mile out from you. Start moving west, mate."

Chris backed the SUV out, then threw the gear in drive, and spun his tires on the wet pavement as we left.

SAMANTHA KNOCKED SOFTLY AND PUSHED THE OFFICE DOOR open and whispered, "Ms. Ross?"

"Come in," Emma said, standing and pushing the desk chair out of the way.

Samantha narrowed her eyes and looked all around the dark office. Totally confused about what was happening. Emma shared the news that Gardner was dead, that his body had been found in his home, that he'd been shot to death. Murdered. She asked if Samantha knew he'd been fired a week earlier. "No," the woman said. "In fact, I just sent him an email an hour ago. It didn't bounce back. He's still active in the system." Then Samantha paused a moment, thinking. "Maybe somebody forgot to revoke his access?"

"Maybe," answered Emma. "But this is the CIA. Mistakes like that aren't made. In fact, I would think access would be revoked before they fire you. Before they walk into your office to kick you out."

Samantha said nothing. Just crossed her arms and nodded her head. A quick, nervous movement.

"Samantha, I need your help. I'm working with some people who believe there was foul play involved in Mr. Gardner's death. They think he had information he needed to share with people. People who wouldn't listen to him. Not here, and not at the Bureau. I've just spent the last thirty minutes searching his office. There's nothing here. Nothing that tells us what he tried to warn everyone about." Emma paused a beat; then she pointed at the flashing voicemail indicator. "But that might help us. I need to hear his messages."

Samantha shook her head slowly. "You need his passcode," she said.

"I know."

Samantha thought a moment longer, remembering something. Then she smiled and said, "I have an idea."

## 25

CHRIS REED SWERVED AROUND TWO CARS AND PICKED UP speed as Jami gripped the grab handle, and I craned my neck around her seat to look out at the road. The heavy rain was making it hard for Chris to maneuver the vehicle, though he proved himself to be a competent driver as he weaved in and out of traffic. Morgan was focused on the map in the Stingray program and watching the two points moving across his screen and barking updates as the dot we were chasing moved away from us. Jami worked as Chris's navigator, looking out the windshield, the side window, over her shoulder, finding spots where Chris could turn left or right or accelerate down a clear straightaway in response to Morgan's directions.

"Where's this guy headed?" I asked.

Morgan said, "Seems to be north and west."

Jami thought about that and said, "Bethesda? Are we crossing the Potomac?"

I said nothing. Nobody spoke. We just sat in silence as Chris stepped on the gas and drove even faster.

. . .

EMMA ROSS LOOKED OVER SAMANTHA'S SHOULDER AS HER assistant flipped through the pages of a manual for the CIA's phone system. Samantha said it had been in place for over ten years. Well before Emma was at the Agency. Even before Samantha had joined herself. Her predecessor had handed over a series of three-ring binders and instruction manuals and detailed notes on how everything worked. Emma looked on and asked, "But how can we get past the passcode?"

Samantha kept flipping through the pages and said, "I believe there's a way to reset it."

Emma checked her watch, making a mental note of how long it had been since she'd met with Adam Stine, and wondering if the young man would actually follow through with her request, or if he'd go straight to Ethan instead and tell him about her visit. Emma decided she'd need to call him soon to check on him. She didn't like leaving things to chance. And didn't like waiting around. She'd need to apply some pressure. And the sooner the better, before Mr. Malone checked in with her to ask her for an update.

Samantha said, "I think this is it," showing a page in the manual to her.

Emma said, "Does it say how to reset it?"

Samantha didn't respond. Instead she stepped forward two paces and clicked a button on the phone to get a line. A dial tone sounded, and Samantha hovered a finger over the dial pad, glancing back to the instructions. She did what the manual said to do. She punched the buttons in the right sequence to attempt to reset the password. She paused and turned back to Emma, wide eyes, both of them holding their breath. Then a recorded voice said: Enter your new passcode. Emma raised a fist in the air, and Samantha smiled, then she punched in a new passcode. The recorded voice then asked her to reenter the passcode. She did as she was asked and waited. The voice said the command was successful, and Emma and Samantha gave each other a high five.

Then the line disconnected.

Emma said, "See if it will let us hear the voicemail now."

Samantha got a dial tone and punched in the new passcode to access the voicemail and waited.

I HELD ON TIGHT AS CHRIS NAVIGATED TWO TURNS, A LEFT, then a right; then he found another straightaway and accelerated hard. Jami had accessed DDC's Maps application on her phone as he drove and was using the app to look ahead and find the best way to get us closer to the black sedan using side roads and live traffic updates superimposed on the screen. Since it was a Saturday, traffic was lighter than usual. But the wet roads and the torrential downpour negated any advantage we might've had with the lighter traffic. Both Morgan and Simon were still on the line. Simon said, "Okay, I have access to the satellite, and I'm moving it into position. But the rain is a major problem, guys."

"How so?" I asked.

"The clouds are making it hard to see much of anything. There are pockets of visibility here and there, but overall, I really can't see a whole lot. When things clear up, I should be able to see things a lot better."

I said, "Morgan, are we gaining on the guy at all?"

"Yes," he said. "But you need to go faster if you want any chance of catching up."

Then we all went quiet again. Jami would point left or right or straight, speaking in a low, calm voice. Morgan and Simon fell silent on the call, too, Simon monitoring the satellite, Morgan watching the two dots on his screen as ours grew closer to the bad guy's. I didn't speak, either. I just held onto my cell phone and stared out the windshield, watching the road, thinking about the trajectory of our movements. My thoughts drifted back to what had happened a week earlier. The assassination attempt on two presidents, one Russian, one American. The Bureau guy I'd taken out, and the CIA guys working for him.

Chris drove on as I thought about the black sedan. How it was government looking. And what that might mean, thinking, trying to connect dots. I broke the silence and said, "Guys, what's north and west of us?"

Chris spoke up and said, "A lot of things."

Jami said, "Not Bethesda," since we'd already crossed the Potomac.

I paused a long moment, thinking hard, putting it together, and said, "Then what?"

Nobody spoke. Silence on the phone. Then Jami turned her head slowly and twisted around to look at me.

EMMA STEPPED AROUND SAMANTHA SO THE TWO WOMEN WERE standing side by side next to the desk phone. They stared at each other as the recorded voice said: *You have two new messages and one saved message; first message.* The saved message was from Mr. Malone, asking Gardner to come down to his office. Short and to the point, as Malone usually was. The first new message was from internal affairs. A woman, who said her name very quickly—too quickly to make sense of it—said they had received his message and asked Gardner to return her call at his earliest convenience. Neither message was useful.

But the second new message was useful. It was from a man named Murray. The message was cryptic. Somewhat vague. The guy just stated his name and said he was sorry for taking so long to get back to him, but said he would help Gardner any way he could. But that was all he said. No further details. No last name unless Murray was his last name. No contact information. No way to get a hold of the person. Samantha moved her hand above the keypad. Emma furrowed her brow, watching her assistant. Samantha dialed two numbers and the pound key and found a pen and a notepad on Gardner's desk and held her breath. A moment passed. The recorded voice spoke ten numbers.

Samantha wrote them down, and Emma smiled.

## 26

Adam Stine stood patiently outside Meyer's door. His boss's office wasn't too far from the Oval Office. Just down the hall. Stine didn't knock, but he also didn't enter freely. He had learned from working with Emma Ross that the best way to connect with your superior was to mirror the way they interacted with you. If they sent you emails when they needed something, you sent them emails back. If they called you on the phone, you called them. Ethan Meyer was prone to stopping at Stine's desk periodically throughout the day. Usually at the most inconvenient times. But for being a senior aide to Keller, he still was respectful. He did not knock and did not barge in. So neither did Stine. He just stood silently, waiting.

But Meyer's door was open, and he noticed Stine before long as he wrapped up a phone conversation. Meyer motioned with his hand for him to step inside, and Stine acknowledged the gesture by nodding and obeying. He took a seat at one of two chairs positioned across from Meyer and crossed one leg over the other and leaned back, looking around the office. An office he envisioned might very well be his one day. Meyer ended the call and looked across at him. He said, "Adam, it never ends."

Stine offered a small laugh and nodded knowingly. "You tried to warn me," he replied.

"I did," answered Meyer. Then the room grew quiet. Meyer interlaced his fingers. "What can I do for you?"

Stine stared across at the man, gauging the best way to explain his predicament, weighing a few different approaches he had considered before walking down the hallway, then deciding the best way was the only way, and that was to be fully transparent. "Mr. Meyer, please don't be mad at what I'm about to tell you."

Meyer furrowed his brow. "I don't like the sound of that."

Stine nodded, looked away; then his eyes moved back. "Emma Ross has been trying to get a hold of you."

"You don't think I know that? I have a phone full of voicemails. The best thing to do is ignore the woman."

Stine said, "She reached out to me, sir."

"You spoke to her?"

"I met with her."

Meyer raised his eyebrows. "You went to Langley?"

"No," he said. "She insisted on coming here. I knew we wouldn't want her on the visitor logs. Not after all of the drama she brought to the White House over the years. So I called down to the guardhouse. I told them not to let her in. Instead, I went down to see what she wanted, and we took a walk together."

Meyer leaned forward. "Adam, before you go any further, you need to understand something—I think I made myself perfectly clear when the president brought me on board that I needed full loyalty from you. Anything less than that is unacceptable. I can't have people seeing you out and about with this woman." Meyer's face grew red, but not out of embarrassment. Out of exasperation. Stine looked on. He knew what buttons to push and which not to push. Ethan Meyer continued, "There's one thing Emma Ross and I agreed on, one thing she understood better than anyone I've met in Washington: optics are everything."

Stine uncrossed his legs and sat up straight. He lowered his head and looked up. He said, "Mr. Meyer, please let me finish."

Meyer paused a moment, then nodded for him to continue.

"Her superiors at the CIA have her looking into the assassination attempt from last week. They think we were involved somehow."

Ethan Meyer stared. "We? As in the White House? Adam, that's utterly preposterous."

"I know, sir."

Meyer stared at him a moment longer. Then he looked away and blinked, trying to calm himself down. Then he leaned back in his chair and glanced at his aide. *Emma Ross's* former aide. "What else, Adam?"

"I made a deal with her."

Meyer said nothing.

"She knows we don't want her around, sir. She was desperate. As if her job depended on this assignment, somehow. So I told her I'd help her. I decided I'd talk with you and whoever else you believed might need to be aware of this information. Maybe we talk to Agent Rivera so he knows his team might be compromised. Or maybe we go to the president himself."

Meyer leaned forward again. He looked across at the young man. "I need you to be direct with me," he said. "What specific accusation is the CIA making of the White House? What did Emma say? Or imply?"

"They believe someone within the president's administration leaked the motorcade route to rogue agents within the CIA and the FBI. The men involved in the assassination attempt last week. The men who died."

"So the CIA had people involved, and now they're trying to deflect? Trying to get us to take the blame?"

Stine stared back. Thinking hard. "Mr. Meyer, with all due respect, I don't believe you want a yes-man working for you. One day, if I'm ever in your shoes, I know I wouldn't. I would want people to challenge me. To play devil's advocate. So tell me it's not possible that someone here leaked the motorcade route."

Meyer said nothing. The room grew quiet. Only the sound of muted conversations coming from somewhere outside the office could be heard. Stine recognized one of the voices. The president was out in the hallway, talking with someone. Meyer stared. He breathed in and breathed out. Then he said, "Anything is possible, Adam. But only a few people would've known the motorcade route. Not even the entire Secret Service team would've known. Only a few of Rivera's men. And only a few people close to the president. Routes change often. They have to. There would only be a select few who could've known for sure that day last week, when and where the presidential limo would've been. Okay?"

There was a soft knock at the door. President Keller popped his head in. He pointed at Meyer and asked if everything was set for later. Meyer said that it was. They were prepared to leave in a few hours. Keller nodded his appreciation and glanced at Stine. He asked how he was, and the young man said all was well.

Then the president disappeared back into the hallway. Back down to the Oval. Ethan Meyer stared at him and said,

"Adam, my father taught me something a long time ago. He said: respect is earned, honesty is appreciated, trust is gained, and loyalty is returned. The people Keller have working for him have earned his respect. We're just about as honest as we can be in Washington. And we have gained his trust." He paused for a moment. Then he added, "But our loyalty is what really matters at the end of the day." Meyer shrugged. "If you're asking me if it's possible that someone within the administration leaked the motorcade route to those rogue agents, then yes, Adam. It is. Anything's possible. But not from the inner circle. The people who work for the president are as loyal as they come. I just don't see it being one of us."

Stine nodded and stood. He reached his hand across the desk, and Meyer shook it. Stine said, "I'll let Emma know that I ran this down and came up empty. By the way—what's happening later with Keller?"

Meyer smiled proudly. "The president's kicking off his reelection campaign. An impromptu rally. We just notified his most ardent supporters. The news will break soon." He paused. "Apparently, he isn't content with an eight-point lead over his opponent. James Keller is a very cautious man."

Stine nodded vaguely and went to the door.

Meyer said, "Adam, what was the deal you made with Emma Ross?"

Stine turned back from the door. "Mr. Meyer, Emma has been a thorn in our side for a very long time now. I told her I'd look into her concern. But I also said, if I find nothing, she can never reach out to us again."

## 27

The man with the silver hair was in his vehicle again, headed back to his office as his cell rang loud and bright in the otherwise quiet car. He slid his thumb across the screen and answered, "Yes?"

"It's me," the caller said.

"Good news, I hope?"

"Excellent news," the caller answered. "I've had an interesting morning. Emma Ross is poking around."

"And?"

"And she's going to come up short. There's nothing to tell her. Our bases are completely covered."

"I should hope so." The silver-haired man paused. "What else?"

"The president is preparing for his campaign rally later today. They're announcing it now, but we've known about it for a week."

"Which is when we'll make our move."

"Agreed," said the caller. "And based on recent conversations, nobody knows anything."

"So it will be a complete surprise."

"Yes. Will your people be in position?"

"You don't need to question me," the silver-haired man said.

"I do, actually. I'm taking a big risk here. If you actually take this guy out, there'll be a lot of confusion."

"I should hope so."

The caller continued, "The administration will be turned upside down. Nobody will see it coming."

He said, "That is the point. We failed last week. Failed to take both presidents out. The peace treaty was signed, and both Russia and our country have moved on. This is our plan B, and we don't have a plan C."

"I understand. My point is, I need some guarantees from you. Not promises. There is a difference."

The silver-haired man said nothing.

"I want another hundred grand sent to my account should there be unexpected fallout. I have mouths to feed, and if this goes south, if they haul me off to Guantanamo, my family will suffer. I'm sure you understand. I'm doing your dirty work here; I'm making sure this goes according to plan. It's only fair."

The silver-haired man said, "You're close to Keller. You play a critical role. Without you, none of this will work." He paused and thought for a long moment. "Make sure the president is in the designated spot and you will be rewarded, but I will not enter endless negotiations with you." Then he clicked off. And then he smiled as he drove on, because if they failed, he'd make sure the caller would take the blame.

## 28

Emma took the notepad from Samantha and stared at the ten numbers her aide had written down. Samantha raised her eyebrows and made a face that said: *Well, are we going to call the number or not?* Emma answered by moving closer to Gardner's desk phone and opening a line. Loud and bright. She punched in the ten numbers carefully, one at a time, her eyes flicking back and forth between the notepad and the keypad. Then she dropped the notepad on the desk and crossed her arms and stood back. The line started to ring. One ring in, Samantha smiled and nodded. Three rings in, the smile faded. Five rings in, she furrowed her brow. By the seventh ring, it was clear there wasn't going to be an answer. And there was no machine to leave a message on, either. After close to a minute of waiting and hoping, Emma clicked off.

Samantha said, "Why wasn't there a voicemail?"

Emma said, "It must be a landline without a machine."

"What do we do now?"

"We call in a favor." She dug into a pocket for her cell phone. It would not work inside the Original Headquarters

Building. No reception. But she found her contacts and scrolled through with her thumb until she found the number she was looking for. She opened another line and dialed the number and waited.

The call went straight to voicemail. Simon Harris's voicemail. So she tried Morgan Lennox out of Chicago, with the same result. Emma tried Blake Jordan. Voicemail. She whispered to herself, "What is going on?" as she ended the call and kept scrolling through her contacts list, looking for any other options. Then she tried Lynne May, out of DDC's Washington field office. The woman answered the call on the first ring.

"I need your help, Lynne," she said.

May hesitated for a moment and said, "What's going on?"

"I don't know who else to call. I have a phone number. I think it's a landline. Can you trace it for me?"

"Trace it how?"

Emma looked away, thinking. "I need an address. I believe it's for a man named Murray. It's important."

May said, "The phone system tells me you're calling me from Alex Gardner's office. Is that right?"

Emma said that it was. She quickly brought the DDC woman up to speed with what was going on. May responded by saying that she was aware of Gardner's death and offered her condolences. Then May asked Emma for the phone number, and she told her to give her five minutes to look it up, then call her back.

Which she did, exactly five minutes later. May answered and immediately said, "I have the address."

"For Murray?"

"Yes, Daniel Murray, lives in Reston, Sixty-year-old white male, former Army, former FBI, now retired."

Emma asked for the address and wrote it down. Lynne May asked if she was going there now, and Emma said that she was. May told her she shouldn't go alone. Emma thanked her and clicked off. She thanked Samantha for her help and warned her assistant not to talk to anyone about this. Then she left.

BETHESDA WAS NORTH AND WEST, BUT SO WERE A MILLION other things. And I was worried about one place in particular. But before I could think any more about it, Morgan broke the silence and said, "Guys, we have a slight problem. The driver stopped moving. The phone's stationary about a mile out from you."

From the front Chris said, "That's a problem?"

"Maybe," said Morgan. "Maybe not."

"He's probably at a traffic light."

I said, "You think bad guys obey traffic lights?"

Chris said, "Then he parked somewhere. Guide us in, Morgan. We'll pull up and watch from a distance."

Jami nodded her agreement as I held my phone in my hand and continued to stare out the windshield. The rain was starting to let up some. It was still coming down hard, but it wasn't a downpour anymore. Simon said it was still too cloudy to see much of anything, but he was in lockstep with Morgan and moving the satellite to our location in case the sky cleared. Jami stopped giving directions, and Morgan took over. He said we were close enough to the other dot on his screen that he was able to zoom in some and offer detailed guidance on what the best approach would be. Morgan told Chris where to turn, offered an estimated distance from our target, and finally brought us to the street where Mark's cell phone was pinging from. Chris turned his wipers on low, and the three of us looked out, searching for the black sedan.

Chris rolled to a stop as we turned at the street where Morgan said the cell was pinging from. But we saw nothing. A few vehicles were parked along the curb, a few more cars were ahead of us on the street and coming toward us from the other side, but only a few of them were dark. Fewer black. None were a sedan.

"Are you sure this is it?" I asked. "Maybe we're off by a block?"

"You're on the right street," Morgan said from the phone.

"We're not seeing anything."

"Keep moving," he said.

So Chris let his foot off the brake and gently tapped the gas, and we picked up speed. Slow at first. Just a crawl. He let the truck glide across, ignoring traffic behind us as frustrated drivers pulled around and sped off down the street. We stared ahead and saw nothing. Jami craned her neck to the left and to the right. I glanced right and looked out the window and down the street. No sedans with a broken window.

Morgan said, "Keep going, you're almost there."

"We're not seeing anything," I said again.

"Just keep going, mate."

Which we did. We kept gliding and looking and moving slow and easy. Chris's windshield wipers pushed the rain back and forth. We looked all over. There was no sedan. Then Morgan told us to stop and look.

But there was nothing there.

"It should be," Morgan insisted. "Trust me, guys; the two dots are basically right on top of each other."

Chris kept his SUV crawling forward, and then a moment later, Morgan told us that we had passed it. Chris picked up speed, and Jami helped him navigate around the block, and we came back from where we had started to try again. We repeated the same process, Morgan navigating us closer, the three of us scanning all around as we moved; then Morgan told us again that the two dots were on top of each other.

Chris pulled to the side of the road and put the vehicle in park. "It's not here," he said.

Morgan said, "And I'm telling you guys that it is."

I said, "Morgan, something's off. There aren't a lot of vehicles on the street. We're not missing it."

"Well, I don't know what to tell you, mate."

"Simon, any luck with the satellite?"

He said, "I've got it overhead, but there are still too many clouds for it to be useful. Sorry, guys."

Chris looked forward, craning his neck, looking all around. There were three cars parked in front of us. None were a sedan with a broken window. Jami turned back from the passenger seat and looked past me. Nothing behind us. Nobody parked to the left of us on the other side of the street. Jami remained facing me. The wheels were spinning. She said, "Morgan, what if the bad guy found the phone and turned it off?"

"What do you mean, love?" he asked.

Jami shrugged. A small, little movement she made as she was thinking. "The dot you're looking at would stay on the screen, wouldn't it? Showing the last location where it had been, even if it's not there anymore?"

"That's a good thought, Jami, but I don't believe it works that way."

"Meaning what?"

"Meaning, I wouldn't be seeing two dots overlaying each other if it wasn't there. If the guy had removed the battery, there would only be one dot. Yours. But there isn't one dot. There are two. So he didn't remove the battery, and he didn't turn it off. I honestly don't know what else to tell you people. It's there."

Simon asked Morgan if there was another cell phone moving along with Mark's. Meaning, if the driver had a cell, could Morgan identify it moving along the same route the guy had taken as he drove away, and if that cell phone was still turned on, see if it had been at the same location as Mark's, which was here.

Morgan told Simon that was also a good idea, but it was a little late to do that. He had scrambled to lock onto Mark's cell using Stingray, and while that was happening, he had tracked my cell phone, so he could help guide us closer to the vehicle as it sped away. Stingray could do a lot of things, but it couldn't track more than two cell phones at a time. Then the car got quiet. Chris put the SUV in park and sighed heavily.

Jami looked away, thinking again. Morgan and Simon grew quiet on the line. Nobody spoke. We all just sat in the silence, thinking, trying to understand what was happening. Chris had said: *It's not here*. And Morgan had answered: *I'm telling you guys that it is*. Then something caught my eye. A small glimmer of light from the corner of my eye. I turned to look and saw a small light shining in the gloom.

## 29

It was a cell phone, small and tiny from where I sat, standing upright against the side of the building, leaning against the outer wall, lighting up from a call coming through. I stared at it for a moment before I knew what I was looking at. Then I understood, as the screen grew dim and turned black. "Look," I said.

Chris glanced over his shoulder and followed my gaze. Jami looked at Chris, turned to her right; then she looked out the window, too. She stared for a long moment with us and said, "Is that what I think it is?"

I said nothing back. Just handed my cell phone over to Chris and opened the back door and climbed out. The rain fell down on me. I closed the door hard and faced forward. The rain wasn't coming down as hard as before, but it was steady and cold and relentless nonetheless. I walked to the building. Jami and Chris stayed inside the vehicle, watching me move as I stepped forward to where the phone was.

Then I reached down and picked it up and stood close to the side of the building where it was dry and protected from the rain. As I stared at it, the screen lit up bright. A sharp ringing sound. The caller ID showed UNKNOWN CALLER. I slid my thumb across the screen and brought it up to my ear. I took a breath and said, "Who are you?"

A voice said, "Do you think I'm stupid?"

"I'm not the one driving in the rain without a window." I turned and looked all around to see if the driver of the black sedan was parked somewhere, or driving by, watching me, but I saw no one there.

"I know who you are, Agent Jordan," the voice continued. "And your wife. And your friend Agent Reed."

"Who are you?" I said again.

The voice made no reply.

"Why are you following us?"

"Your friend has something I want."

"Which is what?"

There was a long pause. He was thinking, debating; then he decided not to answer. Instead he said, "You failed us, Jordan. When this is all over, you're going to regret not cooperating with us a week ago."

"How so?" The guy didn't answer. So I said, "We tracked you a long way. I saw the trajectory. I have a good idea where you were headed now. So I'll know where to find you. I just need to find a way inside."

The guy paused. A sudden realization about something he hadn't considered.

"So which building will I find you in? Original Headquarters or New?"

No reply. Not at first. Then he said, "It'll take you all day to find me. There are a lot of us."

"Thousands," I said. "But I doubt you're a desk clerk. You didn't have the look. So that narrows it some."

"You won't find me in time."

"In time for what?" I said, but he didn't answer. The guy

just breathed as he thought about it. Then he wished me luck, and the line went dead.

I POCKETED MARK'S PHONE AND TREKKED BACK THROUGH THE rain and climbed into Chris's parked SUV. He was still holding my cell phone, and I could hear Morgan and Simon still conferenced in. Jami turned around in her seat and stared back at me. Chris handed my phone back and said, "What happened, man?"

"He called me," I said.

"The guy from the sedan? What did he say?"

"A lot of things." I paused and stared back at my friend. "He said you have something he wants."

Chris narrowed his eyes. "Which is?"

"Knowledge," I said.

"What does that mean?"

"You were his partner. They killed him because he knew something. Or maybe because they thought he did. Maybe they think you do, too. Maybe they're assuming he told you what he knew. You're a loose end."

Jami said, "How were they following us?"

I patted my pocket with my free hand. "Mark's phone. They were tracking him. Maybe Mark knew that. Maybe that's why he left it in his office. Maybe they were tracking him before. Or maybe afterwards. Maybe they were still monitoring it, and they saw it moving and assumed that Chris had it. But he didn't."

"You did," said Chris.

I nodded. Said nothing.

"We need to remove the battery."

I said, "I'm not worried about him finding us. He should be worried about us finding him."

"Which we're not going to be able to do," said Simon from the speakerphone. "The satellite is of no use."

I shifted my eyes from Chris to Jami. I said, "What's north and west of us?"

Jami said, "Bethesda. But we know that can't be it because we crossed the river."

"Then what?"

She thought about that long and hard. Then her face changed. An understanding. She said, "Langley."

I nodded again. "I told him I knew. He was taunting me. I told him I'd find him, but he said I wouldn't. There were too many like him. He's probably thinking we'd never get into CIA HQ." I smiled. "But we can."

Chris said, "Emma Ross."

I nodded a third time. I told Morgan and Simon we'd be in touch. Then I clicked off and dialed a number.

## 30

Emma answered on the first ring. She told us she'd tried to call us earlier. She'd tried to reach Simon and Morgan as well, but nobody was taking her call. So I told her why we'd been busy. I filled her in with everything that had happened over the last forty-five minutes since we'd last spoken to her.

Then she brought us up to speed with things on her end. Emma said she'd searched Gardner's office like I'd suggested. She told us how she'd wasted a lot of time and almost came up empty. But then she didn't. She told us about a voicemail from a guy named Daniel Murray, how she'd called Lynne May at DDC for help to get an address for the guy, and said she had gotten it and was headed there now. Emma told us that May had warned her not to go alone. Chris looked at Jami, and Jami nodded her agreement with that.

Jami said, "Where are you going?" and Emma told her Reston.

I said, "Text us the address, and we'll meet you there." Then I removed the battery from Mark's phone.

. . .

IT TOOK CLOSE TO THIRTY MINUTES TO GET OUT THERE. CHRIS wasn't driving with any sense of urgency. No need to. Our lead had dried up, the sky was too dark for Simon to have tracked the guy, and aside from a general understanding that the bad guy was CIA, the only person who could help us get into Langley needed us in Reston. Chris was quiet. I figured he was thinking a lot about his partner. The kinds of things you think about when you suddenly lose someone close to you. Jami and I had a shared understanding. We didn't talk to him at all. We just let him drive in silence and come to terms that Mark was gone and wasn't coming back.

We passed Langley along the way, and as we drove by it, I thought about the conversation I'd had with the guy on the phone. *There are a lot of us*, he'd said. *Thousands*, I'd replied. He was right. The CIA employed thousands of people. Many of them reported to work at their HQ. Of those, hundreds must've driven black sedans and SUVs, going in and out, passing checkpoints as they entered or left.

Then my thoughts grew darker as I looked back at Chris as he drove. He had something they wanted. *Knowledge*, I had said. And I truly believed that. Which meant they had the same end in mind for Chris as they had with Mark. Then I remembered something else the guy had said: *You won't find me in time*. I looked out the window as we moved and wondered what that meant as we drove on down the highway.

AS WE ENTERED RESTON CITY LIMITS, MY CELL PHONE CHIMED. So did Jami's. It was Emma Ross sending us her location. Jami slid her thumb across the screen and tapped on the address, and the Maps application began navigating us to where Emma was waiting. That seemed to snap Chris back out of it. He became fully present. He was alive again and checking his surroundings and looking out the windows as we moved through the city. I was thinking hard as we moved. I should've believed Chris. *I knew him*, he'd said to me. We pulled up to the address and parked behind Emma's car. She stepped out and met us.

We all stood huddled together. The rain had stopped, but the streets were wet. Chris said, "This it?"

Emma nodded slowly and turned to look at the house. I followed her gaze. It was a sprawling home. Much like the one in Fairfax. An older, distinguished property, back before enterprising builders squeezed as many homes together as they could. There were two large oak trees out front. There were more behind the residence. Spanish moss hung low from their branches. There was an old winding path that led to the front door.

I said, "We don't know who this guy is? Aside from his name?"

Emma said, "He's a white male, older gentleman, former Army, former FBI, now retired. Per Lynne May."

Jami said, "What's the connection to Gardner?"

"I didn't ask. I needed Lynne to get me an address, and that's what she did. I headed right over."

"What do you think we're going to find inside?" asked Chris.

Emma glanced back at the large home and crossed her arms and shivered a little, thinking about it. "Answers," she replied after a long moment. "I believe it was a friend, based on the message on Gardner's machine. I got the feeling he was returning a phone call. That's the only explanation I can give. The message was too short to be anything else. It sounded like a guy calling back saying, *Yes, I'll help you.*"

Jami turned to look at me. So did Chris. He stared a moment longer and said, "Plan, boss?"

I moved my eyes back to the home and the winding path that led to the door. I answered the question by moving past them, leading Chris, Jami, and Emma across the wet grass and onto the easement, past the sidewalk, and to the walkway. I followed the same general steps as I'd taken at the residence in Fairfax. Only this time I didn't have Jami going around the side and Chris going to the back. No need to. As far as I knew, this wasn't someone who wanted to hurt Gardner. It was someone who wanted to help. A friend. But someone we had to talk to nonetheless. Someone who might be able to help put the puzzle together.

I put my ear to the jamb and listened. I heard nothing. No televisions, no muted conversations, no sounds at all. But it felt different from earlier. Different from the home in Fairfax. I sensed someone inside. I glanced over my shoulder briefly at the others. Then I turned back and knocked on the door three times. Jami rang the doorbell. She was anxious to get inside and talk to the man named Murray. We all were.

But nobody answered. Not a man named Murray, not anyone else. I knocked again, three more times. Then in a loud voice I said, "Federal agent; please open the door." Then I did hear movement. Small and subtle but definite. It sounded like floorboards creaking. I imagined fifty- or sixty-year-old wood floors spanning the massive expanse of the home, with a lot of use by the door. Warping over time. Harsh winters, hot summers, in and out every day, month after month, year after year, for decades. Chris and Jami heard it too. I glanced at both of them, and they nodded. I said, "My name is Blake Jordan, Homeland Security. We need to talk to you about one of your friends. A man named Alex Gardner."

We stood there for a long moment, but there was no reply. Then Chris tried. Then Jami gave it a shot. No luck. No response. Just the vague understanding that someone was on the other side of the door, listening but not acting. Not opening up for anyone. Especially not for a bunch of federal agents wanting to talk.

Then Emma tried. She stepped forward. She cleared her throat and spoke softly but with composure and authority but also with compassion. She explained how the guy's friend had been killed that morning. Emma said she'd heard a message from a man named Murray. She was here to help find Gardner's killer. Then something changed. Movement. Low voices. A conversation. Maybe he was on the phone. Or telling a spouse to go to a back room. Then the door opened. An older man stood in the doorway. He looked us over for a long moment, then he stepped aside, and another man appeared from behind. He stepped forward. Emma stared, trying to understand. Then she did and turned to introduce us to him.

It was Alex Gardner.

## 31

ETHAN MEYER STEPPED OUT OF HIS OFFICE AND WALKED DOWN the long hallway inside the West Wing. Keller had the door to the Oval Office shut. He could hear the president talking. Low voices through the door. Two Secret Service agents stood watch outside it. Ethan gestured toward the door, and the man on the right of it opened it up and stuck his head inside. The agent said, "Ethan Meyer is here for you, sir."

He heard the president tell the man to give him a moment; then the agent closed the door quickly. The man started to tell Meyer, but the chief of staff just said, "I heard him; I'll wait here," pointing at a spot a few feet away. Meyer took two steps back and stood with his arms in front of him, his right hand cupping the back of his left, and he listened. The muted conversation continued. The unmistakable low tones of James Keller's voice along with another voice, also familiar, but too soft and muffled to be able to tell whom it belonged to.

But then he knew, because the door opened on its own, and the two Secret Service agents stepped to the side, and two men stepped out: Agent Bryant and Adam Stine. The young man glanced to his right and saw Ethan standing there, waiting. Stine raised his eyebrows as a look of surprise fell on his face. But he didn't speak. He just nodded and walked past him, headed to his desk at the other end of the long hallway.

Meyer turned back, and the agent to the right of the door gestured inside with the open palm of his hand. He nodded his appreciation and stepped through the doorway as Agent Bryant followed him in and stood by the door.

"Ethan, please sit down," said Keller, motioning to one of the two chairs across from the *Resolute* desk.

Meyer stepped forward and walked across the tan carpet with an American eagle emblazoned on it. He pulled a chair out and sat down in it. Keller watched him carefully, but made no further remarks. He was waiting for Ethan to speak. Then he did. Meyer pointed behind him with a thumb. "What was that about?"

The president took a deep breath and let it out. He sat down and leaned back in his chair and eyed him carefully. He said, "Ethan, would you want me telling him what our private conversations are about?"

"I have my doubts about him."

"I know you do. You shouldn't."

"He's not my guy," Meyer said. "He's Emma's."

"Which is why you should stop worrying."

Meyer said nothing. Just tilted his head to the side and stared.

Keller took another deep breath and let it out as if he was growing weary and maybe a little irritated. He said, "Adam told me he met with her a little while ago. He wanted to make sure I knew about her concern."

"So he wanted to make sure I had told you about it? In case I forgot? Or in case I intentionally forgot?"

Keller shrugged. "He's ambitious, Ethan. I can see it in his eyes and the way he works. Reminds me a lot of you. You were his age once. You remember what it was like. You want facetime with the big boss, the guy in charge. It doesn't hurt for me to give him a few minutes of my time. What's the worst that can happen?"

"Other than undermining my authority?"

Keller smiled warmly. "He wasn't doing that, Ethan. I knew you'd tell me about Emma eventually. And I also knew that if you didn't, you'd have a damn good reason why." Keller paused a long moment. "He told me the CIA believes someone in the White House may have leaked the motorcade route last week."

"Pure speculation, sir."

"But possible, correct?"

Meyer relaxed in his seat a little. He loosened his posture and leaned back and crossed one leg over the other. He made a face and looked away, past Keller, out through the tall windows behind the Oval. He said, "Like I told the kid, anything is possible. It's true that only a few people close to you would know the exact route that you and President Stepanov would've taken to the airport last week."

"How many people?" asked Keller.

Meyer shook his head slowly as his eyes danced around, looking up and around as he was thinking. "Five?"

"Has to be more than that. The driver, the agents inside the vehicle, Agent Rivera himself, you, Adam, a few others in our circle, countless Metro PD officers who go on ahead of the limousine clearing the streets. It's got to be close to twenty people, thirty, maybe even more when you think about it. And every one of them is a single point of failure. It only takes one corrupt person to leak something like that. It would be an egregious abuse of power to have that kind of knowledge and leak it to people wanting to hurt me, Ethan."

Meyer's eyes fell back to Keller's. "I agree, sir."

The president smiled again. Warm and bright and welcoming. "I have to trust the people closest to me. What other choice do I have? I'm not going to be one of these paranoid leaders who's constantly firing and replacing everyone all of the time. We'd never get anywhere. We'd never find our stride. I might be the president, but it takes all of us moving together in lockstep if we're going to create lasting change."

"I agree," he said again.

"Good. Now, can we talk about tonight?"

Meyer stared.

"Agent Rivera is making the final preparations. It'll only take a few minutes for us to head over there, so I plan on working from here until it's time to leave." Keller paused and grew quiet, sensing something was wrong. "What is it, Ethan?"

Meyer thought about it for a spell, and then he said, "Sir, it's just that you're kicking off your reelection campaign here, in DC." He paused. "Don't you think you should be doing that in Chicago?"

"No, I don't."

"Your home state is Illinois. Your residence is in Chicago. That would've been more natural, sir."

"Ethan, you need to understand something. I enjoyed my time in the senate, and I absolutely love the people of my state and my city." He shook his head. "But I don't belong to them anymore. So, no, I don't think I should be doing this in Chicago. I'm doing it right here, in the city I'm determined to change from the inside out, one way or the other, whether the people here want me or not."

"I guess we'll find out if they still do," he said as Agent Bryant opened the door to the Oval, maybe sensing the conversation was over.

Keller nodded and said, "I guess so," and watched Meyer step back out into the hallway and disappear.

FIVE MINUTES LATER A SECURE CALL CAME THROUGH. THE MAN with the silver hair answered it. The caller said, "Nobody knows anything. Not even the president himself. They have no idea about today." Then the call ended, and the man with the silver hair smiled as the things he had planned played out in his mind.

## 32

President James Keller remained seated behind the *Resolute* desk. His mind was racing, and he was unable to focus on getting his work done. He had planned on wrapping a few things up, then mapping out what he would say at his impromptu reelection campaign rally. He hated using the teleprompter. He hated giving canned speeches. It was best to speak from the heart. He believed that if you couldn't speak off the cuff about the things that mattered to you, then they must not matter that much.

But his lack of focus and concentration bothered him. For a man in his early sixties, he'd had plenty of energy. And since his wife had passed away a short time after he took office, he had little to do besides work. Which was both a blessing and a curse. Having a loving wife and a family to retire to had been the highlight of his day. Now his days did not end when he left the Oval Office for the residence upstairs. They just bled over to a new location. There was work, and then there was thinking about work. The presidency was by nature a twenty-four-seven job, but even presidents took time off. There was golf and vacations and planned outings. But not for him. He had no interest in such things anymore. Not since Margaret passed. Occasionally he'd make a trip to Camp David to show that he wasn't a complete workaholic, but it was the same thing, just a different place: work all day, then think about work all throughout the night.

Keller blinked hard. He became present again, realizing his mind had wandered, and was bothered by his inability to stay focused. He tried to understand why and stood to pace the room and think it all through. Then his thoughts moved back to the two conversations he'd just had. They bothered him. Both of them.

The fact that someone within his inner circle could've leaked the presidential motorcade route, allowing CIA men to make an assassination attempt with the help of a rogue Bureau agent, was appalling. Those truths had never made it to the news outlets. It had been decided in consultation with Meyer that this would weaken the public's view of the nation's government agencies. And they already had a negative view of them to begin with. So the assassins had been identified, but the facts about who they were and where they worked had been intentionally omitted. Even Rivera, head of Keller's Secret Service detail, agreed with the idea. Then Keller thought about what he had told Meyer and the fact that so many people outside of the White House and his own inner circle knew about the motorcade route. He did believe that. But he'd also learned to trust his instincts when they were trying to tell him something. And his were sending up plenty of red flags now.

Keller walked back to his desk, but he did not sit. Instead he punched a line on one of his desk phones. After a brief pause, an operator asked what she could do for the president. He said, "Get me Agent Rivera."

"I'll patch you in, sir."

"No," he replied. "I want him to come to my office. Right now, please."

There was another brief pause. Then the voice answered, "Yes, Mr. President."

Then Keller clicked off and stood up straight, resting his hands on the back of his chair, thinking hard, waiting. Rivera didn't take long. Two minutes passed, and the president heard two soft knocks at the door. It opened, but unlike earlier, the agent posted outside didn't duck his head in to announce the presence of someone at the door. Instead, Agent Rivera himself stepped through and closed the door behind him. The president stepped around his desk and motioned to the two couches on the opposite side of the room. Rivera took a seat, and Keller joined him on the opposite couch. Nothing between them except for a coffee table.

Rivera said, "What is this about, Mr. President?"

Keller stared across at the man. He said, "Agent Rivera, I believe there will be another attack on my life."

Rivera stared back, trying to understand where this was coming from.

"And I think it will happen today."

KELLER TOLD RIVERA THAT EMMA ROSS HAD MET WITH HIS people regarding concerns the CIA had about a White House leaker. Keller told his head agent his own concerns about security. Agent Rivera assured the president that his team had taken the appropriate precautions. He explained that what had happened a week prior would not happen again. Instead of one exact route for the presidential motorcade to take, there would be multiple options. Therefore a much smaller chance of potential issues. Of course there was one official route they would take, but that wouldn't be fully known by those who needed to know, including Metro PD, until they were on the road. Too hard for potential bad guys to double back and regroup. And there'd have to be a lot of them to cover all of the various routes, should there actually be a White House leaker passing information along. Besides, Rivera and his men had adopted a new protocol: none of their protectees would know which route they'd take before they left. Which included Ethan Meyer and Adam Stine. Which meant if Keller's suspicions were correct, it would not matter. By not sharing plans ahead of time, they'd be heading off any leaks before they could happen, thereby mitigating the risk in its entirety.

Keller thought about that for a spell. Then he said, "I agree with your approach, but you should wait."

Rivera narrowed his eyes and shook his head. A small little movement. "Wait, sir?"

"Yes, wait."

"I'm sorry, I'm not following you, Mr. President."

"I need to know who's loyal and who's not. Therefore you need to hold off on your approach for now."

"And do what instead?"

Keller breathed. "Draw up two versions of the plan. Hand them to both men. Instruct them not to share the details with anybody. As a matter of security. Tell them we'll be exposed. Tell them where; show them the points of exposure. Then bring us in an entirely different way. The actual route you select." He shrugged. "Maybe send a decoy motorcade along the route you give them. Maybe we can prove which one of them may be leaking things. Then we can know for sure if they're in bed with people they shouldn't be."

Rivera thought about that for a long moment. Then he said, "Mr. President, I believe I have a better idea."

Malone waited at Gardner's home until his people showed up. He spoke to them in hushed tones, explaining what had happened and what they were dealing with. Then he made the appropriate introductions with Mulvaney's Bureau guys. Then he slapped his men on their backs and told them to keep him updated as needed; then he ducked out through the open garage and headed to his parked vehicle.

He called Emma Ross on her cell, but the woman did not answer. He figured she might be sitting inside her office at Langley. The one with thick windows and therefore no cell service. So he tried her there but got no answer. He left a message and decided to give her some time to get back to him. He had urgent news to share with her. News he hadn't shared with the Bureau guys. And that news was that the dead man inside the Fairfax home was not Alex Gardner. It was the body of someone else entirely. Someone he knew well. Someone he had not heard from for close to twelve hours. And now he finally understood why.

The Bureau guys would figure it out eventually. They were running the show, after all. Malone had already agreed to that. After the pictures were taken and the crime scene was documented and the coroner took the body, the Bureau would run the prints to positively identify the body but would be unable to. Their systems would identify the body as another man entirely. A CIA guy for sure, but not one named Gardner.

And that created a problem, because he had things he needed to see done, and because the clock was ticking.

## 33

THE MAN CALLED MURRAY USHERED US INSIDE; THEN HE closed and locked the door behind him. Chris, Jami, and I stood across from Emma and Gardner as Murray turned and stepped between us and motioned for us to follow him through the foyer and into a large family room. There was plenty of seating. I saw two large couches. Jami and I sat on one of them. Chris and Emma Ross sat on the other one. Gardner took a seat in a recliner, and Murray stepped away to the kitchen for a minute to make coffee for us. Then he returned and sat down in another chair close to his friend. We all stared at Gardner in silence. Then the man spoke. He eyed us for a spell, then turned to Emma Ross and said, "How did you find me?"

"Mr. Malone told me you were let go from the Agency. I had no idea and, frankly, didn't even notice. Our paths hadn't crossed much lately." She paused. "Then I learned you were dead. They found your body. They said somebody killed you at your home in Fairfax. I needed to know why." Emma took a breath and let it out. Then she continued, "I started poking around your office. My assistant helped me get into your voicemail. I heard the message from your friend offering to help you. I assumed he was calling you back."

Murray glanced at Gardner. A concerned look. He turned to Emma and said, "How'd you track me down?"

"Through a friend."

Murray narrowed his eyes. "Does anyone at the CIA know you're here right now?"

Emma said, "Not yet." She shifted her gaze from Murray back to Gardner. "Alex, what's going on here?"

Gardner asked Emma if she trusted Chris, Jami, and me. Emma said that she did, and therefore so should they. Then Gardner took a deep breath and let it out slowly and sat a little more relaxed in his chair. He said, "The whole thing started a week ago. After the assassination attempt, when we found out that two of our own CIA guys were involved along with that Bureau man who supposedly orchestrated the whole thing. There was an internal investigation. Fast-tracked, of course, with the intent to understand who the men really were, and who they were associated with, the idea being that there had to be more people involved."

Emma said, "We believe someone within the White House leaked the motorcade route to the CIA."

Gardner nodded. "Which is what I told my superiors. Someone needs to be running that down."

Emma said, "I'm doing that. Mr. Malone asked me to. I met with the deputy chief of staff a few hours ago."

"Are they cooperating?"

"We'll find out."

Gardner nodded again. Then he got back into it. He said, "I offered to help figure out who the CIA guys were working with. I had done those kinds of investigations in the past. But I was told to stand down. First by David Malone, then by internal affairs, who told me they were handling it. They sidelined me. And I didn't appreciate that very much. Not after thirty years of service. So yeah, I ignored orders. I started looking into it even though I'd been asked specifically not to so I wouldn't interfere with their efforts."

I said, "So what happened?"

"David Malone fired me," he said. "That's what happened. He called me into his office and sat me down. He said internal affairs had reached out to him. They said I was accessing files I shouldn't have been looking at."

"Were you?"

"You're damn right I was. I felt like I was making progress, too. I explained that to David, but he wouldn't listen to me. He doesn't like people below him making him look bad. So he gave me his usual speech on following orders, respecting the chain of command, all that nonsense. But I told him this was different."

Emma said, "Then what?"

"Then David told me to leave. He didn't even let me get my stuff from my office. He escorted me right out. Two security guys went back for my wallet and my keys and met me at my car and sent me on my way."

Emma said, "If he fired you, then he forgot to put the paperwork through. You're still active in the system."

Jami nodded. "I can confirm that. I logged in at DDC earlier and saw your name in the org chart. It still shows Emma as reporting to you and you reporting to Malone." She paused and said, "Please continue."

Gardner nodded. "So I sat around there for two long days, steaming, irritated, pissed off, quite frankly. Then I decided to do something about it. I tried to file a complaint, but the Agency wouldn't talk to me. They basically told me to lawyer up if I had a bone to pick with them. They wouldn't return any more calls. I went through my files, stuff I had brought home over the years, and found a number for Peter Mulvaney. I figured if the CIA wasn't going to listen to me, I'd talk to the Bureau. But Mulvaney wasn't an easy man to get on the phone. I eventually got a hold of him, and we spoke briefly. He said he was running late to something. He invited me to come down to the Hoover Building, but I said no. It had to be at my home, after midnight. It took some convincing, but he eventually agreed to send a few guys out to talk to me."

"Why after midnight?" I asked.

"Because I felt like I was being watched." Gardner paused, eyeing each of us closely, then seeming to remember what Emma had said about being able to trust us. "There was a vehicle parked down the street. I could see it out the window. It was parked far enough away that it could keep tabs on me. I guess the driver thought he was hidden enough, but he wasn't. He was there twelve hours a day, morning to night." Chris asked if it was a black sedan, but Gardner shook his head. "SUV. A Tahoe, I believe. Either way, it was very concerning. I hadn't done anything wrong. Or maybe I had. Maybe the research I had started triggered something with internal affairs. Either way, the person watching me was why I told Mulvaney to send the two guys after midnight. After the SUV would've left for the day, as it had done the prior two days. One of the Bureau agents called me a few hours ahead of our meeting. He wanted to know if it was really necessary to come after midnight. So I explained why. He was patient with me. I told him about the vehicle down the street. I think the guy thought I was crazy, but I told him I had worked at the CIA for thirty years, and I was a very senior guy there. I wasn't some mailroom clerk with conspiracy theories. The Bureau agent told me he and his partner would be over in a few hours, but then I went to the window, and I saw the SUV again. After hours. I recognized the headlights. A guy climbed out."

Emma crossed her arms and leaned forward. With a soft voice she said, "What happened after that, Alex?"

"I turned the lights off and watched. The Bureau guy said he was on his way, but he was twenty minutes out. He suggested I call MPD, but there wasn't time. As they say, the police aren't the first responders. You are. So I grabbed my weapon and told the agent to leave his phone behind. I told him I'd explain why later, but he needed to stay off the grid starting that very moment now that he was involved with me. So I clicked off and waited. I set the phone down and came back to the window, but the guy wasn't there. Then I unlocked the front door. No use delaying the inevitable. He would've found a way in, and I wanted to nudge him to enter that way. I kept the lights off and saw him out back. I tracked him moving to the front. He stepped inside. Once he was in the foyer, I flipped the lights on, taking him by surprise. I made him drop his weapon and sit on the couch. Twenty minutes later, the door opened again. It was the Bureau agent. I told him to hide his SUV in the garage. We interrogated the guy. Then someone else showed up."

## 34

WE SAT TOGETHER SOLEMNLY, GLANCING AT EACH OTHER AND listening to the man named Gardner as he told his story. Gardner stood and put his hands together as if he were praying and touched his mouth with them, thinking through what had happened; then he glanced around as if his friend's home were his own. The layout was almost the same. He was replaying the whole thing in his mind. He pointed to where I was sitting and said, "That's my couch"; then he pointed to the left of me and said, "And that's the front door to my home. The second guy came in that way. I was standing right here, holding my firearm, aiming it down at the first guy, who I had sitting on the couch. The second guy came through and saw me. He pulled his weapon and held it steady, and I told him to put it down, or I'd take his friend out. The man on the couch told him to listen to me. But the guy wouldn't. He stepped forward, approaching me slowly, his gun still drawn." Gardner paused, thinking about it. "Once he was close to the entrance to the room, the Bureau guy snuck up from behind. There was a struggle.

The guy on the couch started to get up to help, so I shot him in the chest."

"One bad guy down," I said.

Gardner nodded. "So it was me who killed the guy in my home. Then it was two against one. But not really. Because then the Bureau guy told me to get out of the house. But I just stayed there, aiming my weapon at both of them. But the man insisted I leave. This was during the struggle, so there was lots of shouting and punches flying. Both of the men lost their weapons during the fight. So I moved toward the garage and grabbed my keys and left." He paused again, remembering what had happened, and looked at the guy called Murray. "I called my friend from my cell phone. I was in a panic. I didn't know what to do. He didn't answer, so I left a message. Then I started to worry about using my cell phone and being tracked, so I tossed it out the window and just showed up."

Then Murray spoke for the first time in a long while. He said, "I was asleep when Alex first called me. I got up and heard his message. I tried him on his cell and couldn't get a hold of him. So I called his office. Fifteen minutes later, there was a knock at my door. I asked who it was and heard my friend's voice. So of course I let him inside. Then we hid his vehicle in my garage. I made some coffee, and Alex told me everything that had happened. Earlier this morning we heard the news about the dead Bureau agent. We had the news channel on the TV. They showed a picture of the man, and Alex told me it was the same guy."

Gardner said, "I don't know what happened to the other guy in my house. Obviously the agent got away. Maybe the bad guy did, too. Or they would've found the body. Or maybe he kidnapped the Bureau guy."

"His name was Mark Reynolds," Chris said. "And he was my partner."

Gardner stared at Chris for a moment, then nodded solemnly. "I'm sorry."

"I am, too." Chris rubbed his face, thinking. "Any idea who the guy you shot and killed was?"

"Yes," he said. "He was a CIA guy. A special agent. Same unit as the rogue CIA guys who died last week."

Chris turned to me and said, "That Malone guy came to the house in Fairfax. He studied the body. He could clearly see the face. Therefore he knew the dead guy wasn't Alex Gardner, but he didn't say a word. Why would that be?"

"I can answer that," said Gardner. "My assumption is he knew it wasn't me. Was the FBI at the home?"

Chris said, "Yes. Malone wanted to take over the crime scene, but my boss said it was his jurisdiction."

"There you go. If David thought something was off, he wouldn't want the FBI to figure it out. He'd want to do that himself. There's somewhat of a competitive nature between our agencies. He wanted to control the situation."

I said, "He was obstructing justice."

"You guys know how the game works. The Bureau is always trying to one-up the CIA. David knew full well that wasn't me dead on that couch. He's probably trying to figure out where I am at this very moment."

"So why don't you call him and tell him?" asked Jami, trying to understand his thought process.

But Gardner shook his head. "Not yet. Not until we figure out where the other guy is. The second intruder. Until then, I need to lie low." Gardner then turned to Emma and glanced down at her as she sat. Then he said, "You need to check in with David before he starts asking questions."

She pulled her cell phone from a pocket and looked at it. "He tried calling me a few minutes ago."

"You should call him back. But not from here." Gardner looked at each of us in turn. "I would like to ask you to please not say a word about my whereabouts. Not until I figure out what the hell is happening."

The man named Murray stood and moved over to his friend. The rest of us stood and joined them.

I said, "I know why they're after you." Silence in the room. Everyone turned and stared at me. "The files you accessed. You weren't supposed to do that. Internal affairs wanted you to stay out of them. But you didn't. The bad guys must have people in that department. They got tipped off somehow. Maybe they were monitoring who accessed what. They saw you doing some digging, so then they called Malone. Maybe they told your boss he had to let you go. For insubordination. Maybe that's what caused all of this."

All eyes turned back to Gardner. He thought for a spell and nodded vaguely. "Maybe you're right," he said.

Then Murray spoke again. He turned to Chris and said, "You mentioned something about a black sedan?"

Chris nodded. "It's been following us all morning. We figured out they were tracking me using my partner's cell phone." Then he paused, catching himself and what he had said. "*Former* partner, I mean."

Gardner furrowed his brow. "Where's the phone now?"

"In our vehicle," I answered. "Don't worry. I removed the battery. They can't track us anymore."

Murray turned to Gardner. Gardner said, "You need to find the guy. Find him and you'll find the people responsible." He thought some more. "I'll give you an address. Go there. Put the battery back in and wait."

I said, "What's at the address?" as Gardner found a piece of paper and a pen and wrote down the address.

"It's kind of like a safe house of sorts. Or maybe more like a black site. No longer operational but useful."

I thought about that and studied the man and glanced around the room. "And what are *you* going to do?"

Gardner said, "I'm going to stay here. I'm going to lie low. Until this is all over. Until these people are off the streets. The Bureau will figure out that wasn't me in that house soon enough. Probably by end of day. Then they'll start looking for me unless Malone tells them not to. Until then, I'll be here. If you need me."

I nodded and shook his hand. Gardner and Murray stayed where they were, and the rest of us left the home. We huddled by our two vehicles. Emma said she was going back to Langley. I told her she needed to find out which vehicles had passed through the checkpoints in the last hour, if she could. She ducked into her sedan and drove off. Jami and I climbed into Chris's SUV, and I told him to drive us back to the diner.

## 35

Emma Ross called her assistant on the way to Langley, and Samantha answered after the first ring. Emma explained what had happened and how she needed help accessing the historical video feed from the checkpoint at the guardhouse. She said if anyone knew how to get access to the footage, it would be Samantha. But the woman couldn't help. She said there was no footage. They'd turned the cameras off years earlier. They often received guests for meetings held at the Original or New Headquarters Building who had insisted on remaining anonymous. Their visits didn't need to be documented. Therefore, instead of having to take the cameras offline whenever this happened, agency heads had long since decided it would be best to just not have them on to begin with. Easier that way for plausible deniability. Therefore there was no way for Emma to confirm or deny if a man in a black sedan with a missing window had arrived there within the last hour. So Emma clicked off and stopped short of the Langley entrance. She pulled off to the side of the road leading to the checkpoint but did not enter. Just put the sedan in park and left the motor running as she thought long and hard about what her options might be. Which were basically none. Then her cell buzzed, breaking her trance. Emma picked it back up and stared at the caller ID. It said UNKNOWN CALLER. Which pretty much gave away who was calling. "Emma Ross," she said, answering.

A woman with a monotone voice came on the line. She said, "Please hold for the president," then silence.

"Emma," President Keller said ten seconds later, "I need to speak with you regarding an urgent matter."

"Mr. President, with all due respect, I'm a little tired of this being a one-way street."

Keller said nothing.

"Because whenever you need me, I take your call. But when I need to speak with you, I can't. My phone calls get redirected to Ethan Meyer instead. I needed to meet with you today, and I knew I couldn't. I didn't even try Ethan. He just flat out ignores me now. So I had to reach out to Adam Stine of all people."

"I know," he said. "That's why I'm calling."

Emma shifted her eyes to the left and noticed a vehicle buzz past her, headed for the Langley checkpoint. On the opposite side, a vehicle appeared, exiting at the same time. She sighed and said, "How can I help?"

"I met with them a short time ago. Both of them. Ethan and Adam. They had questions about my reelection campaign kickoff rally happening later." He paused and said, "*Inappropriate* questions."

She narrowed her eyes. "Why inappropriate?"

"They were probing, seeing if I had any concerns about my security after what had happened last week."

"Do you?"

"I didn't until I spoke with them."

"If I may, sir, I believe you're being paranoid. They were asking questions on my behalf. That's all."

Keller grew quiet. She could tell he was considering her appraisal of the situation. "But what if I'm not?"

Emma ignored the question and said, "Did Adam tell you what I met with him about this morning?"

"Indirectly."

"My superior at Langley believes the CIA agents involved in the assassination attempt were tipped off."

"By White House staffers who told them about the presidential motorcade and the route it would take."

"That's right," she said. "So Adam explained our concern to you?"

"Indirectly," he said again. "Adam told Ethan, and Ethan told me. Which is why I'm calling you, Emma. I've already spoken with Agent Rivera; I believe one of them may have been involved. Just a gut feeling."

"It's Ethan," she said without any hesitation.

"Now hold on a second. How could you possibly know that for sure?"

"The man refuses to have anything to do with me. He avoids me. He ignores my calls. He stopped taking my meeting requests. It's obvious the man has something against me. Maybe he has something to hide."

"He succeeded you, Emma. He doesn't want to look weak. And he doesn't want to do things your way."

"I can understand that," she said. "However, it's foolish not to consult those who have gone before you."

"Then it's Adam."

She sighed heavily. "Now you're questioning my ability to read people. I had him vetted. He was my guy."

"He's just a kid. He doesn't know any better. Someone may have coerced him."

"Which is why it would have to be Ethan. He's been in the DC echo chamber for years. He knows people. And they know *him*. If you think one of them leaked the route last week, you should look at Ethan Meyer."

Keller made no immediate response. Silence on the line between the two of them. Ten seconds passed. Then twenty. Then he said, "Emma, I find it very odd that I had these conversations with them today. A few hours before my rally. Which makes me think they were testing the waters, maybe checking to see if anything had changed with our security protocol since last week."

Emma said nothing. There was no reason to speak. The president had alluded to Adam Stine being involved, and Emma had pointed a finger at Ethan. Neither would budge. She knew that much was true. Some things would never change. Then she finally spoke. She said, "I've been given clear instructions by David Malone at the Agency. He believes that someone close to you leaked the information. You clearly believe it, too. And I agree, it has to be someone close to you. Someone within your inner circle. But here's the thing: I've essentially been given an ultimatum. I have to figure out who did it, or I will lose my job."

"That's ridiculous."

"But that's what he said, in so many words."

The president thought about that for a spell. Then he said, "I think you should come to the rally."

"I just told you I have an urgent assignment I'm expected to run down."

"You will be running it down. Up close and personal."

She thought about that. "What about Ethan? He doesn't want me anywhere near you. He won't be happy."

"I'll deal with Ethan Meyer. Come to the White House now; we're leaving soon. You'll ride with me."

## 36

Chris drove Jami and me back to the diner. I said I'd feel better if I had my SUV. Two vehicles were better than one. When we arrived, Jami said that three would be better than two. Because her vehicle was parked there, too. Chris had tried calling Mulvaney but didn't get an answer, so he said he wanted to stop by and check in with him. I reminded Chris that his boss had told him to take the rest of the day off. He reminded me that this was personal. Which I understood. He wasn't going to rest until we found out who had killed Mark Reynolds. Jami said she wanted to touch base with Lynne May for a few minutes; then the three of us could regroup.

I climbed into my parked SUV and turned back. They drove off fast, and I watched them over my shoulder until they became two tiny black dots and turned a corner and disappeared from view. Then I thought about what the guy on the phone had said to me: *Your friend has something I want.* A bad move on his part. The guy was frustrated with his lack of progress. That was clear. Later, Chris had asked me what I thought that was, and I had told him: *Knowledge*.

But what the guy really wanted was his life. The guy wanted Chris dead. For what Chris knew or might have known.

I dug into my pocket and found the paper that Gardner had given me. I studied the address. I started the motor and programmed the address into the GPS; then I dug Mark Reynolds's phone out from my pocket. I put the battery back in. To start the clock. To draw them in.

I backed up fast and put the vehicle in drive and headed out to the address alone to deal with them myself.

EMMA ROSS CLICKED OFF AND HELD HER CELL PHONE IN HER hand for a moment; then she scrolled through her phone log. She remembered the missed call from Malone. She'd seen the call come through while she was at the home in Reston, but out of an abundance of caution, had decided to honor Alex Gardner's request for staying off the grid and not return the call yet. The last thing she'd want was Malone to ask her where she was and Emma have to lie about it. No telling how good he was at detecting those kinds of things. She decided it would be best to call back later, after she made some headway. And now she had.

She tapped the number with her thumb and brought her cell to her ear as she watched another set of vehicles buzz past her, headed to the checkpoint at Langley, along with cars driving out opposite to them. She wondered if Malone was inside his office at the New Headquarters Building. He answered, "Ms. Ross?"

"Yes, I'm sorry I missed your call."

"Understandable," he said. "There's a lot going on. Have you made any progress?"

"Some," she said. "I met with someone who's willing to help me, my former aide, Adam Stine."

"I know the man," Malone said. "I'm afraid you're not going to get far with him. Not connected enough. You might as well be working with a White House intern. Why aren't you working with Ethan Meyer?"

"Sir, if you'll let me finish," she said in a measured tone, "I'm also working with the president himself."

Malone did not speak. Not immediately. Emma shifted her eyes away and furrowed her brow as she waited. Then he said, "Well, that's good to hear. Are you aware of the president's rally happening today? He's kicking off his reelection campaign. Right here, in Washington, DC. I understand it will be televised."

"He invited me to it," she said. "I was going to come back to the office, but he just called me. I'm headed to the White House now to do some more digging and see what I can find out about a possible leaker. In fact, I might be onto something." She watched more vehicles buzz past her and added, "I'll be in touch."

Emma clicked off and dropped her cell into her purse. She made a U-turn and headed to the White House.

Two minutes later, the man in the black sedan exited the checkpoint at Langley. He drove right past where Emma Ross had been parked. He pressed a phone to his ear to answer a call and said, "What is it?"

The man with the silver hair said, "I understand the president is getting ready to leave for his rally."

"So soon?"

"He's starting earlier than expected. He enjoys throwing off the media."

"The television networks won't be ready."

"I've spoken to my contacts. They'll cut to it early if they have to."

The man in the sedan drove on, thinking hard. "I need to take care of something. But I will be in position."

I WAS TEN MINUTES OUT FROM THE ADDRESS GARDNER HAD given me. I had Mark Reynolds's cell phone turned on and set on the seat next to me as I drove. The man in the black sedan had been relentless in hunting down Chris Reed. He seemed convinced that Chris knew something he shouldn't. But he didn't. Not as far as I could tell. But the man in the sedan was gutsy. He'd called Mark's cell when he realized I was tracking him. He had made it a point to talk to me and tell me exactly what he was doing. He wanted to take out my friend. That was clear. Which meant I needed Chris out of the picture and safe.

And it meant I needed to hunt the hunter and take the guy out first before he could do something to Chris.

I called Simon and gave him the address Gardner had given me. I asked if the satellite was working now, and he said that it was. The rain had left and so had the clouds. I told Simon to watch the perimeter for me. He said he'd need a few minutes to reposition the satellite. I clicked off and, five minutes later, arrived and looked at the building ahead of me. I parked on the street and checked my Glock. I reached for Mark's cell phone, and I stuffed it in my pocket. Then I stepped out and headed to the entrance to the building.

It looked like a small warehouse, chained up and abandoned. I got to the door and tried the handle. Locked. I looked down both sides of the street. One car had just passed and was headed the other way. Another was headed in my direction but was fifty yards out. Not black. And not a sedan. I faced forward and set the muzzle of my Glock against where I thought the locking mechanism would be, and I fired twice.

The shots echoed off the building across the street, but nobody was around to notice. The door opened, and I pushed it in the whole way and stepped inside. I looked all around and felt there was nobody there. I guessed there hadn't been for quite some time. I wondered what Gardner and his people had used the building for. Not a safe house. That was for sure. I moved to the center of the room. Long chains hung down from the ceiling. I felt them with my hands. The metal was cold and smelled of rust. I turned and looked all around the room. Beams of sunlight streaked through broken windows. Dust caught the light as it traveled inside. Then I moved to a back room, and I waited.

## 37

I WAITED FOR FIFTEEN MINUTES. NOBODY CAME. CHRIS REED called, but I didn't answer. Same with Jami. I ignored both of them, but when Simon called, I answered, and he said he had an update for me. Simon told me a dark vehicle had just arrived, and the driver had parked behind my vehicle. I asked if it was a black sedan. He said it was either black or dark blue. He was too zoomed out to know for sure. But either way, a person had exited the vehicle, and they were headed straight for me. I moved to the entrance to the back room and looked out. From where I stood, I could see Mark's cell phone where I'd left it, sitting on a table in the middle of the room. Simon told me that Jami had called him a few minutes earlier, asking about me since she couldn't reach me. He said he'd given her my location and said she was on her way. I cursed under my breath, figuring she would call Chris, and they'd both head over. Before I could tell Simon to call Jami back, he said, "The guy's almost there."

"Copy that," I said. "I'll be in touch."

I clicked off and thumbed my way through the contacts

on my cell phone and found the number I wanted. Then I moved my phone to my left hand and reached for my Glock with my right. I peered around the corner and waited. Ten seconds after that, I heard the door creak open, and I ducked back behind the wall.

I could hear the person step through. He closed the door as quietly as he could, and he started to move. The man said, "Agent Reed, I know you're in here. Enough of the games. Step out with your hands up." His voice echoed all around the empty space. I waited, hidden inside the back room, listening intently. The man's footsteps grew closer. He said, "Do you know what this building was used for?"

I said nothing.

"This was a black site not too long ago. An off-the-books location used by the CIA. Deserted once it was compromised. The Agency found another location to use." He paused. "Know what the chains were for?"

I made no reply. Not yet. I could hear the guy getting closer. I could imagine him with his gun drawn, leveled, aimed steady, looking over his shoulder, checking his surroundings, moving forward cautiously.

Right to where I was waiting. A sitting duck, but an intentional decision. The only place that made sense.

Because taking the guy at the door was a fifty-fifty proposition. Either I was quicker than him, or he was quicker than me. Same with stepping out of the shadows. I might take him out. Or he might take me out.

He continued, "This building was used for—" he paused for dramatic effect "—enhanced interrogation. That's the more politically correct way of stating it, isn't it? But let's just call it what it really is: torture."

I used my left hand to wake my phone up.

Then I tapped the number with my thumb and dropped my cell into my pocket.

Then I gripped my Glock with two hands and waited, ready to move, trying to time it just right.

Mark's cell phone started to ring, loud and bright. Half a second later I stepped out from the shadows. And half a second after that, the guy, who was glancing over his shoulder, turned back to face me and saw me with my left eye closed and my right index finger squeezing the trigger. The weapon the guy was holding fell from his hands after the first shot, and then he was holding his bleeding right hand with his left after I fired a second shot. I yelled, "Don't move!" and my voice echoed throughout the expanse of the empty room as I approached, my eyes scanning left and right and all around, making sure it really was just one guy and not others as Mark's cell phone finally stopped ringing. I moved forward until I stood in front of the man, and using the butt of my Glock, I struck him on the side of the head.

WHEN THE MAN CAME TO, HIS WRISTS WERE SECURED TO ONE of the long chains hanging from the ceiling. His arms were straight, and he used his feet to stand to take the pressure off his wrists. After I'd knocked the man unconscious, I had found clips near a dusty table. I'd holstered my weapon and grabbed the man and pulled him over to one of the sets of chains and wrapped it around his wrists. Then I used the clip to secure it in place and found a lever that would've retracted the chain up into the ceiling. But it didn't work. No electricity in the abandoned building. So I cranked it myself. A hard manual effort, but it worked.

He struggled to break free, but his feet were barely touching the floor. Only the tips of his toes touched. The guy forced a smile and said, "Agent Reed," believing I was someone I wasn't. Then he sucked in air, clearly in a lot of pain from the pressure on his wrists and from the wound on his hand. "We finally meet."

I stepped forward. I stood two feet away from the man. I stared across at him, sizing him up. He looked just like me. Not a desk guy at Langley. That was clear. But I had figured that much out already. I said, "Why are you following us?" but the guy said nothing in return. Just smiled and stared. "Start talking."

The guy didn't start talking.

I said, "What do you do for the CIA?"

"Mr. Reed, you know I can't talk about that."

"What can you talk about, then? Want to tell me the truth about what happened to Mark Reynolds?"

He tried to smile again, but it came across as a grimace instead. He was in a lot of pain, and I felt good about that. He said, "I read your file. Earlier today. Just before I drove out here. I know your history. You've worked for the Bureau for years. Before that, you worked out of the DDC field office in Chicago. Before you were fired." The guy paused for a beat. "I know your background. You don't torture people."

"There's a problem with your analysis," I said, taking a step forward. "I'm not who you think I am."

The man narrowed his eyes and stared across at me. I stepped closer and punched the guy in the face. When he faced forward, I punched him again. Then I leaned in close, and I said, "Who do you work for?"

The guy eyed me carefully. Then he realized who I was. He said, "You're not Reed. You're Jordan."

I leaned in closer still and yelled, "Stop wasting my time! Who do you work for? Give me the name!" Then he spit on me. I wiped the blood from my face with the back of my hand. I looked straight ahead and said, "The man your people killed this morning was a federal agent. And he was a friend of mine. I want to know why he was killed and who else is involved." I breathed. "I'll give you one minute."

The guy looked me over but said nothing. I checked my watch and waited, knowing Chris and Jami were on their way. The man just stared at me, unwilling to speak, sensing I was in a hurry. Realizing, possibly, that all he really needed to do was wait me out. So I didn't wait for the full minute to pass. Instead, I punched him twice in the gut, yelling for the guy to talk, but he wasn't going to. Not then. Maybe not ever. So I struck him in the head again, and the guy went limp and hung down from his wrists.

When he came to for the second time, it was because I was tapping his face with my free hand, trying to wake the man up as I held onto his body. Then I let go of him completely and stood back, letting him stand on his own. His eyes grew wide. He gasped for air. He looked at me and understood what I'd done. His wrists were tied behind his back with my belt. Now he hung from the chains by his neck. He stood up tall to counteract gravity. I said, "I think you're going to talk to me now." Then I walked over to the lever.

## 38

THE GUY SHOOK HIS HEAD SLIGHTLY. JUST A SMALL, FRANTIC little movement as he stared at me and stood up tall. "Are you going to talk to me?" I asked, but he made no reply. Just stared. So I squatted down and grabbed the lever and pushed it forward. It unlocked something, allowing for manual operation. Next to the lever was a big metal wheel the size of a bike tire, but thicker and rusted and clearly never used. I reached across with both hands and gripped it tight. Then I leaned back and pulled on it with all my strength.

The chains moved a foot. The guy was now on his toes, struggling hard to stand up and balance himself. He kept his head straight but moved his eyes to his left and looked at me and said, "Let me down, Jordan."

"In a minute," I said. "First I need to convince you."

He looked on and managed to get out, "Convince me of what?" with a labored, breathless voice.

"That I will do whatever it takes to get answers."

He danced around through thirty excruciatingly long seconds; then he said, "Okay, fine. I'll talk to you."

"You sure?"

"Yes," he said. "Please let me down."

I looked on for another moment; then I gripped the wheel from below and pulled up. The chains lowered back down a foot. The guy was now standing freely, moving his neck, sucking in air. I walked back over to where the man was standing and said, "I want you to tell me everything you know."

He said nothing. Just looked at me, debating with himself. Or maybe buying time again.

I shook my head and took a step closer. "Trust me," I said. "You don't want to go down this road with me." I swept his legs, and he was back to gasping for air until he stood up tall again and caught his breath.

Several moments passed as he composed himself. He said, "First I want to know who I'm dealing with."

"I already told you. You know who I am. You people tried to get me to kill the president a week ago."

He shook his head, the best he could. "No," he said. "I mean who are you working with? Who else knows?"

I looked on and said, "DDC and the FBI. Three federal agencies are involved." I paused. "Your turn."

He paused and said, "I'm not going to give you my name, but you've already figured out who I work for."

"Why did the CIA kill Mark Reynolds?"

"Because he was a loose end. Because he got involved."

"Involved with what?"

"With what we have planned." I raised my eyebrows as if to say: *Which is?* The guy took the hint and looked away, debating again. Then he said, "Contingency plans from last week. We failed. This is plan B."

I tilted my head to one side. I said, "Plan B, meaning,

there's going to be another assassination attempt?" The guy said nothing back. Just made a face as if to say: *What else could I possibly be talking about?*

There was a rumble of vehicles from somewhere out on the street. I could feel the vibration as a couple of big SUVs drove by. The sound of motors diminished some as the vehicles passed the building; then it abruptly stopped. Engines were being cut. People were stepping out and making their way to someplace. The guy's eyes gleamed. He smiled broadly. Clearly he thought his people had shown up to help him out.

But clearly he was wrong, because the door was pushed open, and Jami stepped through with Chris following her. They held their guns level and approached. "Building's clear," I yelled, my voice echoing all throughout the empty space as they holstered their weapons and walked toward us.

Jami hung back a ways, and Chris stepped up next to me. He looked the guy over and said, "Who is he?"

"He's the guy who's been following you around," I said. The guy I had chained up stared at me. His face changed. He'd made a realization and looked at Jami briefly, then fixed his eyes on Chris Reed and stared. I said, "He was just telling me about what he and his people are planning, a contingency from last week."

Jami said, "Another assassination attempt?" taking a few steps closer.

I stared at the guy and said, "Let's continue from there. Who do you work for? I want a name."

"I'm not going to tell you that no matter what you do to me. If I did, he'd kill me. I'd be a dead man."

I asked the guy when it was happening. He was reluctant

at first; then his face changed again. As if he realized he was still in danger, but maybe not as much now that two other agents were in his presence. Less of a chance for me to do something I shouldn't. Then the guy became brazen. Then indignant. He stopped talking altogether, and I had to set the stage again by going back over to the lever and hauling the heavy wheel back to remind him of the stakes. Jami wasn't so sure about the approach. Chris didn't speak. He just stood there and watched, his eyes flicking back and forth between the guy and the lever and me.

The bad guy got the message. I was in charge. He was wheezing and sucking in air and dancing on his toes again. I lowered the chain back down and moved back to where he was standing. I reached for my Glock and shoved it hard against his neck. I said, "Enough games; tell me when and where this is happening."

He held out for several seconds, thinking about what to tell me. Then he gave up. He said, "Sometime today. That's all I know. I don't know specifics; I don't know when or where. I wasn't in charge of that."

I narrowed my eyes and took a step back and lowered my weapon. "What were you in charge of, then?"

"Taking care of the agent."

Chris stepped forward. He stood right next to me and turned to glance at me as Jami stayed behind us, watching from a distance. Chris looked the guy over. Staring. Thinking. He said, "You killed that agent?"

"Me and this other guy. We were just following orders."

I said, "How'd you do it?"

He paused. "We took him to the top of a building. We forced him to the edge; then we pushed him off." Then he stopped talking. There wasn't anything else to say. Chris looked at the guy for a long moment. Blinking hard, conflicted, clenching his jaw. He looked at the lever. Then he turned to me and nodded. I went over to the wheel, and I hauled the chain upwards, and I kept it there until the guy stopped breathing.

## 39

Jami was watching everything play out. She didn't encourage us, but she didn't tell us to stop, either. My thoughts went back to Emma Ross and the conversation we'd had. *Sometimes there's just us.* Chris walked over to the man and patted him down for some kind of identification. I told him I'd already done that when I'd first knocked him out. He was clean and had nothing on him. But it gave me an idea, so I walked over to the guy's body as he hung there, and using my phone, I snapped a picture of his face.

"I'll send it to the guys," I said, and I sent Morgan and Simon the image, and I got them conferenced in on a call with us. "Can one of you ID the man in the picture I just sent over to you?"

"I'll handle it, mate," said Morgan.

While we waited, Jami moved closer to Chris and me. She glanced up at the hanging body as she moved. She said, "We should've kept him alive. Now we have no way of knowing what's going down later."

"We do," I said. "It's the president's reelection campaign rally. Has to be it."

"Would've been nice to know specifics."

"He wasn't going to tell us anything," said Chris. "He told us everything he knew except for his coconspirators and the person he worked for, but he wasn't going to give that up, Jami." He paused a moment, thinking. "Mark wasn't just my partner; he was my friend. I wasn't going to let this guy rot in jail while Mark has a funeral. The way things are going lately, he would've been back on the streets in no time."

"I worked for the Bureau once," she said. "A long time ago. And I left because of this kind of thing." She stared at Chris, then turned to me. "It's an abuse of power. We were his judge, jury, and executioner. And we shouldn't have been any of those things. Like I said, we should've kept him alive."

I said nothing back. I just stood there thinking about the picture frame and the question Emma had asked.

Chris said, "Now we just need to find the other guy. He said two of them were ordered to kill Mark."

"And I might be able to help you with that," said Morgan from my cell phone. "I just completed a reverse image search in one of our interagency databases. The man in the picture you sent us is a guy named Jacob Freeman. He's been with the Central Intelligence Agency for just over three years. And for the last eighteen months, he's been here. Stateside. No explanation why; I assume those details are for CIA eyes only. My point is he's been partnered up with a man named Michael Ramsdale. Might be your guy."

"Background?" I asked as I heard Morgan typing.

"Similar to Freeman. The guy's also been stateside for quite some time, it seems. Both men have the designation of special agent, so they're trained for the field. Not sure why he wouldn't be overseas though."

Jami said, "Because whoever they work for needed them here."

Morgan stopped typing for a moment and said, "What do you mean, love?"

"Think about it. If you have an agenda to take down a sitting president, and if you have people in your inner circle who believe the same things you believe, do you want them overseas? Or here, ready to help? The CIA can't operate domestically. That's why they created DDC. That's why these people are stateside."

I thought about that for a moment. I said, "You're right. Someone at the top is orchestrating all of this. They have people right here in DC carrying out assassination attempts. And they're doing it in plain sight. Because nobody's expecting them to. They could have a whole army of rogue agents, and nobody would be the wiser. We thought it was just a few rogue agents from last week, but maybe we were wrong."

"So there's two of them," Chris said, looking up at the dead guy. "His friend and their boss."

"Best-case scenario, yes. Worst case, there are a lot of them. Huddled in a room, right now, plotting away."

Jami said, "And I'm assuming we can't see who these guys worked for at the Agency, can we?"

Both Morgan and Simon agreed from the phone that they could not. They could see working relationships horizontally, across teams, but not vertically. Reporting hierarchies weren't included in the interagency database. I told the guys I'd be in touch, and Simon asked if I wanted him to keep the satellite in our area. I told him yes, for now. Then I clicked off and dropped my phone into my pocket, and Jami, Chris, and I huddled together. Chris glanced at Jami; then his eyes flicked back to me. He said, "Plan, boss?"

I looked at him and said, "What do we know?"

"The target is the President of the United States."

I nodded. "What else?"

Jami said, "It's happening today."

"And?"

"President Keller is kicking off his reelection campaign."

I nodded again. "So we know the target, and we know when, and we know where. That's all we need."

But it wasn't all we needed. We knew the what and the when, but we didn't know the how. And that was key. We took one more look around the large room, and I picked up Mark's cell phone, then we headed for the door. Jami stepped out first, followed by me, followed by Chris. We took a moment to plan. I told them we needed to get to Keller and call off the rally. Jami said we needed to find out where it was taking place and make our way over there. Knowing the president, he wouldn't let anything make him look weak, especially cancelling something as important as a reelection campaign rally. Chris nodded his agreement and suggested we check in with Emma Ross. She would know where the rally was taking place. To my left I saw my SUV parked against the curb. A black sedan was parked directly behind it.

Chris and Jami followed me over to the sedan to check it out. I stepped into the road and moved to the driver's door and pointed at it. "The window's intact. The guy in the building wasn't the one following us."

Chris rubbed the back of his neck as he looked. The three of us stood next to each other, staring.

Then a shot rang out from somewhere behind us.

A second after that, Chris Reed fell to the ground.

## 40

Emma Ross parked at the Ellipse for the second time in one day and headed back toward the covered guardhouse. The lead man noticed her coming and made a face that told her he was thinking: *You again?* She ignored it and stepped up to the guy and said, "Emma Ross, Central Intelligence Agency."

She showed the man her credentials, and he looked them over. He said, "You were here earlier."

Emma said, "Now I'm back." She pointed at the White House behind him. "At the president's request."

This time when he checked the log, he found her name with no special annotation. And no one had called down to him ahead of time with special instructions. He looked up and said, "Know where you're going?"

"Don't worry about me."

The man nodded and fished a badge out from a box, made a note of the number, had Emma sign next to her name in a big three-ring binder, then handed the badge over to her. She pinned it to her lapel, and the guy gestured to another man standing off to the side wearing a dark suit and sunglasses. The agent nodded to her, and she walked with him into the White House grounds, and they headed to the entrance.

Within ten minutes, Emma was entering the West Wing. She thanked the agent who had escorted her, and told him she was fine to go the rest of the way on her own. The man started to disagree, but then President Keller himself emerged from his office and saw her in the hallway. Keller told the agent to ask Rivera for an ETA. The guy checked using his wrist mic and a few seconds later said, "Twenty minutes."

Keller thanked the man and escorted Emma down to the Oval, where the two agents posted outside nodded at her as she entered. She knew them well. And they knew her, too. But neither of them spoke. Just allowed her and the president to step inside the room; then they quickly closed the door behind them.

"Please have a seat," he said, motioning to the couches.

She sat on one, and he sat across from her. She leaned forward and stared at him and said, "We're running out of time, Mr. President. If Ethan or Adam is leaking specifics about your whereabouts—"

"Emma," he said, interrupting her, "I'm well aware, and I've already spoken to Rivera about my concerns. I know you're not a fan of Ethan, but it was my decision to choose who would replace you. And Ethan was my first choice. Behind you, that is." He paused. "But it's also possible it could be Adam Stine. Correct?"

She made a face and narrowed her eyes. "And what is Rivera doing about all of this?"

"We have a plan," he said.

"Which is?"

He paused and took a breath. "What's the old saying? Keep your friends close and your enemies closer?"

"Only *one* of them is your enemy."

President Keller nodded vaguely. "If that's true, we'll know soon enough."

SOON ENOUGH ENDED UP BEING FIFTEEN MINUTES LATER. The door to the Oval opened, and Keller wrapped up his conversation with Emma and stepped over to the *Resolute Desk* to grab the notes for his speech. A speech he planned to give without the need of a teleprompter, but one he wanted to review one more time. Keller joined Emma and walked her into the hallway, where everyone from his inner circle who was heading over to the rally was huddled together with lead agent Rivera standing dead center in the huddle.

Ethan Meyer noticed Emma first. She watched his eyes grow wide as his predecessor moved closer to him. A sudden realization as he saw that not only was the woman in the building, but she was going with them. His eyes then flicked over to the president; then he crossed his arms, clearly not happy with her presence.

Adam Stine's reaction was not much different. It started out the same way as Meyer's: wide eyes, an awareness of Emma's presence, remembering the earlier conversation outside the White House, an understanding that he had never really followed up with her afterwards, just blew her off and moved on. Stine stood easy, hands in his pockets, leaning against the wall, as other aides and staffers stood close by.

Agent Rivera remained standing in the center of the huddle. He looked around as if he was confirming he had everybody he was aware of. Then he said, "Listen up. I'm assuming all of you are headed to the president's reelection rally. If you have not heard already, I will share with you the location now: it will be held at the Marriott Marquis. The president has held events there before, as you may remember, so it's a very quick trip over. Less than a mile and approximately five minutes. We will head up Fourteenth and then cut across K or L. There's a secured covered area out front. Streets to the north and to the south will be blocked off with Metro PD assisting. My team is already in place and set to receive us when we arrive."

Emma glanced at Meyer and Stine. Both men were staring at Keller's lead agent. But she could sense both of them watching her out of the corner of their eyes. Then she thought about the president and what he had shared with her minutes earlier. *We have a plan*, he had said. And she had asked, *Which is?* Emma assumed she was about to find out. She fixed her eyes back on Rivera as he continued with instructions.

He said, "We're leaving in ten minutes. Same general assignments as usual. Whichever vehicle and agent you normally ride with, you'll be riding with this time. Except for one change." He looked around, scanning the room. He pointed to Ethan Meyer, then Adam Stine, then directly at Emma. "You, you, and you," the lead agent said as he glanced at each of them. "You will all ride with the president and me."

Then he clapped his hands twice and said to the group to get ready to head out.

The president asked everyone to wait a minute. He waited until everyone had turned to face him. Keller smiled, looking out across the team of his closest and most loyal supporters. Then he looked at Emma and held her gaze for a moment before looking at someone else and continuing to scan all of his staffers' faces. "I just want to take a moment to thank each of you personally. The last three years have been extremely trying. There's one person I wish dearly could be here with us." Keller paused for a very long moment. He tried to speak but gave it up and blinked several times, willing himself to not let his emotions get the best of him. Emma understood whom he was talking about. They all did. Keller confirmed it by adding, "Margaret would've been so proud. Not of me, but of all of you. Truly. She loved you dearly, and so do I."

The staffers began to clap, and it was clear to Emma that the president wasn't going to get much more out. He had become too emotional. Keller glanced at her, and then she followed his gaze as it set on Meyer and then Stine. Then Agent Rivera waited for the celebrations to subside and told everyone to start moving downstairs, and then he hung back to escort the president to his car, along with Ethan, Adam, and herself.

Emma leaned close to the president and asked, "Is this your plan? Forcing them both to ride with you?"

He nodded vaguely.

"Why? Do you think the motorcade will be attacked again? Like last week?"

Keller shrugged. "If one of them is involved, then nothing will happen. Not if they're with me. I hope."

## 41

THE SILVER-HAIRED MAN HEARD A TEXT MESSAGE COME through. He dug his phone out from a pocket and stared at the screen. It read: *Leaving now*. The man smiled to himself. He swiped up to unlock his phone, then dialed a memorized number and waited through two long rings until the call was answered.

"Yes?" a voice said from exactly ten miles away.

"Are you in position?"

"Yes," he said again. "I'm looking through the window now. It's a clear shot."

"Good," the silver-haired man said. "They're about to head over. ETA is five minutes."

"When do you want me to do it? Before the rally or after? When he enters, or when he exits?"

"Your call," he said, and then he clicked off.

SIMON HARRIS RETURNED TO HIS DESK WITH ANOTHER CAN OF Mountain Dew and cracked it open. The sound filled the large expanse of the room where his cubicle was located. He was the only one there. Alone. He dropped back down into his chair and took a long drink and then almost spat the liquid out.

On the computer monitor was a live feed of the street outside the abandoned building he was monitoring. There was a man on the ground and two people dragging his body behind a parked vehicle. Then shots were fired—bright flashes on his screen. Then a vehicle started to drive away and picked up speed. Simon took his mouse and clicked on an icon that looked like a target; then he clicked on the moving vehicle. The screen started to pan to the right, slowly, awkwardly, not fast enough to keep up with the car.

But it would catch up eventually.

In the meantime, he kept his eyes on the mad scramble happening on the screen. One person was firing back. Then they gave it up as the vehicle drove away, and the shooter focused on the one who was hurt. Simon reached for the landline and cradled the receiver against his shoulder and dialed a number.

He gave a woman the location, and Emergency Services said they'd dispatch an ambulance immediately. Then Simon watched as the screen panned slowly to the right, chasing the target he'd set, and his view of the street and the two people huddled over the third moved offscreen. He opened a line and dialed another number. A tired voice answered, and Simon gave Morgan Lennox an update on what had happened.

EMMA LOOKED ON AS THE BACK DOOR TO THE PRESIDENTIAL limousine was opened, and President Keller slid inside. She was next, followed by Ethan Meyer, followed by Adam Stine. She sat next to Keller, and Meyer and Stine sat across from them. She sat through two awkward minutes as the rest of Keller's inner circle climbed into other vehicles in the motorcade. Then the signal was given, and Emma watched through the tinted glass as Agent Rivera climbed into the front passenger seat, and then he pulled the door closed hard.

They pulled out onto H Street and headed east. Meyer and Stine were on their phones, preoccupied, avoiding an awkward conversation. To one, she was a predecessor, and to another she was a former boss.

Emma turned to glance at Keller, thinking to herself that if the presidential motorcade was going to be attacked again, like it had been a week earlier, it would happen within the next several minutes. Or it wouldn't. Not with a coconspirator in the vehicle with him. Unless it would. A sacrifice offered for the greater good. Keller glanced at her, and they shared a look. She could tell he was thinking the same thing.

In the end it was the president himself who spoke up and broke the silence. As the motorcade turned north on Fourteenth, he said, "Ethan, Adam, I need the two of you to know something." He paused. The limousine sped up as it approached Franklin Park on the right, and then it quickly started to slow as the driver approached L and turned east. "It's come to my attention that there may be an attack on my life. Sometime today. Maybe even in the next few minutes." He paused again and eyed both men closely.

Both of them seemed surprised. Neither of them broke a sweat. Nobody spoke; just glanced up and stared.

Keller said, "Agent Rivera has assured me that the building is secure. They've cordoned off the section we'll walk through to get to the waiting area, which means entering and exiting will be potential points of failure. Keep your eyes open and stay vigilant to your surroundings. Let Rivera know if you see anything out of the ordinary that we should be aware of." Then he offered the same warm expression he'd given them when they were huddled together in the West Wing. "Don't worry. It's going to be a good day."

Emma forced a smile herself and faced forward.

Ethan Meyer nodded vaguely and looked out the window.

Adam Stine said nothing.

Up front, from the driver's seat, a Secret Service agent put away his cell phone.

FIVE MINUTES PASSED, AND THE MAN IN THE WINDOW BEGAN to worry. The street had been cleared out thirty minutes earlier by Metro PD, but checking his watch, he decided something had changed. Because the presidential limo should've been pulling up tight against the Marriott Marquis right then.

But it wasn't.

He checked his watch again and looked back out the window. It was possible that he was off by a minute. Maybe longer. Or maybe he had miscalculated. Maybe they wouldn't be bringing the president in through the entrance on L Street. Maybe the Secret Service had Massachusetts Avenue blocked off, too. More disruptive to DC traffic, but anywhere the president traveled was disruptive. Even inside the DC bubble.

Then his concern disappeared as quickly as it had arrived.

Because to his right, turning east from Tenth, he saw the lead car with American flags on its hood appear. The lead vehicle swung a wide turn and crawled slowly until it got to the eastern edge of the Marriott. Metro PD officers were blocking the road and turned to look. Then they nodded at each other: *It's go time.*

Behind the lead car, another black, glossy, spotless Secret Service vehicle pulled up tight, nose to tail. Behind that one, the presidential limousine pulled up and stopped in place as two other vehicles followed.

The man behind the window opened it just a hair. No more than an inch. He kept the curtain drawn and watched through the thin cloth. Then he reached for his rifle and checked it one final time before kneeling down on the floor and easing the barrel out the window, using the sight to aim down at the street below. Then he waited. He was a patient man. As long as his getaway driver was in position, he'd get off scot-free.

## 42

Jami and I crouched behind the black sedan. Not the one with the busted window. A different one. The sedan with the broken window had been parked half a block away, and the driver had taken a shot at Chris. I had dragged my friend behind the parked car, and then I returned fire, as had Jami. We managed to sink a few rounds into the back of the sedan before its tires spun on the pavement and the driver sped away.

In that moment, I had a decision to make: Stay or go?

I had stayed.

Chris was sitting with his back against the parked car, holding his upper left arm. "I'm okay," he said.

"Are you sure?" I asked.

He let go briefly, removing pressure, and ripped part of his shirt and took a look. There was a lot of blood. That was clear. It was a big gash. The bullet had grazed him, but it hadn't done any real damage. That was also clear. Chris was trying to ignore the pain. He held his hand up for me to grab, and I helped him stand. My cell phone was buzzing loud in my pocket. I ignored it as Jami stepped closer to us to inspect the wound. We heard an ambulance warble in the distance. My cell buzzed again, and I answered, "Jordan."

"It's me," said Morgan. "I've got Simon on the line, too; he watched the whole thing happen."

Simon said, "EMS should arrive in a few minutes, Blake."

"Thanks, but we don't need it."

Once I was sure Chris was okay, I moved my gaze over to where the black sedan had been parked. The driver had been facing away from us, the nose of his vehicle facing east. The direction he needed to go in. Not just to make a quick getaway. He needed to head in that direction for another reason, I guessed.

Jami and I walked with Chris along the sidewalk, toward their parked vehicles, as we decided what to do. Simon told me he'd locked a target onto the black sedan using the satellite before he drove away. He said the vehicle had gone offscreen, but it would only be a few more minutes for the satellite to catch up to it. He had been zoomed in too much, which was why he had seen what had happened outside the abandoned building. I asked if the satellite would still have a lock on the vehicle even though it was offscreen, and he said that it would. What he was seeing wasn't a true representation of the tracking the satellite was doing.

Morgan said he was getting a call and told us to hold on. Jami, Chris, and I stopped moving. We were standing close to the entrance to the abandoned building. My car was back where we had come from. By the dead guy's parked sedan. Chris's and Jami's were farther west. I could see both of them parked there.

I said, "We need to head east. That's the direction he was

headed in. We should take all three vehicles. If we can catch up to the guy, it'd be best if it was three against one."

Chris looked at Jami and said, "Two vehicles is better than one, and three is better than two." She nodded, and I patched both of them in to the call I had going with Simon and Morgan. The three of us stood huddled together for another minute until we could all hear each other; then I left them there and headed back to my SUV, and they turned to climb into their own vehicles.

Then Morgan came on the line and said, "I just spoke with Lynne May; we know who those guys work for."

THE MAN WITH THE BROKEN WINDOW ARRIVED AT M STREET and parked with his car facing east. Well past the cordoned-off streets south of him on L and again on Massachusetts. The Secret Service and Metro PD had only blocked off the first set of streets in every direction. No need to go farther out than that. Had the president been meeting with a world leader, or signing a controversial executive order into law, or giving one of his signature addresses where he criticized the other side of the aisle, it might have been necessary.

But not for a rally kicking off a reelection campaign.

The president had plenty of detractors. About half the country. But the people inside the Marriott Marquis were friendlies, as he and the Secret Service called them. People within his administration, their friends, their families, people of the same mind as him. Not people who were against him. Not overtly, anyway.

The driver checked his watch and looked out the rearview and side mirrors.

Then he sent a text message that simply read: I'm here.

. . .

ONE BLOCK SOUTH, THE MAN AT THE WINDOW HEARD A CHIME on his cell phone. Keeping his weapon in place, he dug into a pocket and brought the screen to his face and read the message. Then he put the cell away and glanced around the room, making sure everything was in order and he had nothing left to pack.

Because he wouldn't be firing the shot after the president's speech.

He would do it now.

"TALK TO ME," I SAID TO MORGAN AS I SLID INTO MY PARKED SUV and closed the door hard and watched Jami and Chris climb into their vehicles parked farther ahead of me. "Who do they work for, Morgan?"

"Based on the reverse lookup of the image you gave me, we figured out who the dead guy was. I called Lynne May earlier, and she looked up the hierarchy in the system at DDC. And due to her level of seniority and clearance, and due to the fact that DDC is a subsidiary of the CIA, she was able to find out for me."

"Who is it, Morgan?" I heard Jami ask from the phone.

Morgan cleared his throat and said, "David Malone, love."

Chris said, "Blake, that's the guy who was in Gardner's home, in Fairfax."

"I know," I said as I started the motor.

"The CIA guy who showed up after the Bureau. The one who wanted Mulvaney to give him jurisdiction."

"I know," I said again as I put the vehicle into drive.

"What are we going to do?" asked Jami as I pulled a wide U-turn and stepped on the gas.

I said, "Call me back in five minutes," and clicked off as I picked up speed and dialed another number.

## 43

Emma Ross sat quietly, on edge, her senses heightened, adrenaline pumping through her veins as she waited to exit the presidential limousine. But they weren't exiting. Not yet. Ethan Meyer and Adam Stine were staring across at her, their eyes flicking between her and Keller, then back to her again. Emma turned to her left and asked, "What's taking so long?" but the president just shook his head and glanced out through the partition, through the windshield, at the Secret Service vehicle parked in front of the limo.

There was no movement. None at all. Emma figured they were still trying to confirm the area was clear. Which she thought should've been done hours ago. But she also understood that since nothing had happened during the short drive over from the White House, maybe something was going to happen here.

Then there was movement. Agent Rivera stepped out from the lead car, and she watched as he looked all around the surrounding area, turning to the hotel on one side, then glancing at the other building with windows on the other, scanning each one quickly, looking for anything out of the ordinary as he moved. More agents stepped out, including the one inside their limousine, Agent Bryant. The man climbed out from the driver's seat up front and joined Rivera and a few more agents, and they spoke in hushed tones.

Ethan Meyer lifted his arm and moved it so that his watch fell from inside his coat sleeve, and looked at it. He said, "What the hell are they waiting for?" as he glanced left, looking over his shoulder, past his aide. Stine said nothing. He just stared out briefly, seemingly uninterested, just annoyed that Emma was there.

Then Rivera wrapped up the conversation with his men. He pointed at the vehicles, barking some kind of order as he stepped backwards; then he did a full-on turn and headed toward the hotel. Emma watched as Rivera opened one of the doors and held onto it for the awaiting president. Then she saw Agent Bryant walk back to their vehicle. He opened the door and held onto it with one hand and cupped the other hand and brought his fingers toward him rapidly as the man nodded at the president. Keller shook his head and motioned for Emma to step out first, and as she did, she heard her cell phone ringing.

I PRESSED MY CELL TO MY EAR AS I CONTINUED DRIVING EAST, not sure where I was going, just heading in the direction Simon had said the black sedan had been traveling. As I waited through five long rings, I thought about the target Simon had set, knowing as soon as the satellite had zoomed out far enough, my analyst at Homeland would be able to see exactly where the vehicle had gone to. But before I could think any more, the call was answered. There were muffled sounds. Someone moving awkwardly. Emma said, "Yes?"

"It's me," I said. "The people who killed Mark Reynolds report to David Malone."

She paused to process that and said, "I can't talk right now. I'm with the president."

I narrowed my eyes as I drove and said, "Where are you?"

"Heading to the reelection campaign rally."

"When are you getting there?"

"We just did," she said. "We're entering the building right now."

I drove on, my heart beating hard in my chest, thinking about the direction I was driving in. I said, "Emma, I believe the president is in imminent danger. There might be someone—" Before I could finish, Emma yelled something, her voice muffled, then I heard her cell phone fall to the ground, and I heard a shot fired.

THIRTY SECONDS EARLIER, EMMA ROSS HAD STEPPED OUT OF the limousine and fished around for her ringing cell phone. The president had climbed out immediately after her, followed by Ethan Meyer, followed by Adam Stine. Meyer and Stine were walking together, to the president's left, and Emma had fallen in line to Keller's right as they moved toward the open door where Agent Rivera was waiting for them. As Emma answered the call and heard the warning, she felt the hair on the back of her neck stand on end.

Emma had turned back slowly. She'd kept on walking next to the president, pressing her phone against her ear, scanning the building behind them. She saw the curtains move behind a window on the second floor. She saw the long black neck of a rifle slowly extend from inside, difficult to see because it was aimed directly at them. She stared for two long seconds until she finally understood what it was.

Then she had panicked and dropped her cell phone.

She yelled for those around her to get down and pushed the president forward.

Ethan Meyer glanced over his shoulder quickly, then turned back and landed on James Keller.

Then Adam Stine launched himself forward, protecting Emma, just as a shot was fired from behind.

I DROVE ON, PRESSING MY PHONE AGAINST MY EAR, CALLING for Emma, but the woman didn't answer. Instead I heard muffled voices through the phone. Then I heard men shouting, feet moving fast; then the voices grew quieter. I called again for Emma, but she did not respond. Nobody did. The call was still going, but no one was there.

Another call came through; it was Simon bringing me back into the conference call with Chris and Jami as they followed me toward downtown. I answered fast and said, "Simon, where is the president right now?"

"The Marriott Marquis," he said. "You're headed straight for it."

THE SHOOTER STARED THROUGH THE WINDOW FOR TWO seconds. That was the most he could spare if he wanted to get out of there in time. Just long enough to confirm a direct hit. And he had delivered one. That much was clear. He had seen the blood splatter and the huddled mass of bodies on the concrete. He dropped the weapon and jogged to the door and removed his gloves and pocketed them. The man ran toward the stairwell and took it one flight down and headed north, out back, through a hidden courtyard between the buildings. There was a small community park to his left. Children were playing, and tired parents were watching them. He slowed to a fast walk until he moved past them, looking over his shoulder the whole way, confirming nobody was catching up to him. He smiled briefly because, so far, nobody was.

He found his way to Shepherd Court and started running again through a narrow alleyway between a long row of buildings that faced Ninth and Tenth. When Shepherd intersected with M, he saw the black sedan parked there waiting for him, and he heard the doors unlock as he slowed and walked up to it.

The shooter climbed inside and pulled his door shut fast. He said, "Go, before they block us at Ninth."

The driver put the sedan in gear, and his tires spun as he smashed the accelerator hard. They picked up speed and turned north on Ninth, and then a beat later the driver turned to him and said, "Did you get him?"

The sniper nodded. "I saw blood. There was no movement." He paused for a moment. "One shot, one kill."

## 44

I explained to my team what I'd just heard on the phone. There was silence on the line as the others processed the news. Then Simon and Morgan went back to working on getting the satellite zoomed out so they could see where the target had gone and guide Jami, Chris, and me to the vehicle. I told them one of them needed to focus on that while the other needed to find out what had happened at the Marriott Marquis. Morgan said he'd handle the satellite, and Simon put us on hold to make some calls to find out. From the phone Jami said, "Chris and I are right behind you, Blake. We should split up, don't you think?"

"Yes," I said. "Before the target got out of range, Simon said the sedan was headed east. The hotel is east. These people would want to avoid the area altogether unless it's absolutely necessary. Therefore the guy is part of whatever happened at the hotel. Not enough time to be the shooter. He's driving the getaway car."

The others grew quiet. Then Chris said, "Plan, boss?"

"Chris, I want you to drive toward the Marriott. Jami, I want you south of the hotel. I'll head north of it. We don't know what direction they're heading in. Best-case scenario, one of us is in the area and can take out the target once the satellite is back in position." I thought: *And worst case, we completely miss them.*

They agreed with the plan. I kept my eyes on the road and glanced up a moment later and watched as Jami peeled off right. I glanced over my shoulder and watched her take a side road; then she disappeared. Chris Reed stayed close behind me as I found a cross street and slowed down to take it. Chris sped past me and kept moving east, fast and straight and true as I turned the wheel to the left to go north.

I said, "Simon, are you back yet?"

Silence. Only the sound of road noise could be heard coming from Jami's cell or Chris's, or maybe both.

Morgan spoke up and said, "Bloody hell."

I said, "What's wrong?"

"The target Simon set; I'm not seeing the vehicle anywhere. The target's on the screen, but the car isn't."

"Why would that be?" asked Jami.

"Not sure, love. Hang on a sec."

The three of us drove on, listening to Morgan typing in the background, cursing under his breath, then typing some more. Jami said she was approaching H Street, and I told her to aim for Constitution. Chris asked how far east he should go because he was worried about overshooting it. But I didn't know where we were going, so I told him to stop when he got to North Capitol, and I drove north toward Logan Circle.

Then Simon came back on the line. He said, "Can you guys hear me?"

"Yes," I said.

"I can't get a hold of anyone, but I'm reading the interagency reports and can confirm there was a shooting. It happened outside the Marriott Marquis, northside. But I'm certain of one thing: we have a problem."

Morgan asked Simon what he meant. The rest of us listened hard.

He said, "I think there was a fatality."

I PULLED MY TRUCK TO THE SIDE OF THE ROAD. I KEPT THE engine running and put the gearshift into park. Nobody spoke. The line was quiet. I breathed, and then I finally said, "Tell us why you think that, Simon."

He said, "EMS was called; the call came from the Secret Service."

"But why do you think someone was killed?"

"Because they called five minutes ago. And EMS hasn't arrived yet. There's no urgency to get out there."

"It could've been anyone," Chris said from the phone.

There was a pause, and Jami said, "It could've been the president."

I stared out through the windshield, unable to speak for a long moment. Then I said, "How can we know?"

"Who it was?" asked Simon. Then he answered his own question by saying he'd keep us updated; he'd continue monitoring the interagency bulletins and Secret Service updates. As soon as he knew, we'd know.

Then Jami asked if I'd told Emma about Malone and what she'd said about the news of the people we'd been dealing with all day reporting up to him. I told her I'd mentioned it, but Emma said she couldn't talk. Because she was with the president. *Then I'd heard the gunshot*, I thought. *Then the line had gone silent.*

Chris wondered out loud if it could've been Emma Ross

who'd been shot. "I hope not," I said, thinking about Parker and Elizabeth. I sat there a moment longer, and I decided not to think about it anymore. I put my vehicle in gear and pulled back out into traffic. Because Chris was right: it could've been anyone.

Six blocks south, the driver of the sedan was traveling west at a steady pace. He and his passenger had made it out of the danger zone. The Marriott Marquis was a mile and a half behind them. Now it was a slow crawl to get back to where he'd started from. No reason to speed and bring unnecessary attention upon himself. Then the driver's phone buzzed softly as he moved. He pressed the phone to his ear. "Yes?"

A voice said, "It's confirmed. The target is dead."

The driver smiled and turned briefly to his right and gave his passenger a nod and said, "Good to know."

"Where are you now?"

"Headed back to Langley. We're on K, approaching Washington Circle."

There was a slight pause. Then the caller said, "Pull over to the side of the road. For a few minutes, okay?"

"Why?" the driver asked.

"Because Homeland Security and DDC are tracking you."

The driver tapped his brakes. "You can't stop them?"

"I did already," the silver-haired man said with a smile. "But I have an idea. And I think you'll like it."

## 45

I drove at a slow pace. It was a relatively small area to cover this far inside the DC bubble. Morgan came on the line and said he'd zoomed all the way out, and there was no way to miss the target at this level of zoom. From the phone I heard Jami ask how it all worked and how the target could possibly be missing. Morgan said, "It's simple, love. Simon had the satellite set to a very small area of coverage when he set it. The vehicle drove out of range, and although it takes a while to zoom back out and see a broader view, the target should've still been set. For example, Simon had it set to a two-hundred-foot zoom, so he could see about five blocks in every direction. Now I've got it set to two thousand feet. I should be able to see them."

From the phone, Chris said, "But, Morgan, what would cause the target to just disappear like that?"

Morgan said nothing. Maybe he was thinking. I clarified Chris's question by asking one of my own. I said, "If the driver went into a parking garage, could that do it? Since the vehicle would no longer be visible?"

"I see what you're saying. But in short, no. That's not how

it works, guys. If that happened, the target Simon applied would still be hovering over the last known location. We'd see it on our screen still."

Chris said, "Back to my question; what would cause the target to disappear, then?"

Morgan went quiet again. Like he was thinking. Or maybe finding a way to say what he needed to say without disparaging Simon, because he said, "There are only two ways. If Simon hadn't applied it properly in the first place, or—" Morgan paused for a long moment "—I suppose if someone removed it manually."

Simon immediately chimed in. He said, "Morgan, I know what I'm doing. I set the target correctly."

"I believe him," I said. "Try to zoom out a little more. I think he drove out of range. Maybe east of us."

Morgan told us to hold on. I could imagine him looking at a map of DC and clicking on something that would allow him to reposition the view from the satellite more broadly. He came back a few seconds later. "Okay, mate. It's at one mile. I'm not seeing anything at all. I can see all the way out to Langley now."

"Keep going," I said.

Ten seconds passed. "Now I'm at two miles."

"Keep going," I said again.

"Blake, this isn't going to help us. There's no possible way that vehicle can be at this kind of range. I'm already looking at a coverage area of close to seven hundred square miles. I don't need to go out farther."

I kept one hand on the steering wheel and kept my cell pressed against my ear, thinking about that. I said, "Then we need to assume the target was removed by someone. Any way you can figure out who did it?"

"I can try," he said. "But all it will tell me is a username. That's not going to help much either, I'm afraid."

"Do it," I said, and Morgan said he'd get right on it. Then I thought some more. "Simon, I'm thinking about how your view is separate from how the satellite tracks things. And I know there's a historical aspect to it. Can't you go back in time? So we can see where the target was when it was removed?"

Simon thought about that and said, "You're right, I can do that. Give me a few minutes, Blake."

FIVE MINUTES PASSED, WHICH FELT LIKE AN ETERNITY. IT WAS clear the rest of the team was frustrated. Half of them were sitting behind desks, unable to confirm what had happened outside the hotel, while the other half were driving around aimlessly. I used the time to think things through. The guy with the black sedan had driven east. But if he really was CIA, then eventually he would be headed west again. Back to Langley. After he took care of something downtown.

I decided to hang a left and head west, and I told the others what I was doing. Chris asked what I wanted him and Jami to do, and I told them to go a little farther, then to start heading my way. Best to stay spread out, but I didn't want them too far out in case we somehow found the men in the black sedan. Which Simon told us was a long shot. Even if he was able to find the last known location of the target.

And then he did. He said he'd rewound the historical footage from twenty minutes earlier, and he could see the target moving east from the abandoned building we had been at earlier. He had rewound the footage all the way back to when he'd applied the target on the moving vehicle. Then he said he was fast-forwarding and would let us know what he was seeing. He kept us updated like a sidelines reporter, telling us when the vehicle would move east or south or north until he was approximately one mile north and east of the White House as I stared out the windshield, trying to imagine what was in that specific location.

"The Marriott Marquis," I said.

"Just about," Simon replied. "Very close. A block or two north of it."

Simon said the vehicle had parked and was stationary for approximately ten minutes. As if the driver was waiting on something. Or maybe waiting on someone. *The sniper.* Then everything changed. The vehicle moved, fast at first, hooking a north on Ninth Street; then it drove a strange circuitous route south until it found K Street; then it followed it a long way west, six, seven, eight blocks; then it entered the tunnel underneath Washington Circle and completely disappeared. Jami said, "Is it still in the tunnel?"

"Possible," Chris said from the line. "One of us should check it out. What do you want to do, boss?"

But before I could answer, Morgan came back on the line and said, "It's not in the tunnel, guys."

I said, "How do you know for sure?"

"Because I just confirmed that the target Simon had applied was removed manually by someone."

"And there's no way to get a name from what you're seeing?"

"No, mate. It's just a random username." Morgan grew quiet for a beat, and then he said, "But maybe we can figure out who this person is." Then he went quiet again as he worked in finding some kind of link.

I told Chris I was headed to Langley because that was where the driver seemed to be headed. Chris asked what if it wasn't, and I said it was directionally correct. And I was already west of Chris and Jami. If anyone was going to beat the driver to Langley, it would be me. Jami asked what she should do, and I told her to head to the Marriott Marquis. Chris said he was going to head my way, but drive through Washington Circle along the way, just in case we were wrong and the car was still there, under the tunnel.

Then Morgan had something. He said, "I see the same username logged an after-action report earlier today. After visiting a home in Fairfax. He was required to do so due to jurisdiction made by the Bureau."

My heart was racing. "It's David Malone," I said. "It's not just his people—he's involved in all of this, too."

## 46

Nobody else spoke as I pulled off to the side of the road again. I was thinking hard, but unable to fully believe what Morgan had just confirmed for us. So I said, "But what if it's not him, Morgan?"

He replied, "How many CIA guys were at that home in Fairfax this morning who would be required to file an after-action report?"

Chris said, "Just one, as far as I know. David Malone showed up and met with our Bureau guys. Then he met with Peter Mulvaney and me. Then he checked the body of Gardner and said he wanted jurisdiction."

"Because he wanted to contain the situation," I said.

Chris said, "Blake, David Malone knew full well that the guy in that house was not Alex Gardner. At first I thought it was because he was protecting Gardner. Maybe buying him time if he was on the run. But we were wrong. He knew full well that wasn't his man, and he needed to figure out why, so he said nothing."

"Maybe there's some kind of explanation. Maybe Malone got a request from someone to remove the target

Simon applied to the vehicle. Maybe there's some kind of standing order within the CIA. Maybe they don't like agency cars being tracked. Somebody notified him, and he removed it the moment he got word."

Morgan said, "Think all you want, mate. The fact is, David Malone's people have been tracking you guys all day long using Mark's cell phone. Now that we tried tracking them, their boss went and removed it."

I nodded to myself. Morgan was right. "He's involved, then. More than involved, he's their leader. And if that's true, then David Malone's the one ultimately behind what happened today at that home in Fairfax."

"And the one responsible for Mark's death," added Chris.

"And the assassination attempt last week," added Jami. "And whatever happened at the Marriott as well."

After another long moment of thinking, I said, "Morgan, based on the location Simon found where the sedan had stopped being tracked, is there any way you can try to estimate the vehicle's ETA at Langley?"

"What are you thinking, Blake?"

"Once he gets inside the checkpoint, it's a lost cause. The only one who could've helped us get into Langley is Emma Ross, and she's not answering her phone. I want to know if I have a shot at beating them there."

He paused. More typing. He asked Simon to rewind the footage from the satellite and apply some kind of layer that approximated the target's speed and velocity. Simon did as he was asked and told Morgan that the driver was doing about five miles under the speed limit. Probably to avoid calling attention to himself. Morgan said, "If the guy in the sedan was truly going to Langley, then he would've been taking George Washington Parkway. No other good way to get out there, Blake. I suppose if he maintained a slower-than-normal pace and if you drove out there with a lead foot the whole way, you might be able to catch up."

I thought about it. I said, "I'm going to try Emma again; give me ten minutes, then conference me back in." I clicked off and bumped up onto the Theodore Roosevelt Memorial Bridge and thumbed through my contacts list and tapped on Emma Ross's number. I brought my cell to my ear. The line rang endlessly and went to voicemail. I left a message; then I clicked off and wondered if she had been the one shot. Or was it the president himself? For a moment, I thought about turning back and heading to the hotel. But if it was one of them, it was too late to do anything about it. Then I thought about David Malone. A man high in the ranks of the CIA. A man with total power. Untouchable. If I wanted to get to him, I had to find his man.

TEN MILES NORTH AND WEST, DAVID MALONE SAT IN HIS NEW Headquarters Building office at Langley. There was a digital map on the computer monitor on his desk with four points of interest. Four vehicles. Three belonging to DHS, the FBI, and the Department of Domestic Counterterrorism. The fourth was CIA.

His landline rang. His men were impatient. He liked that. A good quality to have. "Yes?" he answered.

Malone heard road noise. The man named Ramsdale said, "How long do we need to sit under this bridge?"

"Not much longer."

"We're sitting ducks under here."

Malone said, "There are three of them. They've split up. They're driving all over DC looking for you."

"They'll find us soon."

"Trust me, you want that."

The driver paused and said, "Are you doing what I think you're doing?"

Malone smiled. "The one named Jordan is almost here. He'll be arriving at Langley in ten minutes."

"And the woman?"

"She's headed to the hotel. Probably to figure out what happened. Communications are limited."

The driver went quiet for a beat. Then he said, "Enough with the theatrics. Tell me what you're doing."

Malone breathed as he watched the two dots moving closer together. He said, "I did not doubt your abilities. But you need to understand—taking the target out at the hotel was the priority. Now that our work is done, I will allow you to deal with any loose ends as you deem necessary. But you need to do it quickly. As long as you're on the outside, you're a liability. Do what you need to do, then get back here."

"So what's the plan?"

Malone watched the two dots, one representing his men, and the other representing the Bureau vehicle. He said, "The one you've been looking for is heading your way. Feel free to do with him as you wish." He paused and added, "Freeman is dead. My people just found him. So it's up to you now to make this right. Make them pay for what they've done."

"I want to do what we did to the other one."

Malone smiled again. "You're a very cautious man. I still don't think he knows what you think he does. But now they must pay, regardless."

Ramsdale said, "If we want to do what we did before, we have to take him alive."

Malone thought about that. "Your call," he said.

## 47

I ARRIVED OUTSIDE THE MAIN ENTRANCE TO LANGLEY AND parked on the side of the road. I could see the checkpoint up ahead and cars of various makes and models queueing up at the entrance. Others were exiting and buzzing past me. I checked my watch. I had gotten here fast. Faster than the expected arrival time Morgan had estimated for the black sedan if they had continued on their path at the same speed.

There weren't many options for getting to Langley from downtown DC. I'd taken the fastest route here. Other ways would take the driver a lot longer. And I doubted they'd want that. No, they'd want to get back through the checkpoint where they could disappear as quickly as possible. I made a U-turn and parked on the other side of the street so I could look for an approaching sedan with a missing window. I settled in and watched the road and just sat there, thinking. My cell buzzed in my pocket. I dug it out and saw the caller ID and answered, "This is Jordan."

"Blake, it's me," a familiar voice said, speaking softly.

"Emma—is everyone okay?"

"No," she said. I held my breath, waiting, listening hard, pressing my phone to my ear. "Not everyone."

I sat up straight and steeled myself for my next question. "Is it the president?"

Silence. Then she said, "No."

"What happened?"

Emma went quiet again. Then she cleared her throat, trying to compose herself. She said, "Thank God you called when you did. Your warning is what saved the president." Emma paused. "I turned around when I was on the phone with you. We had just exited the limousine. The president had let me exit first; then he stepped out, followed by Ethan Meyer and Adam Stine. Your call worried me. I turned around as we were moving toward the hotel entrance. Just a gut feeling. There was another building back there. Another hotel, I think. I saw movement behind a window."

"What happened?" I asked again, a little softer, a little more understanding.

She said, "The first thing I thought of was the president. He was right next to me. Leading us inside. There were Secret Service agents around, but Rivera was holding the door, and his men didn't see what I saw. There wasn't a lot of time. It all just happened so fast. I didn't know what to do. I just—" she paused again "—panicked, I guess. It felt like slow motion. I turned back and dropped my phone and pointed. That's when Ethan must've realized what was happening. Because he tried to cover the president. And then Adam ran over to cover me. Then we all fell to the ground. Again, it was like slow motion. Like an out-of-body experience. Like it wasn't real. Then the guy in the window took the shot. Blake, he killed Adam."

I turned to look out the window, listening to her, still watching for the sedan. "Where's the president?"

"Inside the hotel with the rest of us. The Secret Service is going room to room to clear the building across the street." Emma took a breath and let it out slowly. "The president wanted me to thank you, Blake."

I nodded to myself as I saw a call coming through. The team was conferencing me back in. I told Emma about David Malone. I told her he was involved. Maybe even more than that. Maybe the leader. I said I had to go but I'd be in touch; then I clicked off and answered the incoming call.

Then everything changed.

There was an argument in progress between Chris and Jami. I was joining the call mid-conversation. Morgan let them talk a moment longer; then he said, "Blake, are you on the line?"

"Yes," I said. "What's the problem?"

Chris and Jami stopped long enough for Morgan to bring me up to speed. He said, "A lot has happened in the last ten minutes. The target Simon applied earlier has reappeared. Like someone maybe reapplied it."

"Why would they do that?"

"I don't know, mate. But they did, and it's in the same exact spot as it was when the target disappeared."

"Under the tunnel?"

"Yes."

"So what's the problem?"

Silence. Nobody spoke. All I could hear was road noise and the faint sound of an engine racing hard. Then Jami said, "Chris is closest to the target. You're all the way out at Langley, and I just parked two blocks out from the Marriott Marquis. I was almost at the perimeter MPD set up when Morgan and Simon noticed the target was back. I'm heading back to my vehicle now, but Chris isn't waiting so we can go in together."

"Chris?" I said, wanting his take, as I looked over my shoulder and pulled into traffic.

He said, "These people killed my partner, Blake. I'm not giving them another chance to get away."

"We know who's responsible," I said as I straightened out and stepped on the gas. "It's David Malone."

"Maybe he gave the order, but this guy was the executioner. Along with the other guy in the warehouse. Besides, I'm five minutes out. You guys are twenty minutes away in both directions." Then Chris thought about it some more. Maybe trying not to let his emotions control his decision-making. "Tell you what, I'll pull up close enough to make a visual. I'll play it by ear from there." Then he clicked off.

Chris Reed arrived five minutes later and entered the tunnel. It was two lanes in each direction, and no shoulder. The black sedan with the broken window was up ahead, less than twenty feet from the tunnel entrance, blocking traffic on the right. Reed decided to pull up close. No other way around it. Vehicles were queueing up on the left. Plenty of witnesses should anything go down, plenty of traffic preventing a fast getaway. Reed put the vehicle in park and kept the motor on and stared out through the windshield. Then his thoughts went to Mark Reynolds. He imagined him being taken up an elevator, forced to the roof, pushed off. He could see it all in his mind's eye. His heart was pounding hard in his chest. He clenched his fists. He checked his watch and decided he didn't want to wait. Not after what they'd done.

Reed stepped out cautiously and drew his weapon as he

approached the sedan. Cars droned by him as he moved. Lots of road noise. Big engines, noisy brakes, a few horns here and there from impatient drivers. He approached the driver's side door and looked inside, through the missing glass. The vehicle was empty. Reed looked in the back. Nobody was there. He holstered his weapon and returned to his SUV and climbed inside. He pulled the door shut hard and stared out at the empty vehicle parked in front of him. He went to dig his phone out as a cold muzzle touched the back of his neck, and a voice said, "Don't move."

## 48

I made the trip back to Washington Circle in under twenty minutes. So did Jami. Just as she said she was about to enter the tunnel from the east, I was approaching the tunnel from the west. I drove through and saw the black sedan parked on my left near the exit, and I stopped, blocking one of the eastbound lanes. I could see Jami on the other side, parked behind the sedan. I asked if she was ready, and she said yes.

We both exited at the same time. We were both blocking a lane on both sides of the tunnel. Drivers with angry faces blew horns as I motioned for them to let me cross in front of them. I drew my weapon with one hand and reached for my DHS credentials with the other. I held them out, and their faces relaxed some. They just watched me glide across as I met up with Jami, and we walked together toward the sedan.

Jami stayed behind the trunk. I moved to the side of the vehicle and aimed my Glock into the window. Just like I imagined Chris Reed must've done minutes earlier. Nobody was inside. And nobody was in the back. All I could see were empty seats and broken glass on the floorboard. I opened the door and popped the trunk and moved to the back. Jami was looking inside. Nothing was there except for a spare tire. She slammed it shut, and we holstered our weapons. She turned to me and said, "Where is he, Blake?"

I said I didn't know as I dug my phone out from my pocket with the conference call still in progress. I said, "Morgan, his truck is gone. The sedan's here, but it's empty." I glanced at Jami. "I think they took him."

"What do you mean, took him?" asked Morgan.

"They took him by surprise somehow. Did you try calling him back after he dropped from the call?"

"Yes, of course. There wasn't any answer."

"I think they're in his vehicle right now. Can you or Simon track it?"

Morgan cursed under his breath. I heard him typing frantically in the background. Jami noticed something behind us, along the outer edge of the tunnel. I watched her walk back to look, and she returned with a cell phone in her hand and showed it to me. It looked just like mine. And hers. Government issued.

"We've got his cell phone," Jami said. "They ditched it when they left so we couldn't track them down."

Morgan came on and said, "Okay, guys, I just need some time to orient myself. I'll do the same thing I did this morning with Mark Reynolds. I'll find his vehicle identifier, then the specific GPS unit inside it; then I'll ping it. Hopefully the CIA guys didn't think of that. Maybe there wasn't enough time to rip it out."

Simon said, "Where do you think they're taking him?"

Silence on the line. Jami stared at me. I said, "Could be anywhere."

Simon asked no more questions. Jami thought for a moment and said, "What do we do while we wait?"

I said, "We should talk to Gardner again. I want to know more about Malone. Maybe he can help us."

Jami glanced past me, across the road. "Meet you there? Two vehicles are better than one?"

I shook my head. "Not anymore. Now we're staying together." I put one hand on Jami's back and held the other one out to stop traffic. We moved to the eastbound lanes and climbed into my SUV and drove off.

Chris Reed drove slower than the traffic around him, trying to buy as much time as he could. Sitting directly behind him was one man, and next to that man was another. Reed wondered who the other guy was as he navigated the DC streets and started putting it all together. After taking a shot at him by the abandoned building, the guy driving the sedan had sped away east. And what was east? The Marriott Marquis. Where the shooting had taken place. And then he was back on the western side of DC. Reed understood that the guy in the sedan had picked up the other man. *The shooter.*

The last few minutes had been a blur, but he thought through his mistakes anyway. Reed had correctly used the traffic and road noise to his advantage, having pulled up right behind the parked sedan, knowing he had the upper hand approaching the vehicle without a clear getaway because of the gridlock. But he had been so focused on what was in front of him that he hadn't thought about the bad guys coming up from behind. Reed figured they must've been hidden outside the tunnel entrance, waiting for him to arrive. They'd climbed into his own vehicle when his back was turned. He hadn't even heard them. Too many loud engines and noisy brakes. That meant someone knew he was coming. Someone had told them.

They made him drive through Washington Circle and hang a right on Twenty-Fifth Street, and another on L, and they continued to navigate from the backseat until he understood where he was going.

He was driving back to where it all began.

As he approached the building where they'd found Mark Reynolds's body, he searched desperately for Metro PD and FBI vehicles. He saw none, and Reed thought through why. MPD was preoccupied now. The president was at the Marriot Marquis for his rally. That was where MPD needed to focus, on protecting someone still living, not blocking the streets over someone who was dead. And the Bureau wasn't here anymore, either. Peter Mulvaney ran a tight ship. Mulvaney would figure out what happened eventually, but no need to keep agents outside the building all day. They had pictures and people out at the Fairfax home, looking into the connection to Gardner. News Reed hadn't shared with him yet and now regretted it. All day he'd been imagining what Mark had gone through. Now he would find out.

The man directly behind him said, "Slow down. I want you to drive around the building nice and easy."

Reed did as he was told. He slowed even more than he was already going and drove his vehicle counterclockwise around the tall building. He drove by the spot where he heard they had found Mark's body. The chalk outline was still visible. He stared at it as he passed by. Then Reed glanced up from the window. It was a long way up to the top of the building. And a long way down. The guy behind him spoke again. He said, "Now enter the parking garage on your left."

Reed glanced up at the rearview mirror and said, "What do you want from me?"

"You'll find out," the man replied as he handed a keycard to him over his shoulder, and Reed took it, drove into the garage, and came to a stop. He lowered his window and tapped the card against a reader.

A light turned green, and a long barrier arm lifted up high, allowing the vehicle to enter the garage. Reed handed the card back over his shoulder and drove through and followed the man's instructions on where to park. He went to a spot by an elevator door and stopped the vehicle. Slow and steady, trying not to make any sudden movements. For a moment, Reed wondered if he was doing the right thing coming here.

But he knew his friends would make every effort to find him; he'd bought as much time as he could. And he wanted to find the man who had sanctioned Mark's death. He wanted to look the man in the eye. The man named David Malone.

And he figured, if they were bringing him here, he'd get to do just that.

## 49

Jami left her vehicle parked inside the Washington Circle tunnel. The black sedan was already blocking traffic. Another vehicle parked behind it wouldn't make a difference one way or another. We decided there was no longer a need for a conference call either. Chris was missing, and Jami would be with me, and Morgan and Simon needed time to find the vehicle's identification number and the GPS unit tied to Chris's SUV. The guys said they'd stay on the line and would call me back when they had news to share.

I clicked off and headed back to the home in Reston with Jami by my side. She played navigator like she had with Chris, telling me which roads to take, telling me where to exit, remembering our first visit to the home earlier in the day. We didn't call ahead. Gardner had seemed hesitant to meet with us the first time. He clearly didn't want anyone knowing where he was. Especially Malone's people. For his own protection.

We pulled up twenty minutes later and parked in the same spot we had the first time. Jami and I climbed out, and I stepped in front of the hood, across the easement, and to the walkway that led to the front door. Jami rang the doorbell, and I knocked three times. We both faced the door and then turned to glance at each other when it wasn't answered immediately. Like last time, I could sense that someone was inside. Just the feeling you get when you know with absolute certainty that someone else is there.

I said, "We're here to see Alex Gardner. We were here before, with Emma Ross."

No response. Not at first. Then the latch was undone, and the door opened an inch, then it was pulled open the whole way. Murray was standing in front of us, and Alex Gardner himself was behind him, looking on from a distance. Murray told us to hurry and ushered us inside, and once we stepped past him, he closed the door fast and quickly locked it behind us. This time, we weren't invited further inside. We weren't offered a seat or coffee or the same kind of hospitality we'd been given the first time around.

Gardner stepped forward. He looked at me, then glanced at Jami and said, "Why did you come back?"

Jami's eyes moved to mine, and I turned to face the man and said, "We need your help."

He furrowed his brow, unsure about what to say at first; then he said, "I'm not sure how else I *can* help."

Murray said, "He's told you everything he knows."

"Maybe so," I said. "But a lot has happened since we were here."

Gardner narrowed his eyes and said, "What are you talking about?"

I looked at the man straight on. I said, "Half an hour ago, our friend was taken by the CIA guys."

"Who was taken? The man who was here with you earlier?"

I nodded.

"Why would they do that?"

"Because they think he knows something. They think he knows what this whole thing is about."

"Does he?"

I thought about it. "He knows a lot." I glanced at Jami briefly. "We all do."

Gardner eyed both of us carefully. Like he was thinking hard, thinking through the implications, and maybe considering what he could do if it was true, if we really did know what this whole thing was about.

Then his face changed. Like something had been activated deep inside him. Like a soldier called to duty or a father being asked advice or a student realizing he had finally become the teacher for somebody else. He said, "I've told you everything I know, but maybe there is a way I can help. Depending on what you know so far."

"We know David Malone is involved."

"More than involved," Jami added.

Gardner's eyes moved back and forth between the two of us. Studying us. Trying to understand. "Explain."

She said, "The CIA guys report up through him. We've confirmed that much already."

"They report up through him," he repeated, looking away. "Which means they reported up through me, too. Which means they also report up through Emma, in a way." He glanced back at us. "Is she okay?"

"Yes," I said. "Which is another problem. One of Malone's boys tried to take out the president. Just a few minutes ago. Emma was there. I called her on her phone and warned her something might be going down. We saved the president's life by warning her. We're assuming it was a CIA guy who tried to take him out."

Gardner thought about that. "This has to be some kind of misunderstanding. Have you spoken with David? He might not know he's got bad people working for him. Just because they report up to him—"

"It gets worse," I said, interrupting the man. "Before the assassination attempt, we were tracking one of the CIA guys' vehicles. We had one of our analysts apply a target to the vehicle so we wouldn't lose it."

Gardner stared. "What happened?"

"We were using a satellite. Someone logged in to remove the target long enough to draw our friend in. Then they reapplied it and captured him. That's how they got our friend."

Jami said, "Our people looked into who did it. A username was logged. But we did a search, to see if that username had popped up before. And it had. Earlier this morning. It was used to log an after-action report after visiting your home this morning, which was required because the FBI claimed jurisdiction. So any other agency visiting the crime scene had to log a report immediately upon returning to their office." Jami stared across at Gardner. "David Malone filed the report. And David Malone removed the target."

Nobody spoke for a very long moment. There was nothing but silence between the four of us. Gardner's friend was looking at Jami. Jami was looking at me. I was staring at Gardner while he looked out at nothing at all, thinking again, trying to understand, trying to put the pieces together. Then he did. Because he came to the same conclusion that we had come to earlier. Gardner said, "David Malone was in my home this morning. He'd been there before. A long time ago. He knew the address. And he knew what I looked like, obviously. I thought the fact that he didn't tell anyone else that it wasn't me was to protect me. But it wasn't. No, he understood everything. He knew who the dead guy was. It was one of his men."

"We need your help," said Jami.

Gardner glanced at her. "What do you have in mind?"

"We're trying to find our friend. We have people working on it. But maybe you can speed things up."

I said, "If you were the bad guys—one of these rogue CIA agents—where would you be taking him?"

Then Gardner's face changed again. From ignorance to understanding. He said, "We need to leave—now."

## 50

We piled into my vehicle and headed out, back toward the DC bubble, back toward downtown. I asked Gardner where we were headed, and he told me to drive towards the building where they'd found Mark Reynolds's body. Emma Ross called me on our way. She asked if we had found Malone, and I said not yet. I told her where we were headed. Gardner didn't seem to like that very much. The less people knew, the better. Emma said they'd taken Adam Stine's body away, and the area had been cordoned off as a crime scene. After the building opposite the northern entrance to the hotel had been cleared, Emma, Ethan Meyer, and the president had been ushered into the Marriot Marquis. Secret Service agents had huddled all around them as they moved, shielding them, protecting Keller from anyone else hiding in the shadows.

Jami asked me to put the call on speakerphone; then she asked Emma what the next steps were with the president. Emma said they were going to reschedule the rally. Date and time TBD. Gardner did not speak. He seemed to be very worried, which I could understand. An attempt had been made on his life. People were out there, including David Malone and his men, who probably wanted him dead and knew he was still alive. Few people knew the truth, and I was okay with keeping it that way to protect the man.

I saw another call coming in and told Emma I had to go and said I'd keep her updated and clicked over. "Yeah," I said, answering the incoming call on speakerphone.

"It's me," said Morgan. "And I have Simon on the line as well."

"What do you have?"

"I was able to track down Chris's vehicle."

I glanced over to Gardner as I drove. "Let me guess; it's somewhere close to the place where Mark died."

Gardner stared at me, then glanced down at my phone.

Morgan said, "Yes, mate. Not just close, it's inside the building somehow."

"We know where the building is," Jami said from the backseat. "We're headed there now."

Morgan paused a beat. "Well then, I want the last half hour of my bloody life back."

I said, "Can you and Simon do me a favor? Can you guys move the satellite and monitor the area?"

"Already done," Simon said, and I remembered the guys had stayed on the conference call without us.

I thanked them both and clicked off.

Gardner sat next to me and helped me navigate our way towards the downtown building. He pointed out which streets to take and gave me a few shortcuts that would get us there faster. As we approached, he had me park on the southern side of the street facing north so we could watch the parking garage entrance for a few minutes. I put the gearshift in park but kept the motor running. I stared at the entrance for a moment; then I turned to my right. Gardner's eyes flicked over to look at me. I said, "What is this place?"

He hesitated for a moment and made a face. The face of a man who had a lot to say but wasn't sure how much he should share. Gardner was a cautious man. He said, "The CIA owns the place. It's off the books."

"The whole building?"

Gardner nodded. "It's like a safe house in a way. Only instead of a residential building, it's commercial."

"Hell of a place," I said, turning back and craning my neck to look as high up as I could.

"We own all of it but don't occupy all of it. It's got to look legit. And it does, wouldn't you say?"

I nodded. It looked like a regular office building. No identifying markings outside it. Nothing screaming *federal building* in any way whatsoever. Just a small marquee with the building number out front.

"Floors toward the bottom and middle are all rented out. We have the top half for the most part."

"What are they used for?"

"Multipurpose."

"Meaning?"

"Meaning it's not a designated office space. It's not like they have warrens of cubicles up there. We have computer servers on a few floors, conference rooms, offices for private meetings we don't want to have at Langley for whatever reason. And the underground parking garage kind of masks the vehicles for those who come here. Again, think of it like a safe house, only nobody lives here. It's just a private office space."

Jami leaned forward in her seat and said, "A federal agent leapt to his death from the top of the building. A building you say is owned by the CIA. That wouldn't throw up red flags with anybody in the Agency?"

"Of course it would," he said. "But David is the highest-ranking person here. The buck stops with him. He's the head guy for the whole Department of Domestic Counterterrorism. Above him is all CIA guys."

Jami understood. So did I. Having led the first DDC field office in Chicago, I knew how it worked. The CIA couldn't operate stateside; they were entirely an overseas operation. But with the increase in domestic terrorism, former president Rouse had not only blessed but encouraged the domestic spinoff of the Agency. She said, "Since it's an off-the-books site, it hasn't hit the papers that the CIA or DDC is involved."

"As far as the press knows, it's just a regular office building. They don't need to know. It's immaterial."

I said nothing back. The three of us sat in silence, thinking, getting a lay of the land, watching the traffic lights toggle from green to amber to red and back again. It didn't take long for nightfall. Maybe fifteen minutes. The streetlights flicked on as we continued to watch and wait. I asked Gardner what we were waiting for. He just checked the time and told me I'd know soon. The sun disappeared, and the streetlights grew bright. They overtook the sunlight a few minutes later. I grew impatient and said, "Mr. Gardner, our friend is in there, and we don't know what they're doing to him. I can't wait any longer. I'm going in."

But Gardner just held a hand up and then used it to point to a dark SUV as it passed by us, then slowed, then hooked north and turned into the garage. It didn't stop. Just rolled forward slowly. Then the SUV disappeared inside. Gardner told us it was David Malone. I asked how he knew. He said he saw the tag. Jami asked how he knew he'd come here. Gardner told us Malone was a creature of habit. He always left Langley at 6:30 p.m. He figured if our friend really was here, Malone would want to talk to him himself. Then Gardner pulled a keycard from his pocket and handed it over and said, "Use this to get inside. Twentieth floor. They have an interrogation room there. That's where they have your friend. Good luck."

He dug out his phone and started to climb out, but I grabbed his arm and said, "I need you to go with us."

## 51

Alex Gardner seemed hesitant about that. He said, "You don't understand—David Malone and his people—they want to kill me. That should be obvious by now."

"It is," I said. "But we don't know the layout inside the building. Easier for you to show us the way."

Gardner turned his gaze from me to the building. He stared at it through the windshield. He said, "Okay."

I put the gearshift in drive and craned my neck to look over my shoulder. I waited for a break in traffic; then I buzzed across three lanes and made the turn to head up the western side of the building; then I turned in. I could see a long barrier arm out in front of us and a card reader. No humans were involved. Not like the other government buildings around town. I figured they might notice a pattern with black sedans and SUVs with federal plates. Or they might catch a glimpse of visitors attending clandestine meetings that needed to remain secret. Gardner told me to use the keycard, and I buzzed my window down and tapped it against the reader, and the barrier arm lifted up high, giving me clearance.

I accelerated fast, past the raised barrier, into the garage. Gardner navigated me around a corner as I handed the keycard back to him, looking for a good place to park. We passed a number of SUVs, and Gardner told me to slow down. We found Malone's vehicle parked in a space close to an elevator, and he said this was where we needed to be. Jami watched from the back and suggested I pull around so we could face the parked vehicle from two rows back. I found a spot and asked her what she thought of it.

"Perfect," she said.

Gardner stared out and said, "What's the plan?"

I followed his gaze and watched the elevator and said, "You'll get us inside. You'll show us where to go."

"I told you where to go. Twentieth floor."

"I still need you to go with us."

"Why?"

"In case of unforeseen circumstances."

Gardner grew quiet. I turned and studied the man. He looked nervous. Like he was steeling himself, mentally preparing for what was to come. I looked at Jami through the mirror. She said, "Question." Gardner did a half turn and looked over his shoulder. "If Malone fired you, why is your keycard working?"

I said, "Sloppy work," answering for Gardner. "Malone was too busy plotting an assassination attempt." Gardner made a quarter turn forward and stared at me as I added, "That's why his voicemail wasn't reset. And that's why he's still showing up in the org chart. Malone didn't bother processing the paperwork yet."

Gardner nodded. He said, "I should have a weapon. In case something goes down up there. In case they take the two of you out. I haven't fired one in a very long time, but I know how."

"I only have one," I said.

We all grew quiet. Nobody spoke. Then I heard Jami unholster her weapon, and she handed it to Gardner.

Gardner took the Glock and craned his neck, looking at Jami over his shoulder. "You sure?"

"I'm going to stay here," she said. "Hopefully I won't need it."

I stared at Gardner for a beat, then turned back and glanced at her over my shoulder and said, "Why?"

"If you miss Malone for any reason, then I'm your failsafe. I'll hang back in case he leaves unannounced."

"You won't be able to engage."

"I hope I won't need to. Cut the motor. I'll sit up front. I'll follow him if I have to."

"You'll still be on your own. We don't have another car."

Gardner said, "We do. We always keep a few spares here. I know where they keep the keys if we need one."

I nodded and turned to face the man. "You ready?"

He nodded that he was. I cut the motor, and we both climbed out. Gardner moved toward the elevator and put his weapon in a pocket and waited for me. Jami climbed out and took my place in the driver's seat. She stared up at me as I stood by her door, and she told me to be careful. I told her I would.

I shut her door for her and joined Gardner. He led the way. We moved past two long rows of vehicles and made our way to the elevator along the far side of the wall. Gardner pulled his keycard out from a pocket and held it against a reader. The light on the reader changed from red to green, and then he pushed the button to call the elevator. We stood there together waiting, and I glanced back across at my parked SUV. Jami stared at me. She nodded her support, and I nodded back. It was parked perfectly. A good vantage point to surveil Malone should he exit from here and get into his car. As we waited, I turned to envision the path the man would walk. He wouldn't notice Jami. She was one in a sea of a million similar vehicles.

I turned back and looked at Gardner. I said, "Put the keycard away and get your weapon ready."

"Hope we won't need it," he said, tucking the keycard into a pocket and awkwardly pulling out the Glock.

The elevator doors chimed open. We stepped inside. Gardner pushed the button, and the doors closed.

EMMA ROSS PLACED A CALL TO GET AN UPDATE ON THE situation unfolding a few miles out from her, but the call did not go through. Just a fast transfer to voicemail. She stood alone inside the Marriott Marquis, separate from everybody else in the president's entourage, scrolling through her contacts, and then she stopped at one. She dialed and pressed the phone to her ear, and Jami answered on the first ring. She told Emma where she was and what they were doing with Emma's former boss. Emma said she'd been there once, with Alex Gardner, when she first joined the CIA, touring facilities. She asked, "Why are you there?"

Jami said, "We think Chris Reed is here somewhere. And we saw Malone arrive a short time ago."

Emma grew quiet, thinking through the implications. Then she said, "That building is used for meetings, but it's also used for other things." Emma glanced up and saw Agent Rivera appear, talking on his phone. "I'm going to find someone to drive me there. I think they could use my help."

# 52

The elevator rocketed upward. But we weren't going to the twentieth floor. Gardner had pushed the button for the twenty-first floor. He must've seen the confusion on my face because he said, "We'll go one floor up and take the stairs down one. Safer that way. We don't know what we're dealing with yet."

I nodded and glanced up at the digital board that was showing which floors we were passing as we moved. I glanced back down and checked my weapon, counting how many rounds I had, and I said, "Best guess?"

Gardner said, "We know there's at least one. The guy who must've forced your friend to drive him here. Plus Malone. Plus a few others." He paused a beat and said, "Maybe five total to deal with."

The elevator started to slow. I told Gardner to get ready and to stay behind me. The man looked worried. Like he was about to engage in a battle he wasn't entirely sure he wanted to be involved in. Then he lifted Jami's Glock and aimed it at the floor and stood to the side of the elevator, taking a second-in-command position behind me. I aimed my own weapon to the floor for a brief moment, standing straight on. Ready.

The elevator stopped. I leveled my weapon and aimed it straight ahead, waiting for the doors to open. Then they did. I stepped out fast and stared straight ahead. I saw nobody there. We crossed a hallway and entered a room. I aimed my Glock to the left. Then I swung hard to my right. Then I straightened out and moved farther into the expanse of the large room. I could see Gardner whenever I'd glance left and right, gripping Jami's gun tight, mirroring my motions behind me. I saw two meeting rooms up ahead, one on the left, one on the right. I let go of my Glock with my left hand and used two fingers to point across my extended arm, motioning to our right.

Gardner understood. He broke off and moved toward it to clear the room. I mirrored him on the left side. A light flicked on from a motion sensor as I stepped inside and looked all around. Nobody was there. Then I stepped out and saw Gardner do the same on his end. We joined each other in the middle again.

We kept on moving, clearing four additional rooms, two on each side, following the same process. Nobody was there. But the last two rooms along the far side of the wall were different. They had equipment that reminded me of a hospital room. Large screens used for monitoring heart rates, breathing, oxygen levels.

I lowered my weapon and held it loose in my hand.

Gardner watched me closely. He said, "Nobody's here."

I nodded and glanced around the room. "What is this place?"

"I didn't tell you about this part. Occasionally we have to bring people here who won't cooperate."

I narrowed my eyes. "Meaning?"

"It's like the place downtown you went to. The address I gave you before. For enhanced interrogations."

"Okay," I said as I turned and glanced back down to the other side of the floor. "Where's the stairs?"

"We're not going down yet."

"Why not?"

Gardner lifted his weapon fast and rested the muzzle against my temple. "Unforeseen circumstances."

## 53

I stood perfectly still, staring across at Gardner. He said, "Drop it, Jordan. Nice and slow." The man's face had changed. He no longer looked like a man not used to handling a weapon, out of practice, relegated to a desk job at Langley after growing too old to be out in the field. Now he looked ruthless, cunning, more than capable. He pushed the muzzle harder against my temple. "Do it now."

My Glock was still loose in my hand. I thought about my options and realized I had none. Jami was downstairs sitting inside my car. No weapon. No way to even get inside the elevator, let alone help me. Chris Reed was one floor below me. Unarmed himself, I imagined. A prisoner. Enduring enhanced interrogation, maybe. Gardner narrowed his eyes, growing impatient. So I crouched low and dropped it.

I stood up slowly and raised my hands halfway up. I said, "Who are you?"

"You know who I am." The guy paused. "I'm Alex Gardner. Assistant director of stateside CIA operations."

I said, "How are you involved in all of this?"

"Now that's a different question."

"David Malone is a very dangerous man," I said. "So are the people working with him."

Gardner smiled.

"What you're doing is an abuse of power, using your authority to sanction two assassination attempts."

"One attempt," he said. "Today's was successful."

I shook my head. "Your people missed today. The president is alive and well."

"Yes, but Adam Stine isn't," he replied.

I narrowed my eyes. "How was Stine involved?"

Gardner stared at me. "He wasn't, actually. But we'll make it look like he was. He was our backup plan. We've already planted things on his phone. Changed text messages, altered conversations to frame him."

"Frame him for what? The assassination attempt on the motorcade?"

"What else?" he asked.

I said nothing. Just stared back in silence.

"And now that he's dead, he can't say he didn't help us. He can't prove he wasn't the leaker. He can't bring us down in any way; all of this goes away."

"I'm familiar with the hotel downtown. That building on the north side is very close to the entrance. If your people had the ability to take out Stine, then you had a chance to take out Keller. A do-over from last week. So why not do it? Why not finish the job? You've gone this far already. Why take out Stine instead?"

Gardner thought about that for a long moment, gauging how much he should share with me. Then maybe realized he had nothing else to hide. Not anymore. Which also told me everything I needed to know about what his plans were for me once he was done. He said, "You're right. The president was our target. Along with the Russian president.

There were a lot of people involved. People in the CIA, people within the Bureau, even people within Keller's inner circle. Which caused a lot of problems when we failed—thanks to you, I might add." He breathed in and let it out slowly as he studied me. "But that ship had sailed. It was just a matter of time until someone talked. We ran the risk of being exposed. We had to act."

"What are you saying?" I asked. "Are you telling me that everything that happened today was just so you and your people could cover your tracks? That three people died today so you could avoid being caught?"

"More than that," he said. "Agent Reed will make four. You and your wife make six."

"You son of a bitch, leave her out of this."

Gardner shook his head. "Can't now. As soon as I deal with you, I'll have to go down and take care of her."

He nodded past me, telling me to turn around and move. I watched him a moment longer; then I turned. It was clear he wanted me in the back corner room. The one with the medical equipment. The one used for enhanced interrogation. I started to walk and glanced over my shoulder. I said, "Who's your informant?"

"What do you mean?"

"You told me there were people inside the president's inner circle. Was it Stine? Or someone else?"

Gardner smiled again and said, "Agent Bryant, United States Secret Service. He's one of ours."

I stopped at the entrance to the room and turned around. "Who else?"

"Besides Bryant? No one. We had to take a need-to-know approach."

I stood there, hands raised, a question on my mind. "What really happened with Agent Reynolds?"

Gardner thought about it. He said, "My name had been circulating around as someone potentially involved in last week's assassination attempt. David was informed. We had our suspicions on who had started talking. So he put me on administrative leave, but told everyone he had fired me. The plan was for me to act like a whistleblower. To change the conversation. To get people to think I couldn't be involved if I was making all these phone calls, trying to talk to internal affairs within the Agency and then the Bureau. And if I wasn't involved, then David couldn't be, either. He wanted me to pin everything on the guy we suspected of talking." He looked away. Lost in thought. Remembering everything. "So I made some calls. Nobody would listen to me. So David found the direct line for Peter Mulvaney and gave it to me. I called the guy up. I left messages. Then we finally spoke on the phone. He agreed to send a few of his guys out to talk to me. So I played the part. I told Mulvaney it had to be after dark and in the middle of the night."

"Then Agent Reynolds called you."

Gardner shook his head. "I called *him*. Ahead of our meeting. Because I had just killed a guy in my home. The guy we wanted to pin everything on." He paused, looking away, remembering. "He knocked on my door ninety minutes before I was supposed to meet with the two Bureau agents. I thought he just wanted to talk, but he was there with a gun. He knew I was involved, not just in framing him, but with the first assassination attempt. He tried to force me to admit it. He wouldn't give it up. So I did. There was a struggle. I knocked him out. I positioned him on my couch."

I said, "And when he came to, you shot him."

Gardner nodded. "I wanted him to know that he hadn't won."

I said nothing.

"Then I called Agent Reynolds, telling him I saw someone outside my home."

I thought about that. "Why did you wait until now to deal with Chris Reed?"

Gardner shrugged. "He didn't arrive with Reynolds. It was hours ahead of our designated meeting time, after all. I figured he didn't know anything. But one of our men thought he might. He got the ball rolling, so now we're finishing what we started. No loose ends." Gardner motioned to the room with the weapon. I turned and looked at the equipment inside the room and clenched my fists as I moved, thinking through what I had to do, trying to time it right. But Gardner was one step ahead of me. He must've been studying me, because he brought the Glock up high and struck me on the back of my head.

Everything went black.

# 54

When I opened my eyes, I was on the floor, facedown, my hands cuffed behind my back. I blinked several times as I started to become aware of my surroundings. Gardner was standing over me. He told me to get up, but I couldn't. The pain on the back of my head was unbearable. He stepped up close and kicked me hard. It knocked the wind out of me. Ten seconds passed; then I gasped for air. Thirty more seconds passed, and I managed to turn over, knelt, and balanced myself. Then I stood, uneasy at first, then tall as I stared straight at the man.

Gardner had the keys to the handcuffs in one hand and Jami's Glock in the other. He said, "I was going to make it quick and painless. But instead I think I'll take my time and enjoy it."

I glanced over my shoulder at the room behind me. Then I turned back and stepped closer to the guy. Gardner dug a phone out from his pocket. He dialed a number. He said, "I need you on the twenty-first floor"; then he clicked off and dropped it back into his pocket. I felt my heart beat hard in my chest. So far it was one against one. In a moment

I'd be outnumbered. No way of saving Chris and Jami. Game over.

Then the lights went out. A brief flicker, then off completely. I lowered my head and led with my shoulder. I hit Gardner hard; then we both hit the wall. I heard the keys hit the floor but not the weapon. Not yet. The lights came on again, but only the floodlights in the corners of the room. A backup generator must've kicked on, programmed to start ten seconds after losing power. Typical in a government building. I stepped to the side and brought my right knee up hard, landing a blow against Gardner's stomach. Then I kneed him again, then again. Gardner held onto the gun but curled forward, the wind knocked out of him. I slipped his head through my arms with my wrists locked together. A reverse headlock. I squeezed hard. Gardner tried to turn the weapon toward me, but I jerked quick and felt a snap.

Gardner fell to the floor.

THE SNIPER WAITED FOR THE BACKUP GENERATOR TO KICK ON; then he headed to the elevator and stepped inside. He pressed the button for the twenty-first floor and rode it up and stepped out into a hallway. The man smiled. A smug expression on his face as he moved. Not only did he have his man, but it seemed he was now getting the other one. Agent Reed's friend. The one his prisoner had said would rescue him. Instead, his people had apparently found the guy first. Alex Gardner had made the call. He'd recognized his voice instantly. Which meant he was now out of hiding. Which also meant they were close to tying up all remaining loose ends. The man reached into his pocket as he approached and pulled out a keycard. He held it to the reader, and the light changed from red to green as he gripped the handle and twisted it open.

I STOOD NEXT TO THE DOOR AND HEARD A TONE OUTSIDE IT. Then I heard someone twist the handle, and the door opened. Not fast, not slow. Not cautiously, either. A confident man entering a room. He stepped inside. Then he noticed Gardner's body. I held my gun to the back of his head and said, "Take me to him."

## 55

The guy froze and didn't move for a long moment. Then he turned his head to look at me. I said, "Find your weapon and drop it on the floor. Then I need you to turn around slowly and exit the room."

The guy did as I asked. Then he made a slow turn, eyeing me the whole time, and moved. He reached into his pocket for his keycard and held it to the reader on this side of the door. A light turned green. He twisted the handle; then I followed him out. We moved across the hallway, toward the elevator. I didn't recognize the guy. It wasn't the one with the broken window. The one who'd followed us all day. The one named Ramsdale. The guy glanced over his shoulder as he moved and said, "It's too late. Your friend isn't here. You missed him."

"Shut up," I said, following, holding my weapon out with one hand, walking steadily.

The man kept moving and slowed as he got to the elevator. But he didn't push the button. Instead, he turned back and stared straight at me. He said, "Your friend didn't know much. Just like the other one."

I eyed him for a moment, deciding if I wanted to engage. Then I said, "Why'd you bring him here?"

"Who? Agent Reynolds?"

I nodded.

"I was at Gardner's house. He called me. After one of our colleagues went over there to confront him. Before the Bureau guy showed up. Gardner was taken by surprise. He killed the CIA agent, and the Bureau guys were going to cause problems. He knew it the moment he killed the guy in his home. He was in a tough situation. Think about it. We were going to frame the guy he ended up killing. We had a backup plan with Adam Stine, of course. But in the meantime, the meeting with the FBI was already in motion. Already set to be happening in a few hours. Two Bureau guys were going to be going to his home. Gardner took the opportunity to take care of one of them. Easier than dealing with two agents at the same time. I promised Gardner we'd take care of the other one." The man studied me a moment longer and smiled. "And we have."

"Where is he?"

The guy shook his head slowly. "I told you, it's too late. Your friend's not here."

I stepped forward and rested the muzzle of my weapon on his forehead. I said, "Take—me—to—him," pausing after each word, pushing my weapon hard against his skin, blinking hard, restraining myself. My heart was racing. I was breathing hard, gripping my weapon tight, clenching my jaw, staring.

Then the guy forced a smile, giving in, not willing to die over it, and said, "Okay."

He turned slowly and reached for the button to call the elevator and pressed it. Then we waited, and I said, "Who does David Malone work for?"

"Nobody who's involved," he replied. "He calls the shots. This was all his idea."

"And whose idea was it to throw a man off the top of this building? A man with a wife and a kid at home."

"It was Malone's idea."

"But why kill him that way?"

"Because shooting a federal agent creates questions. Who did it? Why'd they do it? Means, motive, opportunity. But a man leaping to his death doesn't. Happens every day. The stress of the job does it."

"You don't think an FBI agent falling to his death from a CIA-owned building would create questions?"

"We're framing Reynolds along with Adam Stine. We have access to many tools. We'll make it look like he was helping the Bureau man from last week. The one who died during the original assassination attempt. He worked from here. From this building. This is where he planned everything. We'll make it look like Reynolds had been here with him before. They'll think he couldn't live with himself. Because of the guilt."

I glanced at the digital display above the doors. It showed the elevator car heading our way, counting up. I said, "I killed one of the men who forced Agent Reynolds to his death." I paused. "Who was the other person involved?"

The guy said nothing. Just stared at me.

The elevator doors dinged open. I motioned with my weapon for the guy to turn and step inside, and he obeyed. I followed him in and kept my weapon aimed at the man. The doors closed. I said, "Which floor?"

"One floor down."

"You sure about that?"

"I'm positive, Mr. Jordan," he said, telling me he knew exactly who I was. "But it is a death sentence."

"How so?"

He paused, thinking. "Because Malone will kill you. When he sees I brought you to him, he'll kill me, too."

"I'm going to kill you, anyway."

He paused again. Thinking hard. Calculating what would happen the moment we arrived at the floor below. I could see it in my mind's eye. David Malone interrogating my friend. Chris Reed strapped to a chair, maybe in a corner room like the one on the twenty-first floor. Maybe a few of Malone's men standing guard. I knew I could take them all.

The guy turned back and said, "It's too late for your friend. They took him away already."

"Who is they?"

The man said nothing back.

I motioned to the panel with my gun. I said, "Push the button."

He pushed the button for floor twenty. Nothing happened. He feigned ignorance, and I reached into my pocket for Gardner's keycard, which I'd taken, and held it against the reader. It turned green, and I hit the button myself. I dropped the keycard back into my pocket and used my free hand to grab the guy by the shoulder, and I positioned him right in front of the doors. Then I stood behind him as we started to move.

It was a quick ride. I felt the elevator drop downward for a second; then it jerked to a stop. As soon as it did, I could hear men talking. The man standing in front of me smiled as he turned backward slightly, eyeing me from the side as I started to understand what the guy had done.

Then the elevator doors chimed open. But they didn't open up to a hallway. They opened up into a large room. A conference room. I stared straight ahead and counted three men sitting together, arms crossed, talking casually. One relaxed conversation going on at the end of a long conference room table. I was looking at a boardroom. The men were in a meeting. Or maybe one had just ended. There was laughter and congratulatory slaps on shoulders. The one in the middle was trying to light a cigar.

The man in the center noticed me. He stared ahead and blinked hard, trying to understand what he was looking at. Thirty feet away, I was doing the same exact thing. The others stopped talking. They followed his gaze and turned to me, and I forced the man I was holding at gunpoint to step forward, into the room.

## 56

The man in the center was in charge. That much was clear. He was seated at the head of the table, and the other two had been turned to him. They went to look at him again, and the man in charge pointed and said, "Kill them both," which I wasn't expecting, but should've with men who were tying up loose ends.

I hesitated for a moment, processing his words, watching the men on the head guy's left and right reach into their jackets, pull their weapons from their holsters, and awkwardly try to stand and aim.

I shot them first.

But one of them managed to fire a wild clumsy shot that struck the man I was holding at gunpoint. He hit the guy square in the chest. Center mass. His legs buckled, and he dropped to his knees and then fell facedown on the floor, and he didn't move any more.

Then it was just the head guy and me. The last man standing. A man with silver hair, slicked back and perfect. "Stand up—now," I said, aiming my weapon across at him, realizing he had no weapon of his own.

David Malone said nothing. Just stared at me for a long moment, then his eyes fell downward, and he looked at the lifeless bodies of the two other men.

"I said stand up!" I yelled, repeating myself and moving to the left, around the table, closer to him.

Then Malone became present again and looked at me. He said, "It's too late for your friend. Believe me."

"They keep telling me that."

Malone looked down again. Then he stood. He moved around the other side of the long table, staying opposite from me. Malone lifted his hands halfway into the air and moved to his left, along the wall, taking a circuitous route until we were both standing the same distance to the elevator. Then he grew bolder, realizing he had something I wanted, and if that was true, he had an advantage. Malone picked up a weapon off the floor from the man who'd been seated at his left. and I fired a shot just to the right of him. Malone paused briefly. Then he stood up tall and held the weapon aimed downward but gripping it tight. He stared across and said, "I know who you are, Mr. Jordan."

"And I know who *you* are. Alex Gardner told me all about it. One floor up from where we're standing." I paused, watching him carefully, my eyes moving from his face down to his weapon and back again. "One week ago, you and your men tried to kill the President of the United States. But you failed. Everything that happened today was you trying to clean up the mess you and your people made. But take a look around."

Malone's eyes darted all around. They danced all over the large room, looking at the three dead bodies. Then maybe thinking about one more one floor up. Maybe trying to figure out how he would deal with it, how he'd explain it all away. He was standing less than ten feet from me. Both of us equidistant to the elevator on my right and on his left. He said, "Mr. Jordan, I want you to listen to me very carefully. In a moment, I'm going to step into that elevator, and you're going to let me. I will blame all of this on Alex Gardner. He will take the fall. Then in five minutes, I will call my man. I'll tell him to let your friend go, and you'll forget all about this." He paused and studied me for a moment. His eyes shifted to the elevator, then back to me. "But if you stop me, if you don't let me step into that elevator, I can't make that call."

"I don't believe you."

"You don't have a choice."

"We all have a choice," I said. "Like when you decided to kill Mark Reynolds."

Malone stared. He slowly raised his wrist and glanced at his watch. He said, "Now you have four minutes."

"What happened to five?"

He stared. "I gave the order to kill your friend a few minutes ago. It's already in motion. Unless I stop it."

I said nothing.

"Time marches on, Mr. Jordan. Let me go and your friend lives. Don't and he won't. Believe me." Malone paused. "Like you said, we all have a choice."

I stared at Malone for a long moment, studying the man's face, keeping my Glock leveled, understanding that soon it would be three minutes. I said, "If you're lying to me, I'll hunt you down, and I will kill you."

Malone nodded.

He moved to the elevator and pushed the button. It chimed open, and he stepped inside cautiously, watching me the whole time. He found his keycard and tapped it against the reader. He pushed a button.

Then he disappeared.

## 57

I GLANCED AT MY WATCH TO NOTE THE TIME. NOT THAT I believed what David Malone had told me blindly. But if he was going to make a call, it would be in the next minute or two, once he was out of the building. He'd make the call as he walked to his vehicle, with Jami eyeing the man the whole way. She'd follow him out and track him to wherever he would drive to. I'd have to deal with him later. Right now, my priority was finding Chris.

I checked my Glock. The magazine had a few rounds left in it. Jami's Glock was in my pocket. I'd picked it up after taking out Alex Gardner. I took a look around; then I turned to face the elevator and pressed the down button and checked the time. Two minutes had passed. Two to go. I figured the best play was to start searching, floor by floor, looking for my friend. I knew Chris wasn't on the twenty-first floor, and he wasn't here, so I'd have to start from the nineteenth floor down. I'd use Gardner's keycard. Or the driver of the black sedan's keycard. I had both.

But when the elevator door chimed back open, it wasn't empty. Jami stepped out, followed by Emma Ross, followed by Agent Rivera. Jami glanced behind me briefly; then she gave me a quick hug. Rivera stepped inside and scanned the room; then he looked at the three bodies on the floor, studying them. Emma turned to me and said, "What happened here?"

"David Malone was having a meeting," I said. "Some kind of after-action debrief with his people, I think."

"What were they doing?"

"Talking and laughing, mostly. Until they saw me exit the elevator."

Jami turned slowly to look at me and said, "Did you get Malone?"

"No," I replied as I glanced at Emma Ross. "I let him go."

Emma furrowed her brow and asked, "Why?"

"Because he told me if I did, he'd make a call. He'd phone his boys and tell them to let Chris go."

Emma looked away. "I wouldn't trust what he says if I were you. You really think Agent Reed is still here?"

"Maybe. But I don't know where I'd find him. It's a big building."

Jami said, "Malone didn't pass us. We didn't see him at all."

I said nothing.

"But we had Morgan cut the power to the building. I hope it helped you."

I nodded and looked at Agent Rivera. I said, "Why are you here?"

"Ms. Ross needed a ride; she said it was a matter of life and death."

"It is," I said. "But you shouldn't be here. You should be with the president."

Rivera narrowed his eyes. "The threat is over downtown;

my team is preparing to take him back to the White House shortly."

"You need to arrest Agent Bryant. I just confirmed that he leaked the motorcade route last week."

Rivera stared. He opened his phone but got no signal. He said, "Bryant is driving the president back."

Rivera looked around for a landline and found one. It was in the center of the mass of bodies. He stepped over and around them and hit a button on the Polycom and made a call on speakerphone. One of his men answered, and Rivera asked for a situation report. His man said they were just about to head out. President Keller was already in the limousine. They'd be back at the White House in no time. Rivera told his man to wait for him to return. His man said that wasn't necessary, but Rivera said it absolutely was. He said to tell the others that he'd be there in ten minutes; then he clicked off and walked back toward us. Rivera said, "I don't want to take any chances. I need to be there myself to deal with Bryant. While we still have the roadblocks in place. Once he leaves, we lose control. Fewer restraints if he tries to do something."

I nodded. Said nothing.

Rivera asked if I was absolutely sure that Agent Bryant was involved, and I said that I was. He pushed the button for the elevator. The doors opened and Emma stepped inside for a second and used her keycard so it would work and pressed the button for the parking garage. Emma stepped back out; then Rivera stuck his hand out, and we shook; then he stepped into the elevator, and a moment later Agent Rivera was gone.

I said, "Emma, if Agent Reed is here, where would I find him?"

Emma pointed toward the ceiling. "One floor up," she said.

"I was just up there. Gardner led me there. He wanted to restrain me. Maybe torture me. No one's there."

"Maybe they are now."

"They're not, Emma. I killed Gardner up there a few minutes ago. Nobody else was on that floor."

Emma tucked a lock of hair behind her ear and said, "Then where else could they be?"

"You tell me."

Emma turned and looked out at nothing at all. Her eyes were flicking around as she thought, processing what she had seen. But she came up with nothing and said, "I don't know, then. I'm very sorry."

Jami said, "We need to split up. If he's not above us or on this floor, then he's down on one of the others. I'll check nineteen through twelve. Blake, you take the next six, and Emma, you take the rest. Does that work?" She turned to look at Emma; then she faced me again. "Do you have a better idea?"

I thought about it. "No," I said as I handed Gardner's keycard to Jami and kept the sedan driver's keycard for myself. Emma pressed the down button to call the elevator. I gave Jami her Glock back and found Emma a weapon of her own. In case she needed it. Emma held it loose and aimed it down toward the floor. Jami got hers ready. The elevator door chimed open, and I stepped inside with Emma. Jami hung back. She said she was going to find the stairs. No use holding us up. She'd head down a floor and would start checking. Emma used her keycard and I hit the button for eleven. Then as the door closed, I held my hand out, stopping the elevator door from closing. They fumbled back open awkwardly, and Jami asked what was wrong.

I said, "We're not going to find Chris on any of the floors we check. I was wrong. He is above us."

Jami narrowed her eyes and shook her head. A small little movement. Then she got it. Her eyes grew wide, and she stepped forward, joining Emma and me. I looked at the row of buttons and traced my finger up. Emma swiped her badge again, and I pressed the highest button on the panel, and Jami said, "Rooftop access."

## 58

The elevator dropped downward. Consequences of hitting the button for the lower floor before I realized where we would find Chris Reed. But the minor detour only wasted thirty seconds, which Jami, Emma, and I used for planning our next steps. The elevator doors opened up to a room similar to the one on twenty. Another conference room. Direct access. No hallway. I pressed the close button repeatedly until the elevator obeyed. Then we rocketed back upward, toward the top of the building. I held onto the grab bar to steady myself. Jami and Emma did the same. Then we slowed, and the doors opened up again, and I raised my Glock, unsure of exactly what to expect. I imagined more CIA guys guarding the access point.

But that wasn't what I found. The doors opened up to a short, dark hallway that led to a set of stairs. Nobody was there waiting to take us out. Nobody at all. Just an empty room. I glanced over my shoulder; Jami and Emma stared at me with confused expressions on their faces. I turned back and stepped out.

They followed closely, and Emma said, "I don't think he's up there."

Jami said, "If he was, they'd have a lookout posted here, guarding the access point."

I hesitated for a moment, my heart racing in my chest. Twelve minutes had passed since I had let David Malone go. He'd promised he'd call his men and tell them to release Chris. Maybe they had.

Or maybe they hadn't.

Jami said, "Original plan. We split up and search the floors. We've only lost a few minutes; let's go back."

I said nothing. Just stepped forward cautiously, lowering my weapon as I moved, glancing upward as I approached the stairs and saw they led to a small hatch. Like a half circle. Like a steel bubble on a hinge. "We need to go up there," I said, climbing up a few of the steps and pushing on the hatch with one hand.

But the hatch wouldn't budge. I holstered my weapon and steadied myself on the stairs and used both hands to push up as hard as I could, but it didn't move. Jami said, "Maybe it's locked," and I looked around until I found where the key went and pointed at it for her to see.

"It's not," I said. "Someone unlocked it. It should just open right up."

"Maybe someone's sitting on it," Emma said.

I thought about it; then I nodded. "Which means we need to get them to open it."

Jami stared and said, "Maybe if you ask nicely."

I stared back. "What options do we have? Besides knocking on the hatch and crossing our fingers?"

Emma said nothing. Jami shook her head slowly. Then she said, "I think that's the only play. Maybe they'll think it's one of their guys. If they had reason to believe people like us were here, they'd have a man posted down here to take us out the moment we stepped out of the elevator. Maybe they're not worried. Or maybe one of their guys is tired and resting. Or maybe nobody's up there, and we're just wasting time."

I looked up again, deciding what we should do. Then I said, "Let's find out," and I knocked on the hatch.

WE WAITED THROUGH TEN LONG SECONDS WHERE NOTHING happened. I climbed up two more steps on the ladder and drew my weapon and aimed it up with my right hand and put my left on the hatch and waited. I could feel movement. Someone moving off it maybe. Then I heard a muffled voice say, "Took you long enough," followed by the sound of someone straining to lift the hatch open. I helped push from below and climbed up fast. It was plenty dark outside. Minimal lighting up on the roof was my friend. I decided to take another approach. He had the high ground, and hence, the advantage, so I holstered my weapon and ducked right and just stood there and lifted my hand like I was asking for help. The man offered his palm. I grabbed it and stepped down from the stairs and pulled with all of my strength, and the guy toppled over.

He fell headfirst down into the small room we were standing in and stopped moving. Jami checked for a pulse. There wasn't one. The guy had a broken neck. I glanced back up and started climbing. I was worried about the man tipping off whoever else was up on the roof. I imagined them hearing the commotion, thinking something was wrong.

But it didn't seem to matter. Because as soon as I climbed up high enough, I noticed the loud hum of fans moving.

They were hard to see, but there were rows of air-conditioning units surrounding the hatch, responsible for cooling and heating the big government building. I reached for my Glock and climbed up and all the way out. I felt loose gravel underneath my shoes. I looked around. It was dark, but the moon was out, and the DC sky was lit up bright. I should've seen the faint outline of men walking the perimeter.

But nobody was there. I turned to my left and saw no one. I turned right. Just a dark empty void. Then I crouched down low and moved to the south side of the building. Above where they'd found Mark's body.

And I saw two men standing. Two silhouettes.

One with two hands raised and one with two hands extended outward.

The one with hands extended sensed something. He glanced over his shoulder and stared. Too dark to be sure if I was friend or foe. But the light from the rising moon helped him, and it was clear: I was his foe. The guy stepped backward and grabbed the one with his hands up and pushed him in front of him. He yelled, "Don't move! Don't take another step. If you do, your friend dies." He stared at me. "Understand?"

I couldn't see his face; therefore I couldn't see his eyes. And the eyes tell you everything you need to know. But right now I knew nothing other than two dark figures were twenty yards ahead of me, two silhouettes, one about to do something to the other, and I was the only one able to do anything about it.

The man barked more orders in my direction. *Put your weapon down; get on the ground; don't move.* I just moved slowly in their direction, gripping my gun tight in my hand, aiming to the side of the two figures. Then I thought about Mark Reynolds. Almost twenty-four hours earlier, he'd stood in the same spot. I imagined him looking over the ledge, arms raised, his mind racing. Alone. Then I stopped, and I aimed.

I said, "Lower your weapon, and I'll let you live," yelling over the sound of fans blowing behind me.

The guy said, "I have the advantage. If you shoot, you'll hit your friend." Then he seemed to have another idea. A better idea. He had leverage, and I didn't. I closed one eye and maintained my stance, feeling adrenaline rushing through my veins. I watched as the silhouetted gun moved from the captive towards me. Just one big slow awkward movement. Then the captive did something unexpected. He ducked.

I squeezed the trigger and watched as the second dark figure fell down. I ran over, lowering my weapon but keeping it fixed on my target, and kicked the weapon away from the man's body. I checked his pulse with two fingers. I felt nothing. I turned his face toward me and studied it. It was Ramsdale. The guy with the broken window. I stood and holstered my weapon and turned back. Now I was the one backlit, but the other man wasn't. Chris Reed stepped forward, toward me, and pulled me in for an embrace.

## 59

I slapped my friend on the back twice, and then I stepped back. But I held onto him for a moment longer, my heart still racing in my chest. I asked Chris if he was okay, and he told me that he was. Then I let go and looked him over some more in the dim moonlight. Chris had been beat up. That was clear. He had a bloody nose, and his face was starting to swell. It would be all bruised up in another day or two.

As Chris got his bearings, I stood next to him, wiping sweat from my brow with my hand, and then my thoughts went back to the room up on the twenty-first floor. The room where Malone and his men did their enhanced interrogations. The floor where I'd killed Alex Gardner. I could imagine Chris sitting in that room, his arms strapped to a chair as CIA men tried to beat answers out of him. Answers he didn't have. *Just like Mark Reynolds*, I thought to myself. They'd killed him for no reason. No reason at all. Then my friend's face changed. Chris became present and stared at me. He said, "How'd you find me, man?"

"Long story," I replied. "Let's get out of here."

Chris nodded. Then his face changed again. A confused look. "Where's Jami?" he asked.

Which was a very good question. Because I didn't know. I turned and looked, past the air conditioners. Jami and Emma weren't there. Then they were. Crouching, hiding, the moonlight catching their faces. Then Jami stood tall, stepping out from the shadows with her weapon raised high, and she fired it once.

I FLINCHED AND SO DID CHRIS. THEN I REACHED FOR MY weapon and turned around and saw a body on the rooftop, twenty paces behind me, moving slightly, maybe the guy's final moments. Then he grew still. I moved over to him fast, aiming my Glock downward, and kicked his gun away from him. I crouched down carefully and checked his neck for a pulse and felt nothing. Staying crouched, I glanced up and scanned the rest of the rooftop, looking for others, using the light from the moon coming up over the horizon to help me, but I saw nobody else there other than Jami and Emma and Chris moving toward me.

"Thanks," I said to my wife as I stood, talking loud over the drone of the AC units. "I didn't see him."

"You wouldn't have," she said. "Neither of you would've, the way he was approaching."

"Are there more?" asked Emma, holding her weapon loosely, looking over her shoulder.

I shook my head. "I don't see anyone else." The four of us stood there a moment longer, and I said, "Emma, I need to know if the president's okay." But before she could respond, I heard the faint sound of a cell phone ringing, low and small and dulled. She dug her phone out from a pocket, and she answered it.

. . .

EMMA PRESSED THE PHONE TO HER EAR, BUT IT WAS CLEAR SHE was struggling to make out what the caller was saying. She dropped the weapon she was still holding with her other hand into a pocket and motioned for the hatch and then turned and walked quickly to head back down. It was clear she was talking to Rivera. My heart started to race again as I wondered what had happened, if he'd made it in time, if the man had been able to get back to the Marriott Marquis before Agent Bryant could make a move.

Jami, Chris, and I followed her. We walked over to the hatch, and I let my wife and friend climb down first. Then I followed them. Emma was inside the small hallway, standing next to the dead body, her phone pressed against one ear, another small hand cupped over the other one. Still struggling to hear over the drone of AC units, so I climbed back up the ladder and closed the hatch and pulled it downward until it was sealed. Emma said that she understood. Then she thanked the caller and said she'd be in touch.

"What happened?" I asked as Emma clicked off.

"He got there in time. Agent Bryant has been detained."

Jami said, "So the president's safe?"

Emma nodded. "They're heading back to the White House now."

Chris looked away, thinking. He put one hand on his hip and wiped sweat from his forehead with the other one. He glanced back at me and said, "We're done, then. Nothing else to run down now. The party's over."

I said, "Not exactly."

. . .

I spent the next few minutes bringing Chris up to speed with what had happened in the gap between when we lost communication and when we found him up on the roof moments earlier. I told him about Alex Gardner and how the man ended up being someone other than who we thought he was. Jami filled in the rest of the details. The parking garage, how she hung back, how she'd spoken with Emma, who got a ride from Rivera. Then I told him that Malone was the top dog. How I'd confronted him. How I'd let him go.

"We need to go after him," Chris said.

"We can't," I replied.

"Right here, right now, Blake."

"Chris, listen to me—we're going to have to figure out the best way to play this."

He shook his head. "You're not getting it, man. This guy is responsible for Mark's death."

Jami stepped forward. She said, "Blake's right. David Malone is too high up the food chain."

Chris said nothing.

I stared across at my friend and nodded slowly, but I didn't speak. I didn't know what to say.

But Emma did. She said, "I've met with the man a few times. I know how he works. And they're right." She glanced briefly at Jami and me. "He's high up the chain. And cunning. And shrewd. He's the kind of guy you love to hate. The kind of person who can talk their way out of anything. I wouldn't be surprised if he's on the phone right now, with his own boss, spinning a good yarn. Or maybe he went home. Maybe he's waiting to get a call tomorrow, telling him to get down here, and he'll act surprised about the whole thing. Or maybe he's somewhere right this very moment calling more of his men, telling them to go after us."

"Wherever he is," Jami said, "we're going to have to take him down. One way or another."

"The right way," Emma said.

Chris made eye contact with me. I said nothing and just glanced at Emma.

"I'm going to head back to Langley. I'll find out who he reports to. I'll tell them everything I know."

Jami said, "You need to be careful. You don't know who else is involved. It may go higher than Malone."

Emma nodded. A slow, knowing nod. Something in her eyes. A woman determined to bring a man down. She turned and punched the single button by the elevator behind her. The doors opened, and she stepped inside, followed by Jami, followed by Chris, followed by me. Emma swiped her keycard against the reader.

Then I pressed the button for the ground floor, and the elevator doors closed.

THEY OPENED BACK UP SIXTY SECONDS LATER. I HELD THE door to keep it from closing, and Jami and Emma stepped out first, then Chris and I followed them out. We stood together in a huddle. I glanced around at each of them in turn. Then Emma said, "I can't go back to Langley. Not right now. In case Malone's there."

"He's not there," I said. "You were right before. He's at home, licking his wounds, planning and plotting."

"Then where do I go? What should I do?"

I grabbed my keys from my pocket and tossed them to Jami. She caught them in midair and stared at me. I said, "Your truck's been towed by now. So take mine and give Emma a ride back to the Ellipse."

Jami said, "Then what?"

"Then go home." I turned to my friend. "Chris will take me back. After we tell Mulvaney what happened."

Jami asked about Malone and what we were going to do about him. I said we weren't going to do anything. Not yet. First we needed to get to Mulvaney, if he was still at the Hoover Building, and talk to him. We'd need someone at his level to do something about it. Due process. We'd need him to make some calls to the people above Malone and tell them what had happened. That was the only way it could work. Because Malone would be suspended. There'd be an investigation. It would last for weeks. Maybe months. This wasn't something we were going to solve tonight. So we said goodbye, and Jami walked over to my SUV and climbed inside along with Emma. Chris found where he'd parked, and we moved toward the vehicle. Jami started the motor and backed out. She threw it in drive and buzzed past us and exited fast. Chris tried the door, and it opened up. So did mine. I climbed in and saw he'd left the key in the ignition.

Chris went to turn the key, then stopped. He turned to me. He said, "You know, even if we win, we lose."

I stared at him for a long moment; then I glanced away and nodded slowly but said nothing back.

"There'll be a funeral. Tamara will be there. And Marcus. And Mulvaney. He'll offer his condolences. He'll tell them if there's anything he can ever do for them, to let him know. But there isn't anything he can do. You and I both know that. And a week after that, it'll be business as usual. They'll all forget. But I won't."

"Chris, I know what you're—"

"No you don't, man. You've lost people in your life. I get it. But this is different." Chris started the motor. It came to life, and he sat there for a long moment. Then he backed out and threw it in drive and drove forward, toward the exit. He slowed long enough for the barrier arm to recognize the approaching vehicle, and it lifted up fast. Then Chris turned and headed for the Hoover Building so we could talk to Mulvaney.

I had said that due process was the only way to bring down Malone.

But that wasn't true. Not true at all.

## 60

**ONE WEEK LATER**

I ENTERED THE SECOND FLOOR OF THE LONG-FORGOTTEN building at the Nebraska Avenue Complex. Far down along the middle of the floor, I saw Simon Harris working alone. He must've heard the door click closed behind me because he hesitated a moment, turned and looked at me, then gave me a small wave hi.

I nodded and stepped into my office, holding a cup of coffee, and closed the door. Then I dropped into the chair behind the desk and checked my watch. Just past eight in the morning on a Saturday. Enough time to get some work done before I'd meet up with Chris and Jami and head over for the twelve o'clock funeral. But as I leaned forward and started sifting through the paperwork Simon had left for me on my desk, I found it hard to focus. Then I heard a knock at the door and told Simon to open up and step inside.

But Simon wasn't at the door. Instead, Emma Ross pushed it open and stared down at me.

"Emma," I said, "please come in."

I gestured to the chairs on the other side of my desk. Emma didn't move. Not at first. She just stared at me for a few more uncomfortable seconds; then she stepped the whole way into my office. She was carrying a folded newspaper with her. She unfurled it and tossed it on my desk. It landed on top of the paperwork Simon had left, the front page facing me, a large, bold headline inches from my face. Emma pulled one of the chairs out and dropped down into it and crossed one leg over the other and stared some more. I picked up the paper and read the headline again, then a third time; then I glanced up. "Is this true?"

Emma nodded, but said nothing.

I lowered my gaze and said, "Former CIA deputy director David Malone found dead in apparent suicide," reading the headline out loud; then I looked at her over the newspaper.

Emma maintained her cold stare and remained completely silent.

I said, "When did this happen?"

She looked on for another long moment, eyeing me, judging me, before she finally spoke. She said, "Authorities found his body at approximately one thirty in the morning. They found him in the street. It happened outside his luxury apartment in Arlington. It's called Marlowe."

I nodded vaguely. "I know the place."

Emma tilted her head to one side. She studied me a moment longer. "The working theory is that David Malone couldn't take the pressure from the investigation related to Mark Reynolds's death. The investigation Peter Mulvaney and the Bureau launched at the request of you and Agent Reed a week ago."

"So he took his own life?"

She kept staring. "Like I said, that's the theory."

I thought about that for a long moment. Then I said, "How'd it happen?"

"He jumped from his balcony. He fell thirteen stories. Long way down. They called and woke me up at two o'clock in the morning. I was in Langley working with my people thirty minutes later. By four we had isolated the timeline. By five we had accessed security cameras. By six we had a positive ID."

I said nothing.

"My people sent me what they found. I was in my office, and I watched the whole thing." She tilted her head to the other side and eyed me a moment longer, thinking, debating, studying me carefully. "Two white males parked three blocks away. They got out of a dark vehicle and approached the building. I got a good look at them as they moved, even with their masks. One dark-haired man, and—" she stared at me "—one with brownish hair. They didn't use a keycard to get inside. The door unlocked on its own after the one with the brownish hair made a call on his cell. Almost like he had help from someone with extremely privileged access to be able to do such a thing."

I said nothing.

"They stepped inside, exited fifteen minutes later, walked back to their vehicle, and disappeared."

"We should try to find them," I said.

"I found one of them," she replied.

Emma's eyes were fixed on mine. Unwavering. Just a cold, calculating glare. I stared back, my heart beating hard in my chest, my palms sweating, my fists clenched, as I thought through what this meant. I said, "I've been in that apartment building. They don't have security cameras, from what I remember."

"They don't," she said. "But there's another building on that street that does. Right by the sidewalk. Well lit, too."

I looked away, replaying it in my mind; then I turned back.

Emma looked me straight in the eye and said, "I destroyed the evidence."

I breathed a sigh of relief, and then I nodded. "Thank you."

"Then I spent the last three hours verifying there were no other cameras in the vicinity. You're lucky. There weren't any. Then I told my people they never saw the original footage. The footage I destroyed."

"What people?" I asked.

Emma tucked a lock of hair behind an ear and sat up straighter. "I was promoted. To Gardner's position. After what happened to Malone, I was appointed to acting assistant director of stateside CIA operations. The new liaison between DDC and the CIA. I have a feeling if I get past my first mistake, the job is mine."

I narrowed my eyes. "What mistake is that?"

"I failed in my first assignment. I wasn't able to find the people responsible for killing David Malone."

My office grew silent. Neither of us spoke for a long moment. Only the faint sound of air blowing through the overhead vents could be heard. I looked across at her and said, "Why are you helping me, Emma?"

Then her face changed a little. Her eyes became kinder. Emma leaned forward in her seat and stood. Then she glanced down at the picture frame she had noticed a week earlier, and I followed her gaze. She reached for the frame and lifted it so it was facing up at her. She held it in her hand and read the inscription; then she nodded slowly to herself. Emma set it down and turned it around so it was facing me. Then she turned back and pulled the door open and disappeared. I watched the door for a moment longer; then I looked down at the frame and the face of a younger version of myself and my SEAL buddy. It reminded me of the photo in Mark's office. Then I read the inscription and leaned back in my chair and looked away.

**THREE HOURS LATER**

Chris, Jami, and I were seated together at Mark Reynolds's funeral. Tamara and her mother were sitting in the front row inside the church, with Marcus nestled between them. The place was packed with fellow Bureau agents taking up seats not already filled by family members, a few standing along the walls, arms in front or behind, hands clasped together, solemn, regretful looks spread all across their faces. Little Marcus was wearing a dress shirt tucked into dress pants with what I figured was a clip-on necktie. He'd turn periodically and look at me, then at Chris; then he'd glance at all of the Bureau men and women gathered around, studying each of them in turn, no doubt seeing a little of his father in each of them. Jami grabbed my hand and whispered in my ear how sad the whole thing was. I nodded my agreement, but said nothing back. To my right, Chris leaned in and said, "I wish there was something we could do for the kid."

I thought about that. My mind went back to the last time I had spoken with the boy. We were inside his father's office at the Hoover Building, looking at pictures and books, talking about his birthday while his mother and grandmother met with Mulvaney down on the first floor. I remembered the hope in his eyes. The anticipation, the excitement that he could barely contain, which I doubted would ever come to pass.

I leaned to my right and replied to my friend, "I think there is."

ANOTHER WEEK PASSED AND I SKIPPED MY USUAL SATURDAY morning office tasks to run a quick errand; then I headed over to Chris Reed's apartment. My quick errand ended up taking over an hour. Decisions had to be made. And I had to choose the right thing. But I'd made my choice and pulled up to the complex and found Chris sitting on the steps, watching me park, looking at his watch in an exaggerated manner.

He stood and sauntered over to the passenger door as I buzzed the window down. "Where've you been?"

"Sorry," I said. "Get in."

Chris opened the door and slid into the seat. He looked me over and said, "So what's the plan, boss?"

"We pull up and ring the doorbell and take it from there."

"They're not expecting us."

"Not us, specifically. But they are expecting company. Us showing up won't be a big deal. It'll be fine."

Chris just shook his head and faced forward as I put the SUV in reverse and backed out, then drove off.

IT WAS A RELATIVELY SHORT DRIVE. TEN MINUTES. I PULLED UP to the home, and Chris finally put it together. There were cars lined up and down both sides of the street. There were signs pinned on the front of the home against trees, and balloons taped to the door, and a big HAPPY BIRTHDAY sign consisting of thirteen different letters was stuck into the dirt along a perfectly manicured hedge in front of the home.

Chris looked at me and shot me a worried look. He said, "We don't have a gift."

I turned in my seat and reached back. Chris watched as I lifted a thin blanket off a pet carrier. There was a tiny trill sound from the small cat curled up in a tight ball as it opened its eyes and looked up at us.

"You've got to be kidding me," he said.

"It's what the boy wanted," I replied. "He told me Mark was going to get him one for his birthday."

"What if Tamara already got him one?"

"Then he'll have two."

Chris watched the tiny creature for another long moment, then looked at me and smiled. "Okay. Let's go."

I climbed out and opened the back door. Chris joined me. I reached in and grabbed the carrier and hauled it out and held it out so he could take it. "No," he said. "It shouldn't come from me."

"It should," I said. "Mark was your partner. And Marcus is his son. You're the next man up."

Chris thought about that for a moment; then he nodded to himself and grabbed the carrier. I heard the small sound again and caught my friend's smile as I walked around to the back, opened the hatch, and reached inside for a large bag of cat food.

"What about the litter?" he asked as I closed the hatch.

"You can come back for that later," I said.

Chris shook his head as we walked toward the house.

I saw a large bounce house in the backyard, which I guessed Marcus's mother had rented for the party. As we approached the door, I could hear the sounds of kids playing inside, their parents talking, a community of friends and family and neighbors gathering around a broken family, offering their love and support, trying to help Marcus have a good day in an otherwise dark time in his life. We walked to the door and stood there, side by side. I pushed the doorbell and heard a chime. Then I stepped backward.

Chris glanced back at me over his shoulder, understanding I was letting him take the lead. *Next man up.*

As I stood behind my friend, I thought about little Marcus and what he would remember from this day. I knew he'd remember the family and the friends, the presents, the cake, and being sung happy birthday. He'd remember the gift his dad had promised him, which I hoped would give him joy for years to come. But mostly I hoped he would remember a band of brothers, his father's friends, who made him a priority. Men who looked after each other and held an unspoken promise to have each other's backs, any time, any place. Men who would step in and be present and offer all of ourselves when one of our own had fallen.

Mark and I didn't always see eye-to-eye. But we shared a common belief, that darkness could be driven away only by the light. That the good guys won in the end, knowing that the real battle between good and evil was one that was fought every day inside the heart of every man, whether he realized it or not. As my dad used to say: The only thing needed for the triumph of evil is for good men to stand by and do nothing.

I followed Chris inside and watched him give Marcus the gift. Tamara looked on with tears in her eyes. A promise made, a promise kept, from father to son. As I watched, I thought about something we used to say in the service, a saying I must've said a thousand times, on my hardest days and in my darkest nights:

*Call on me, oh brother, we'll fight them to the end.*

*Because no bullet, no shell, and no demon in hell can break this bond called brothers.*

Mark was gone, but Chris and I would keep his memory alive. We would make sure of that. Because soldiers looked after each other. And because it was in our blood to never leave a fallen brother behind.

I hope you enjoyed book 9 in the Blake Jordan series. Have you read them all? Go to kenfite.com/the-senator to start book 1.

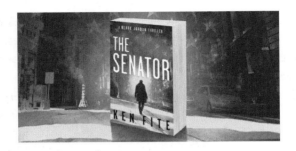

## The senator is kidnapped. Can Blake Jordan save him?

After his wife is murdered in Chicago, by-the-book agent Blake Jordan focuses on the one thing he's always been good at: his job. But Blake is so consumed by grief, he doesn't notice that someone is watching him from the shadows.

When Senator Keller asks Blake to handle security the night he's set to receive his party's nomination for president, he accepts the assignment. But he didn't expect the senator to disappear under his watch.

If he wants to get him back, Blake must break every rule he's lived by. But what the kidnappers are planning to do next is shocking... and it's much darker and far more personal than he could imagine... THE SENATOR is a fast-paced thriller you'll be reading late into the night.

HERE'S WHAT READERS ARE SAYING...

★★★★★ "I was completely hooked start to finish."
★★★★★ "You won't be disappointed."
★★★★★ "...on par with Baldacci!"
★★★★★ "I couldn't put the book down."
★★★★★ "Do not miss this series!"
★★★★★ "The story grabbed me and didn't let go."
★★★★★ "Full of surprises and never-ending twists."
★★★★★ "...great read."
★★★★★ "The ending left me wanting more."
★★★★★ "Fans of Mitch Rapp will like Blake Jordan."

READY FOR A GREAT STORY? START READING IT NOW:
kenfite.com/the-senator

## WANT THE NEXT BLAKE JORDAN STORY FOR $1 ON RELEASE DAY?*

*KINDLE EDITION ONLY

I'm currently writing the next book in the Blake Jordan series with a release planned soon. New subscribers get the Kindle version for $1 on release day.

Join my newsletter to reserve your copy and I'll let you know when it's ready to download to your Kindle.

kenfite.com/books

## THE BLAKE JORDAN SERIES
IN ORDER

*The Senator*
*Credible Threat*
*In Plain Sight*
*Rules of Engagement*
*The Homeland*
*The Shield*
*Thin Blue Line*
*Person of Interest*
*Abuse of Power*

Made in United States
Troutdale, OR
07/18/2023

11377938R00190